Cane Bay Zombies

C.F. Hayes

Published by C.F. Hayes, 2024.

This is a work of fiction. Similarities to real people, places, or events are entirely coincidental.

CANE BAY ZOMBIES

First edition. October 23, 2024.

Copyright © 2024 C.F. Hayes.

ISBN: 979-8223147039

Written by C.F. Hayes.

Table of Contents

Prologue 1
Chapter 1: Calm Before the Storm 4
Chapter 2: Fortifying Home 8
Chapter 3: Trouble, Zombie Trouble 12
Chapter 4: The First Attack 16
Chapter 5: Holding the Line 20
Chapter 6: A Plan of Action 24
Chapter 7: The World Closing In 29
Chapter 8: The Edge of Normal 34
Chapter 9: A Visitor at Dusk 39
Chapter 10: The World Outside Our Door 44
Chapter 11: Fortifying for the Worst 49
Chapter 12: The New Reality 54
Chapter 13: Descent into Chaos 58
Chapter 14: Hold the Line 63
Chapter 15: It's Everywhere 67
Chapter 16: The Gamble 72
Chapter 17: No Way Out 77
Chapter 18: The Plan 81
Chapter 19: Unrest 86
Chapter 20: Gathering Forces 90
Chapter 21: Tensions Rising 95
Chapter 22: The Siege 99
Chapter 23: Into the Unknown 104
Chapter 24: Hard Choices 109
Chapter 25: Routine and Tension 114
Chapter 26: The Broken Grid 119
Chapter 27: Unwelcome Guests 123
Chapter 28: Thin Line Between Trust and Survival 127
Chapter 29: The Hardest Decisions 131
Chapter 30: Beaufort and the Marines 135

Chapter 31: Sergeant Frank Makes a Comeback 140
Chapter 32: Fight, Sleep, Rinse, Repeat 145
Chapter 33: Beautifying Beaufort 149
Chapter 34: Search and Rescue 153
Chapter 35: Contact Front 157
Chapter 36: Interlocking Fields of Fire 162
Chapter 37: Annie and Frank's Day Off 166
Chapter 38: The Boys Are Growing Up 170
Chapter 39: The Work Continues 174
Chapter 40: Next Steps 178
Chapter 41: The Price of Progress 182
Chapter 42: Dawn of the Fight 186
Chapter 43: Actual... Engaged 190
Chapter 44: Building Something New 195
Chapter 45: Love in the Time of Chaos 199
Chapter 46: We Will Survive 206
Chapter 47: Expanding Horizons 210
Chapter 48: Mission to Savannah 214
Chapter 49: Hostess City of the South 219
Chapter 50: The Human Threat 223
Chapter 51: How to Prepare for Unwelcome Guests 228
Chapter 52: A Southern Welcome 233
Chapter 53: Fortifying for the Future 238
Chapter 54: First Line of Defense 242
Chapter 55: Safer, Finally 246
Chapter 56: Going to Charleston 251
Chapter 57: The Ghosts of Charleston 255
Chapter 58: One More Stop 259
Chapter 59: Politics Is Not Polite Dinner Conversation 263
Chapter 60: Storm on the Horizon 268
Chapter 61: Admin Isn't for Everyone 272
Chapter 62: The Mayor of the Clipboard 276
Chapter 63: Impending Nuptials 281

Chapter 64: Gravity 286
Chapter 65: Under Attack 291
Chapter 66: The Aftermath 295
Chapter 67: Wedding Day 299
Epilogue 303

Prologue

Before the world fell apart, before the undead walked and life unraveled, South Carolina was a state of contrasts. History, nature, and progress all blended in a delicate balance. The Lowcountry moved to its own slow rhythm, with the tides and marsh grasses setting the pace. Charleston, with its cobblestone streets and pastel antebellum homes, was the pride of the South, a city that had seen centuries of change but always endured.

The greater Charleston area was a patchwork of old and new. Expanding suburbs like Summerville, just a stone's throw away from the historic downtown, had become a haven for families seeking a peaceful life near the coast. Known for its blooming azaleas and sweet tea, Summerville exuded small-town charm while benefiting from the rapid development that followed Charleston's rise as a hub for tech, tourism, and military operations. The Charleston Naval Base, though a shadow of its Cold War prominence, still held its place as a pillar of the region's defense infrastructure.

North of Summerville lay Cane Bay Plantation, a sprawling, master-planned community nestled within acres of woodlands and wetlands. It was a symbol of the suburban boom. Modern, safe, and carefully designed for families looking for a little more space and a slower pace of life. Cane Bay was the epitome of the American dream, with tree-lined streets, well-maintained parks, and schools that promised the best for the children who grew up there.

This was where Frank and Annie had decided to raise their sons, Colt and Nash. After leaving Pennsylvania three years ago, they found solace in Cane Bay, a neighborhood that offered both security and a sense of community. For Frank, a Marine Corps veteran, it had felt like the perfect place to finally settle down, far from the chaos of his military past, yet close enough to Charleston to feel connected to the heart of the state.

Life in Cane Bay moved at its own speed, its own southern rhythm. Mornings were filled with the sound of kids boarding buses for school, the quiet hum of lawnmowers in the distance, and the murmur of neighbors chatting on their front porches. In the evenings, the sun dipped low over the still waters of nearby lakes, casting golden hues on the tightly knit homes. Families gathered for cookouts, and children played in the streets until the fireflies signaled it was time to head inside.

It was the life Frank had always wanted for his family; stable, peaceful, and predictable. But as the world around them began to change, as reports of a mysterious sickness spread and fear gripped the nation, that fragile peace would soon shatter.

The signs were subtle at first. A neighbor mentioned that someone in Charleston had gotten sick, really sick. Then, there were whispers of panic in the city and strange news about people who wouldn't stay dead. The schools closed without warning, and the highways became choked with cars as people tried to flee the coastal cities. Frank, with the instincts of a warrior, could sense what was coming, even before the chaos reached their quiet corner of the world.

The world beyond the Cane Bay community was descending into madness, and soon enough, even this suburban paradise would be forced to face the horrors that awaited.

South Carolina, with its beauty and history, was no longer safe. The greater Charleston area, once a vibrant center of life and culture, was overrun. Summerville, with its proud traditions and strong community, struggled to hold the line as its people tried to survive the wave of the undead. And Cane Bay, nestled far enough west of it, all should have been safe but would become both a refuge and a battleground.

In the blink of an eye, everything Frank and Annie had built for their family, everything their neighbors had come to rely on, would be tested. The struggle for survival would begin here, in the heart of the Lowcountry, where the marshes met the sea, and where life would have to find a way to endure against overwhelming odds.

But even as the world outside fell apart, Frank knew one thing: Cane Bay was more than just a neighborhood. It was their home. And come what may, they would fight to protect it.

Chapter 1: Calm Before the Storm

The air felt thicker than usual, heavy with the kind of humidity South Carolina's always known for. I stood in the backyard, looking at the tree line behind my house that separated our development from the retirement community next door. It was quiet. Too quiet. The cicadas weren't singing, and even the wind seemed to have gone still. I feel like I've lived here most of my life, though in truth we have only been here for 3 years. In all my 49 years, the stillness always meant a storm was coming.

I wasn't in the service anymore, but some instincts don't fade. The years in the Corps wired me to notice things, pick up on when something wasn't right. And right now, that feeling was gnawing at me like an itch I couldn't scratch.

I let the back door slam shut as I headed back inside. My moccasins slid against the mock hardwood floor. The house wasn't the warm friendly home we had shared in Pennsylvania, it was new construction, but it was home. It was just a place to live with my family. My wife of 20 years, Annie, and our two boys Colt, 18, and Nash, 12. Good kids. Smart, stronger than they realized, but teenagers all the same. Right now, they were in their rooms upstairs, each glued to their own screen. One playing a video game, the other watching something on his phone (probably YouTube).

"Dad, have you seen this?" Colt called, jogging down the stairs, his phone in hand. "There's this virus on the news. It's blowing up."

I paused, halfway to the kitchen. "What virus?"

Nash appeared right behind him. "People are getting really sick, Dad. Like, everywhere."

I walked over to the couch, where Annie was sitting peering over her shoulder. The news channel she had open on her phone was running a live feed of some reporter in New York City. The streets behind her were chaos. Police lights flashing, people running, and...

Was that a body on the ground? The anchor's voice sounded too calm for what they were showing.

"Authorities are urging people to stay indoors and avoid contact with those showing signs of illness. Symptoms include fever, extreme aggression, and erratic behavior..."

I watched for a minute longer, that bad feeling in my gut growing worse. I'd been out of the Corps since I was 24, but I'd seen enough in that time to know when something was going south. Whatever was happening, it was bigger than just another flu outbreak.

"Turn it off," I said, quieter this time.

Colt shot me a look like I was being dramatic. "Dad, seriously? It's probably nothing."

"Turn. It. Off." The edge in my voice cut through whatever argument he had ready. He shut the TV off without another word. Annie put her phone down as well to observe the interaction between me and the boys.

I took a deep breath, trying to settle myself. I didn't want to scare them, but I couldn't shake the tension creeping into my chest.

"Boys, listen to me," I said, sitting down across from them. "We need to be smart about this. Whatever's happening, it's spreading fast. We're gonna stock up on some supplies, just in case."

Nash looked confused. "You think it's that bad?"

I glanced out the window again, toward the backyard. "I don't know," I said honestly. "But we're not gonna wait around to find out."

Colt shifted uncomfortably. "Dad, it's probably just the news blowing things out of proportion. They do that."

"Maybe," I replied, "but better safe than sorry."

I grabbed my keys off the counter and headed for the door. "I'm going down to Publix to get some things. I want you three to stay here and lock the doors. Don't answer for anyone you don't know. Got it?

Nash nodded, but Colt just sighed, clearly still thinking I was overreacting. But he knew better than to argue. "Yeah, okay." Annie said, "Let me get my shoes on, I'm going with you".

The drive down Cane Bay Blvd to Publix was quick, just over 2 miles. We live in the Summerville zip code, but the town of Summerville proper was about a 20-minute drive. As I came to the parking lot, I could see things were already off. There were more people out than normal for a Friday afternoon, and not in a good way. It wasn't panic yet, but it was close. The Publix parking lot was packed, and the shelves inside were starting to thin out. Annie was concerned, but I reiterated that we needed to grab some things, just in case.

Annie and I split up and grabbed what we could canned food, water, batteries, and first-aid supplies then headed back toward the house. As I loaded the truck, my phone buzzed. A text from my parents, "Have you seen what's going on?"

I called and my dad picked up "Are the boys with you? Tell me you've seen the news."

"They're home. Annie and I are picking up supplies. You okay?"

He replied. "It's spreading. Mom's saying people are getting violent. Get the boys and hunker down."

I stared at the dashboard of the truck, the words sinking in. Violent. This wasn't just some flu. This was something else.

As we pulled out of the parking lot, the tension in the air shifted. The wind picked up, rattling the truck's windows, and in the distance, I could see dark clouds rolling in. The storm was coming, and it wasn't just the weather.

The drive back felt longer. Traffic was worse. People were trying to leave, or maybe trying to get home. I couldn't tell. By the time we pulled into the driveway, the sky had gone from gray to an angry black.

"It's real," I said to Annie. "And we need to be ready."

CANE BAY ZOMBIES

The storm had arrived.

Chapter 2: Fortifying Home

The ride back home from Publix felt heavy. The wind had picked up, slapping at the trees lining Cane Bay Boulevard. It wasn't just the sky that was dark, there was palpable tension everywhere. People were on edge, rushing home like they could outrun what was coming. Annie was quiet, her hands resting in her lap, fingers twitching as if wanting to grab her phone again and check the news. But neither of us needed more updates. We both felt it. Things were unraveling.

As I turned into our driveway, I scanned the neighborhood. Kids were still playing outside, riding bikes, and tossing footballs like nothing had changed. But there were fewer of them, and more parents were standing on their porches, watching.

"We need to move fast," I said, cutting the engine. "This thing could blow over in a couple of days, but we need to be ready in case it doesn't."

Annie nodded, her face drawn tight. She opened the truck door, and we both began hauling the bags of groceries and supplies inside. The boys were already downstairs, waiting by the door, eyes wide with questions they didn't quite know how to ask.

"Did you get everything?" Colt asked, trying to sound casual, but his voice cracked slightly.

"Got enough," I replied, setting down a case of water bottles on the kitchen floor. "But we're going to need more than just groceries. Colt, I want you to take inventory of everything we have canned food, dry goods, anything that won't go bad."

He nodded, grabbing a notepad from the counter. Nash hovered nearby, clutching his phone.

"Can I go back outside?" Nash asked, glancing out the window at the few neighborhood kids still playing.

"No," I said, more firmly than I intended. I caught his expression, a mix of confusion and frustration then softened my tone. "It's not safe, bud. We're staying inside for now."

Nash frowned but didn't argue, heading off to help Colt with the inventory. I watched him go, feeling a pang of guilt. It wasn't fair. They were kids, and this wasn't the world they should be dealing with. But this was the reality we had to face now.

Annie leaned against the counter, her arms folded across her chest. "You think it'll come here?" she asked quietly.

"I don't know," I admitted, stepping closer to her. "But we're going to be ready. Just in case."

I kissed her on the forehead, then turned toward the garage. I had some supplies of my own stashed there. Tools, some scrap wood, and other odds and ends I'd kept around "just in case." This was one of those times. I dragged out the boxes and laid everything out on the workbench: hammers, nails, some plywood sheets I'd been saving for who knows what. It wasn't much, but it was a start.

When I went back inside, Colt was reading off the inventory while Nash scribbled in the notepad. "We've got enough canned food for maybe two weeks," Colt said, glancing up at me. "But if things get worse..."

I nodded. "We'll ration what we have, and we can always make another supply run if we need to. But right now, the focus is on securing the house.

Annie was in the living room, pulling the curtains closed. The sun was still up, but the last thing we needed was people peering inside. I headed for the windows, checking each one, making sure they were all locked. I knew the usual security wasn't going to be enough. If things went bad, really bad, we'd need to barricade ourselves in.

"Colt, help me grab some of this plywood from the garage," I called.

He dropped the notepad and followed me outside. Together, we measured the windows, cutting the plywood down to size. The hammering echoed through the quiet neighborhood, and I felt a few eyes watching from the nearby houses. Normally, I'd have felt paranoid, but today I welcomed the stares. Let them see us preparing. Maybe it would encourage others to do the same.

As we worked, I caught glimpses of my neighbors pulling into their driveways, hurriedly unloading their cars. Some of them waved, others just glanced over nervously before disappearing into their homes. No one was panicking yet, but there was an unspoken understanding in the air: we were all bracing for something.

Back inside, Nash was helping Annie gather more supplies: flashlights, batteries, candles, and extra blankets. The boys moved quickly, a sense of urgency guiding them. They might not fully understand what was going on, but they trusted me. I could see it in their eyes.

By the time we finished securing the windows, the sky had darkened, and a cold breeze was rolling through the open garage. The sun dipped below the horizon, casting long shadows across the yard. The neighborhood was quieter now, too quiet, even for the evening. No more kids playing. No more cars driving past.

I closed the garage door and headed back inside, where the family was gathered in the living room. The TV was on, muted, showing the same chaotic footage as earlier. It didn't seem real, even now, watching it unfold. But the fear in Annie's eyes was real. The uncertainty in Colt and Nash's faces was real.

"We're locked down now," I said, trying to keep my voice steady. "We've got enough supplies to last us for a bit, but we need to be ready for whatever's next."

Nash looked up from his phone. "What if... what if they come here?"

I knelt down in front of him, meeting his eyes. "If they come, we'll be ready. We're safe here as long as we stick together and don't panic."

Annie stepped closer, placing a hand on my shoulder. "And what if this isn't enough?" she asked, her voice barely above a whisper.

I stood up, glancing out the window at the darkening street. The storm wasn't just in the sky, it was everywhere, creeping closer with each passing moment.

"We'll deal with that when we have to," I said softly. "But for now, we're as ready as we can be."

And as the wind picked up outside, rattling the windows and howling through the trees, I could feel the weight of it all bearing down on me. Protecting my family was all that mattered now. But in my gut, I knew this was only the beginning.

Chapter 3: Trouble, Zombie Trouble

The next morning, the house was eerily quiet. Normally, we'd be going about our weekend routines. Annie sipping her coffee while reading something on her Kindle, Colt lounging on the couch with his video games, Nash outside messing around with the basketball hoop. But today was different. Everyone felt it.

I was the first one up. I'd barely slept. I kept getting up, pacing the house, checking the barricades, listening for anything out of the ordinary. My body was tired, but my mind wouldn't shut off. Something about the air, even inside, felt too still.

I brewed a pot of coffee and stood by the window, sipping the bitter liquid and watching the empty street. Nothing moved. A few houses down, the Andersons' lights were on, but I hadn't seen anyone outside since we got home from Publix. It was like everyone had taken shelter in their homes, waiting for the storm to pass. Only, this storm didn't feel like it would pass anytime soon.

Annie came down the stairs a little later, her hair pulled back into a loose ponytail, looking like she hadn't slept much either. "Morning," she murmured, heading straight for the coffee.

"Morning," I replied, keeping my eyes on the window. "Sleep okay?"

She shook her head. "No. I kept thinking... about everything. What's going to happen? How bad it could get."

I nodded, knowing exactly what she meant. "We'll be okay," I said, trying to sound convincing. "We're prepared. If things get worse, we've got what we need."

"I hope you're right," she whispered, looking into her mug as if the answer would appear in the coffee.

The boys came down shortly after, both of them moving slower than usual. The tension in the air had hit them too, even if they weren't saying much. Colt had his phone in his hand, scrolling through social media, no doubt seeing the same chaos we'd been watching on the news.

"Anything new?" I asked, nodding toward his phone.

"More of the same," Colt said, sighing. "People are freaking out everywhere. There's this video from Atlanta... it's bad, Dad. People in the streets, fighting, biting. The cops are trying to get control, but it's... it's crazy."

I frowned. "Let me see."

Colt handed me the phone, and I watched the shaky footage. People were running, screaming, some falling to the ground as others attacked them. The cops were doing their best, but the crowd was overwhelming. It wasn't just panic, it was something else. People were turning violent in a way that didn't make sense.

I handed the phone back to Colt. "This isn't just panic," I muttered. "Something's wrong with these people."

Nash spoke up for the first time that morning, his voice small. "Are they... are they zombies?"

We all looked at him, the question hanging in the air. I wanted to tell him no, that zombies weren't real, that this was just a temporary crisis that would blow over. But the truth was, I didn't know. And judging by what I'd seen, the word didn't feel so ridiculous anymore.

"I don't know what they are," I said slowly, "but we're not going to take any chances."

Annie put down her mug and looked at me, her eyes wide. "What do we do now, Frank? We can't just sit here waiting for... for whatever this is to come knocking at our door."

She was right. Sitting around wasn't an option. We had to have a plan, not just for supplies, but for defense, for escape if things got bad.

"We're going to secure the perimeter," I said, thinking aloud. "Check all the exits, reinforce the doors if we can. Then we'll set up shifts. Someone needs to be awake at all times, watching. Just in case."

"Shifts?" Colt raised an eyebrow. "You think people are actually going to come for us?"

"I don't know," I admitted. "But we're not going to be caught off guard if they do."

We spent the rest of the morning working as a team. Annie gathered more blankets and set up a sort of central command in the living room, a place where we could all hunker down if needed. Colt and Nash helped me go over the house's defenses again, double-checking every door and window. I managed to scrounge up some extra nails and screws from the garage and reinforced the back door as best I could. It wasn't Fort Knox, but it would have to do.

While I worked, my mind kept drifting back to what Colt had shown me. The people in Atlanta... they weren't just scared. They were acting like animals, attacking each other without hesitation. It was as if something had taken control of them, turned them into monsters. Zombies. The word felt absurd, but I couldn't shake it.

By the time the sun began to set, the house was as secure as I could make it. The boys were sitting on the couch, their eyes glued to the TV, even though the broadcast was now just a repeating emergency message. Annie was in the kitchen, packing more of our food supplies into boxes in case we needed to move quickly.

As night fell, the uneasy quiet of the neighborhood returned. There were no cars, no people walking their dogs, nothing. Just the occasional gust of wind rustling through the trees.

I was on the back porch, keeping watch. The air felt thick like it had before a storm, but this time it was different. The cicadas had gone silent again, and there was a chill in the air that wasn't from the temperature. My gut was telling me something was wrong.

That's when I saw it. Movement at the edge of the yard.

I tensed, narrowing my eyes. The tree line behind the house shifted, shadows flickering in the fading light. I stepped off the porch and moved closer, trying to get a better look without making a sound.

At first, I thought it was just an animal. Maybe a stray dog or a deer. But then it stepped out of the shadows, a person. A man. He was stumbling, his clothes torn, one arm hanging limp at his side. His face was pale, eyes wide and unfocused like he was in a trance.

"Hey!" I called out, instinctively reaching for the hammer I'd been using earlier. "You need help?"

The man didn't respond. He just kept moving toward me, slow and deliberate, his body swaying like he was drunk. But something in his movements was wrong. Too jerky, too... unnatural.

I backed up, my heart pounding in my chest. "Stay back!" I warned, louder this time.

But he didn't stop. He just kept coming.

I stepped back again, my hand tightening around the hammer. Behind me, I heard the back door creak open.

"Frank, what's going on?" Annie's voice, filled with worry.

"Get inside," I ordered, never taking my eyes off the man.

"Frank..."

"Get inside, now!"

And as the man finally stepped into the fading light, I saw the blood. His mouth was stained with it, dried and caked around his chin. His shirt was torn open, revealing gashes across his chest, but he didn't seem to notice. He wasn't human anymore.

I raised the hammer, my pulse hammering in my ears.

"Get inside," I repeated, my voice low, the reality of what was coming finally sinking in.

The apocalypse wasn't on the news anymore. It was here, in my backyard.

Chapter 4: The First Attack

I stood frozen, gripping the hammer tighter, as the man kept stumbling toward me. His eyes were blank, no recognition, no emotion, just a slow, hungry advance. The blood around his mouth glistened in the fading light. He wasn't the first sign of trouble, but he was the first tangible evidence that everything we'd seen on the news wasn't just happening in distant cities. It was here. It was real. And it was at my doorstep.

"Annie," I called back, not taking my eyes off the man. "Get the boys upstairs. Now."

I could hear the panic in her voice, but she didn't argue. "Colt! Nash! Upstairs, now!" she shouted as she hurried them inside. The back door slammed shut, and I heard the deadbolt slide into place. Good. I needed them safe, and right now, that was inside.

The thing inched closer. Its breath was wet and rattling, sending chills up my spine. Its arms hung loose, one twisted at a weird angle. Broken, maybe. Didn't matter. Pain wasn't part of its world anymore.

"Stay back!" I shouted again, but it was pointless. He wasn't listening. His steps quickened, and suddenly, he lunged.

My Marine reflexes kicked in. I sidestepped, heart pounding, and swung the hammer with everything I had. Crack. It hit his skull, but he didn't go down. He turned, eyes wild, a growl ripping from his throat.

I backed up, keeping my grip tight on the hammer, my mind racing. This thing was stronger than it should've been. No normal man should still be standing after a hit like that.

He lunged again, but this time I was ready. I swung the hammer downward, smashing it against his skull with all my strength. The impact sent a shockwave through my arm, and this time, the man crumpled to the ground.

For a moment, I just stood there, panting, staring at the body. The light was nearly gone, and all I could see was a twisted, broken form lying in the grass, blood pooling beneath him. My stomach churned, but I swallowed down the bile rising in my throat. This wasn't the time to lose it.

I wiped the sweat from my forehead with my sleeve and backed toward the house, keeping my eyes on the still form. When I reached the door, I slid inside, locking it behind me.

Annie was in the living room, arms wrapped around the boys. Nash's face was pale, and Colt looked shaken. I must've looked like hell, blood and dirt smeared on my shirt, but I didn't have time to worry about that.

"What happened?" Colt asked, his voice tight with fear.

I shook my head, trying to catch my breath. "We've got a problem," I said, my voice steadier than I felt. "That wasn't just some drunk guy wandering around. He was... gone. I don't know what to call it, but it wasn't human anymore."

Nash's eyes went wide. "Was it like the people in the videos?"

"Yeah," I admitted. "Exactly like that."

Annie put a hand on my arm. "What are we going to do, Frank? This isn't just the news anymore. It's here."

I nodded, my mind already running through the next steps. "We're going to fortify. We need to secure the house as best we can. I don't know how fast this is spreading, but we can't take chances. Not now."

Colt was already on his feet, his fear starting to shift into action. "What do you need me to do?"

I looked at him, grateful for his willingness to step up, even though he was only eighteen. "We're going to finish barricading the windows and doors. I'll need your help with the front entrance."

Annie turned to Nash. "You stay with me, honey. We'll get more supplies together anything we might need if we have to stay in here for a while."

I glanced out the window, the darkness outside thick and oppressive. The wind had picked up again, rattling the windows like an ominous warning. Time wasn't on our side.

Colt and I worked quickly, hammering plywood across the remaining windows. Every bang of the hammer felt like a countdown, the sound echoing in the stillness of the house. The adrenaline pushed me forward, but I couldn't shake the dread creeping up the back of my neck. That thing in the backyard had been alone—but for how long? And how many more were out there?

We finished with the windows and moved to the front door. I pulled a heavy dresser from the hallway and wedged it in front of the entrance, tipping it sideways to block the door. Colt helped me push it into place, both of us straining under the weight.

"That should hold for a while," I said, wiping sweat from my brow. "But we're not going to rely on just one barricade. We're setting up a watch."

Colt looked at me, his face pale but determined. "A watch?"

I nodded. "One of us stays awake at all times. Two-hour shifts. We can't afford to be caught off guard. Not with... whatever's out there."

"I'll take the first shift," he said quietly, surprising me.

I studied him for a moment. He was scared, but there was resolve in his eyes. "Alright," I said. "But I'll take the next one. If anything happens, anything, you wake me. Got it?"

He nodded.

We gathered in the living room, setting up a makeshift camp with sleeping bags and pillows. The boys stayed close to Annie, but I could see how the day had weighed on all of them. None of us had the luxury of sleep, but we had to try.

CANE BAY ZOMBIES

The emergency broadcast was still flashing across the TV screen, urging people to stay indoors, to avoid contact with anyone showing signs of illness. But I knew, deep down, that wasn't going to be enough for much longer.

As I sat down, my back against the wall, I watched Colt take his place by the front window, his phone in hand, glancing outside every few minutes. I knew what he was feeling that gnawing uncertainty, the weight of responsibility pressing down on him. But he was strong. I had to believe that.

The wind howled outside, and somewhere, faintly in the distance, I thought I heard something else. A low, haunting moan. My chest tightened.

We were prepared for tonight, but I didn't know what tomorrow would bring.

And as the storm raged outside, I knew one thing for sure: this was just the beginning.

Chapter 5: Holding the Line

The house was silent except for the occasional creak of wood settling and the faint whistling of the wind outside. I had barely slept. My body was exhausted, but my mind refused to shut off. I glanced over at Colt, still sitting by the front window, his face lit by the soft glow of his phone. He hadn't looked away from that window for more than a few seconds. I could see the tension in his shoulders, his grip tight around the baseball bat he'd taken from his room. It wasn't much, but it was something.

Nash was curled up beside Annie on the couch, his small frame wrapped in a blanket. I'd told them to sleep, though I knew it wouldn't last long. None of us could really rest, not with what we'd seen. Not with what we knew was out there.

I got up quietly and walked over to Colt, placing a hand on his shoulder. He didn't flinch, but his eyes were wide, a mix of fear and determination etched into his face.

"Anything?" I asked, keeping my voice low.

He shook his head. "No. But I keep hearing things, Dad. Like… noises, but I can't tell if it's just the wind or…" He trailed off, his jaw tightening.

I knew what he meant. The wind carried strange sounds now—things that could be written off as branches scraping against windows or animals moving in the underbrush. But something in those noises felt different. More deliberate. The way the dead man in our backyard had moved played over and over in my mind.

"You did good, Colt," I said. "It's my turn. Go get some rest. We need you sharp for tomorrow."

Colt hesitated, then nodded. He handed me the bat, a wordless exchange between us, before heading over to where Annie and Nash were lying. He sank down beside them, still clutching his phone, but within minutes, his eyes closed.

I took his place at the window, moving the curtain just enough to peer outside. The moon was high now, casting long shadows across the yard. The body was still out there, lying just beyond the tree line, barely visible in the darkness. I knew I'd have to deal with it at some point—move it, bury it, something. But not tonight.

The sky was cloudless, and the neighborhood was eerily still. No lights in any of the nearby houses, no cars driving by. It was like the world had been turned off, and we were the only ones left.

Suddenly, I heard something, a soft rustle, just beyond the window. My grip tightened on the bat, my heart pounding in my chest. I stayed perfectly still, straining to listen.

The sound came again, this time closer. Slow, dragging footsteps, like something was shuffling through the grass.

I glanced back at the others. Annie was still asleep, her hand resting protectively on Nash's arm. I knew I had to keep quiet. I didn't want to wake them unless I had to.

Slowly, I edged toward the back door, bat in hand, keeping my steps light. I could hear it more clearly now. The footsteps weren't wandering; they were deliberate, moving toward the house. I swallowed hard, adrenaline spiking through my veins.

I pressed my ear against the door, listening. The shuffling had stopped. But there was something else... breathing. Ragged, uneven breathing, like someone struggling to stay upright.

With one hand, I carefully unlocked the deadbolt and eased the door open just a crack. The night air rushed in, cool and damp. I kept the bat raised, ready for whatever was on the other side.

Then I saw him.

A man. No, a thing. Stood at the edge of the front porch, its head lolling to the side, its skin pale and slack. Its mouth hung open, revealing teeth slick with blood. For a moment, we stood there, frozen in the stillness of the night, just staring at each other.

But I wasn't sure he even saw me. There was no recognition in its eyes, no acknowledgment of anything human. Just hunger.

Suddenly, it lurched forward, arms reaching out. I stepped back, heart racing, and slammed the door shut, locking it in place.

The creature's body slammed against the door with a sickening thud. I braced myself against it, holding it shut as it clawed at the wood, snarling and growling like a wild animal. Its strength was terrifying, the door rattling with each hit.

Colt was up in an instant, bat in hand. "Dad, what is it?" he whispered, his voice barely audible over the noise.

"One of them," I muttered, pressing harder against the door. "It found us."

Annie stirred, waking up. "What's going on?" she asked, her voice thick with sleep.

"Stay with Nash," I ordered, my tone sharper than I intended. "Colt, grab the hammer. Now!"

Colt sprinted toward the kitchen, where we had left the toolbox after boarding up the windows. The creature outside slammed against the door again, harder this time. I could hear its nails scratching against the wood, desperate to get in.

Colt rushed back, handing me the hammer. "What do we do?"

I gripped the hammer tight, my mind racing. The back door wasn't going to hold if this thing kept pounding against it. We had to act now.

"Go around," I said, my voice steady but urgent. "Through the garage. We'll flank it. You get its attention, and I'll take it down."

Colt's eyes widened, but he didn't argue. "Okay."

I slipped out through the garage, moving as quickly and quietly as I could. Colt followed close behind, both of us armed and ready. We crept around the side of the house, the sound of the creature's growls growing louder as we approached.

When we rounded the corner, I saw it, still slamming itself against the door, its body jerking violently with each impact. Colt and I exchanged a look, a silent agreement.

"Hey!" Colt shouted, his voice ringing out in the quiet night.

The creature froze, its head snapping toward him. Its eyes locked onto Colt, and with a guttural snarl, it charged.

I didn't hesitate. The moment its back was turned, I rushed forward, swinging the hammer with all the force I had. The blow connected with a sickening crack, and the thing crumpled to the ground.

I stood over the body, panting, the hammer still clutched in my hand. The night was silent again, save for the ragged sound of my own breathing.

Colt walked over slowly, his face pale but resolute. "Did we... Did we kill it?"

I crouched down, pressing two fingers to the creature's neck. There was no pulse, nothing. I looked up at Colt. "Yeah," I said. "It's done."

We stood there for a moment, the reality of what we'd just done sinking in. This was our new life now, fighting to survive, protecting each other from the nightmare that had come to our doorstep.

"We need to move the body," I said quietly, already thinking ahead. "Before it attracts more."

Colt nodded, swallowing hard. "Okay."

As we dragged the body toward the tree line, I couldn't shake the feeling that this was just the beginning. There would be more. We weren't safe. Not yet.

But as I glanced at Colt, his jaw set, his hands steady, I felt a small spark of hope. We'd make it. We had to. For Annie, for Nash, for all of us.

We weren't just surviving anymore.

We were fighting back.

Chapter 6: A Plan of Action

The morning light filtered through the cracks in the boarded-up windows, casting faint slivers of sunshine across the living room. None of us had really slept, not since the thing had slammed itself against our back door. I was dead tired, but the rush of adrenaline hadn't worn off yet, keeping me wired and alert.

Colt was already up, sipping from a cup of water at the kitchen counter. He hadn't said much since we took out the creature last night. I could see him replaying it in his head over and over, probably wondering if it was real or just some kind of nightmare.

Annie was next to Nash on the couch, gently rubbing his back as he stirred awake. She hadn't asked for details after the chaos of the night, but I could tell she had questions, ones I wasn't sure I could answer yet.

I ran a hand over my face and stood up, stretching my back. "We need a plan."

Colt set his cup down, looking at me. Annie, hearing the change in my voice, sat up straighter. Nash blinked the sleep from his eyes, sensing the shift in the room.

"What do we do now, Frank?" Annie asked, her voice soft but steady. "We can't just stay here and wait for more of those things to show up."

"I know," I replied. I'd been turning it over in my head all night. "We need to figure out our next steps. We've got supplies for a few days, maybe a week at most. But if this thing, whatever it is, keeps spreading, we'll need more than just food and water."

Colt frowned, arms crossed over his chest. "How bad do you think it's going to get?"

I glanced out the window. The neighborhood was still quiet, but that didn't mean anything. The calm before the storm could last hours or days, and I wasn't about to gamble on either. "Bad. We need to assume that the situation is only going to get worse."

Annie stood up, wrapping her arms around herself. "Do you think we should leave? Maybe we should go to my parents' place. It's farther out, more rural. We could wait it out there."

I shook my head, already knowing what I had to say. "No. Right now, we stay put. We've got more control over our surroundings here. Out on the road, there are too many unknowns. We don't know how widespread this is, and the last thing we need is to get caught in a mess somewhere between here and there."

Annie nodded, though I could see the worry in her eyes. "What about Colt and Nash? The schools are closed. They won't have anywhere to go."

"I don't think this is just about schools or a couple of sick people anymore," I said grimly. "This is something else entirely. And until we know how bad it is, we have to focus on protecting ourselves."

Nash sat up fully now, rubbing his eyes. "Dad, are those people... zombies?" His voice was small, like he didn't want to say the word out loud, afraid that doing so would make it real.

I sighed, crouching down to be at eye level with him. "I don't know what they are, Nash. But what I do know is that they're dangerous. And we're going to do everything we can to stay safe. Okay?"

He nodded, still looking scared but trusting me. That trust was a weight on my shoulders, and I felt the responsibility of it in every fiber of my being.

Colt shifted on his feet. "So, what's the plan? We can't just sit here doing nothing."

I nodded. "First, we fortify this place properly. More than just the doors. I want every window secured. We'll start by taking stock of what we have. After that, I'll show you how to barricade the doors and windows with what's in the garage. We're also going to need to make an emergency exit plan. In case we have to leave fast."

Annie furrowed her brow. "And what if we have to leave? Where do we go?"

"Depends on what happens next," I said, pulling out the map I'd grabbed from the truck. "But my first thought is to head west, away from the city. Find somewhere off the main roads, where people won't think to look. We could try to make it to your parents eventually, but that's secondary. First, we lock down here."

I spread the map out on the table, tracing a finger over the highways and back roads around Summerville. "This development is pretty isolated already, which works in our favor. Fewer ways in, means fewer threats. But it also means we could be cut off if things go south."

Colt stepped closer, looking over my shoulder. "What if more of those... Things show up? We barely handled one."

"That's why we prepare," I said, meeting his eyes. "We're not going to be caught off guard again. We'll make sure we're ready for anything."

Annie touched my arm, her voice low. "Frank, what about the neighbors? The people across the street, down the block. Shouldn't we warn them?"

I looked at her, considering. The idea of going door to door, trying to explain what we'd seen, wasn't exactly appealing. People might not believe us. Or worse, they might panic.

But Annie was right. We couldn't just sit on this. "We'll check on them," I said finally. "At least the ones closest to us. See if they're safe, and maybe form a plan together. But we have to be careful. We can't trust everyone."

Colt raised an eyebrow. "You really think people will turn on each other that fast?"

"I hope not," I said, though deep down, I knew better. Desperation did things to people. I'd seen it in the Corps more times than I wanted to remember. "But we can't take any chances."

Nash pulled his blanket tighter around himself. "Do you think it's just here, or is it everywhere?"

"I don't know, buddy," I said quietly. "We'll have to wait and see."

We spent the rest of the morning preparing the house. Colt helped me move furniture in front of the doors and windows, while Annie took stock of our supplies. We had enough food and water for a few days, maybe a week if we rationed carefully. Nash stayed close to Annie, helping where he could but mostly watching, his wide eyes taking in everything.

By early afternoon, the house was as fortified as we could make it with what we had. The windows were blocked, and the doors reinforced. I'd even rigged up some noise traps, empty cans tied to strings, positioned near the back and front doors. They'd rattle if anything got too close, giving us some warning.

It wasn't perfect, but it was something.

As the sun climbed higher, I stood by the front window again, staring out at the empty street. Nothing moved. No birds, no cars, no people. It was as if the entire world had decided to hold its breath, waiting for whatever came next.

Annie came up behind me, resting a hand on my shoulder. "Do you think we'll be okay?"

I looked down at her, taking her hand in mine. "We'll be okay," I said, though I wasn't sure if I was saying it for her or for myself. "We've got each other, and that's what matters."

She smiled, though it didn't quite reach her eyes. "I just want the boys to be safe."

"We're going to keep them safe," I promised, meaning every word. "No matter what." And as I stood there, looking out over our quiet little corner of the world, I couldn't shake the feeling that something worse was coming.

The storm hadn't passed. It had only just begun.

Chapter 7: The World Closing In

The stillness of the neighborhood was unnerving. The wind that had picked up the day before was now a gentle breeze, pushing dry leaves across the road. The eerie silence of Cane Bay Plantation felt like a warning, like the world had been sucked into a vacuum and all that was left was the ticking of time, inching closer to something we couldn't stop.

After spending hours fortifying the house, we needed to check on the neighbors. Annie wasn't thrilled about it, and neither was I, to be honest, but there was no way around it. If we had any chance of riding this thing out, we couldn't be completely isolated. And if the neighborhood had turned into something out of a horror movie, we needed to know sooner rather than later.

I pulled the door open slowly, my eyes scanning the street as I stepped out. Colt followed behind me, holding the old baseball bat I'd handed him earlier. It wasn't much, but it was better than nothing.

"Stay close," I said under my breath, knowing he would, but also understanding that I needed to say it anyway.

We crossed the lawn, heading toward the Wilsons' house, two doors down. They'd been friendly enough since we moved in, a retired couple in their 60s. I hadn't seen any movement from their place in the last two days, though. Their windows were dark, and their driveway was empty.

I glanced back toward our house, seeing Annie peeking through the front window, Nash beside her. She gave me a tight smile, worry etched into her face.

Colt stepped up onto the Wilsons' porch, hesitating at the door. "You think they're still here?"

"I don't know," I said, giving the door a gentle knock. The sound echoed through the house beyond it, unnaturally loud in the quiet morning air.

We waited.

Nothing.

I knocked again, harder this time. "Mr. Wilson? It's Frank. You in there?"

Colt shifted nervously on his feet. "Maybe they left."

"Maybe," I said, but something felt off. There wasn't the usual clutter on their front porch, the patio furniture was gone, their welcome mat rolled up. I frowned, stepping back to get a better look. "They didn't leave. They're still here."

Colt shot me a confused look. "How do you know?"

I pointed to their front windows. "No one boards up their house and rolls up their mat unless they're planning to stay. It's like they're trying to look like they're not home."

Colt nodded, understanding, his grip tightening on the bat.

"Mr. Wilson?" I called again. "It's Frank. We're your neighbors. We just wanted to check if you're okay."

For a few seconds, there was silence. Then, from inside, a rustling noise. I exchanged a look with Colt and raised my hand to knock again when the door creaked open an inch.

Mr. Wilson's face appeared in the small crack, pale and haggard. He looked like he hadn't slept in days, his eyes sunken and bloodshot.

"Frank," he rasped, glancing behind me like he was expecting someone else to be there. "What are you doing here?"

"I came to see if you're alright," I said, lowering my voice. "You and Mrs. Wilson okay?"

He hesitated, his eyes flicking toward Colt and the bat he held. "You shouldn't be out here," he whispered, his voice barely audible. "You should go back inside."

"What's going on?" I asked, trying to keep him talking. "Have you seen anything strange?"

"Strange?" Mr. Wilson gave a dry, humorless laugh. "This whole thing's strange. But it's more than that, Frank. It's not just sickness. It's something else. People are changing. You can't trust anyone."

"What do you mean, 'changing'?" Colt asked, stepping closer.

Mr. Wilson's eyes darted around again. "I mean exactly what I said. We saw... we saw one of them yesterday. Out in the street. It wasn't human, Frank. Not anymore."

His words sent a chill down my spine. He wasn't talking about a sick person. He was talking about the thing that had tried to break into our house last night.

"You and Mrs. Wilson have enough supplies?" I asked, switching gears. "Water, food, something to defend yourselves with?"

He nodded weakly. "We've got some canned stuff. Water. I've got my shotgun."

"That's good," I said, feeling a little relieved. "Stay inside, keep the doors locked. If anything happens, you call us. Got it?"

He nodded again, but his eyes were distant, unfocused like he wasn't sure how long he could keep it together. "Frank," he said quietly, "if you see them, those things, don't hesitate. They're not human anymore."

Before I could say anything else, he shut the door, the locks clicking into place. I stared at the door for a moment, then turned to Colt.

"We need to be prepared for whatever this is," I said quietly. "Because I think it's getting worse."

Colt nodded, his jaw set in that determined way he had when he was bracing himself for something.

As we walked back toward our house, my mind raced through the possibilities. If the Wilsons had seen one of those things, how many more were out there? How much time did we have before this place became overrun?

The moment we stepped back inside, Annie rushed over. "What did they say? Are they okay?"

"They're fine," I said, but I couldn't keep the tension out of my voice. "But Mr. Wilson confirmed what we suspected. Whatever's happening, it's not just a virus. It's changing people."

Annie's face paled, and she pulled Nash closer to her. "So, what do we do now?"

I sat down at the kitchen table, feeling the weight of the moment pressing down on me. "We do what we've been doing. We stay prepared. We protect each other. But we have to assume things are going to get worse."

Colt dropped the bat onto the floor and slumped into a chair, rubbing his eyes. "How much worse?"

I looked at him, at Nash, and then at Annie. "I don't know. But we're not waiting around to find out. We stay alert. And if things go south, we're ready to move."

Nash, who had been quiet this whole time, finally spoke up. "Dad, if people are turning into... into monsters... are we safe here?"

I leaned forward, trying to find the right words. "We're as safe as we can be, Nash. We've done everything we can to make sure of that. But if things change, we'll adapt. That's what we do. We protect each other, no matter what."

Annie came over, her hand resting on my shoulder. "And if we have to leave?"

"Then we leave," I said, standing up. "But only if we have no other choice."

The room fell into a heavy silence. Everyone knew what that meant. The house we had turned into our fortress might not hold forever. But for now, it was home, and it was the safest place we had.

CANE BAY ZOMBIES

I glanced at the window again, my eyes scanning the street. It still looked quiet, but now, I wasn't so sure. Something was coming. Something darker than the stillness outside.

And when it came, we had to be ready.

Chapter 8: The Edge of Normal

The day dragged on with an unnatural sense of calm that only deepened the tension in the house. We spent the afternoon keeping busy. More fortifications, more planning, more of the same anxious routine that had set in since the news broke. But beneath it all was a current of fear none of us could shake.

Annie was in the kitchen, taking inventory of our food and supplies. Nash helped her count cans and boxes, the clinking of metal on metal the only noise that broke the silence. Colt sat by the window in the living room, his eyes scanning the empty street outside. Every now and then, he'd turn to look at me, like he was waiting for orders.

I stood in the doorway, looking out across the yard. The sky was a dull gray, not quite overcast but far from sunny. The kind of sky that made you feel like something was wrong even if you couldn't put your finger on it. I hadn't seen anyone else in the neighborhood since our trip to the Wilsons'. No kids playing outside, no joggers on the sidewalk. Just stillness.

But something was coming. I could feel it in my gut.

Colt shifted in his seat and cleared his throat. "Dad, you think the Wilsons are gonna make it?"

I turned to him, his face lined with the kind of worry that didn't belong on a 18-year-old kid. "I hope so, Colt. But we've gotta focus on ourselves right now."

Colt nodded, but I could see he wasn't satisfied with the answer. None of us were. We were all thinking the same thing. How much longer could we keep pretending things would be okay?

"I'm going to check on them again," I said after a moment, grabbing the pistol I'd tucked under my belt earlier. Annie looked up from the kitchen, her brow furrowing.

"Frank, you just checked on them yesterday. They know how to reach us if something happens."

"I know," I replied, tucking a spare magazine into my back pocket. "But I need to get a lay of the land. Make sure there's nothing going on we're not seeing."

She didn't like it, but she didn't argue. She knew me well enough to know when I had my mind made up.

"I'll come with you," Colt said, standing up from his chair.

I looked at him, weighing the idea. His eyes were determined, but there was a flicker of unease underneath. I didn't want him out there, not really, but I also knew it wasn't smart to go alone.

"Alright," I said, nodding. "But you follow my lead, got it?"

He grabbed the bat again, giving it a few test swings as we headed for the front door.

"Be careful," Annie called after us, her voice tight with worry.

"We will," I assured her, though I wasn't sure how much that promise was worth anymore.

The street was eerily quiet when we stepped outside. Not a single car passed by, not even the usual sounds of distant traffic from the highway. Just the wind rustling through the trees and the occasional distant bark of a dog.

We walked in silence toward the Wilsons' house again, my eyes scanning every corner, every shadow. There was no telling what was hiding out there now. The thought made my fingers twitch around the grip of the pistol.

When we got to the front porch, I noticed something was different. The front door was cracked open, just a sliver. My heart sank.

Colt noticed it too. "Dad..."

"I see it," I said, motioning for him to stay close behind me. I stepped up to the door, pushing it open with the barrel of the gun.

The house was dark, the air inside thick with the smell of something foul. I held my breath, waving Colt to follow me in as quietly as possible.

"Mr. Wilson?" I called, my voice barely above a whisper.

There was no answer. The only sound was the creaking of the floorboards beneath our feet and the faint hum of the refrigerator. We moved through the hallway, careful not to touch anything. It felt like we were trespassing on a grave.

In the living room, I found what I was afraid of. Mrs. Wilson was slumped over on the couch, her body limp and pale, eyes half-open but unseeing. Her hands were coated in dried blood.

"Jesus..." Colt whispered, stepping back. His face had gone white.

I knelt beside her, checking for a pulse, though I knew it was a futile effort. She was long gone. And whatever had done this wasn't far behind.

"Come on," I whispered to Colt, pulling him toward the hallway that led to the back of the house.

The door to the master bedroom was open. Inside, I could see Mr. Wilson, lying face down on the floor, a shotgun beside him. The stench of blood and death hung heavy in the air.

"Dad..." Colt's voice wavered as he stared at the scene. "What happened here?"

I moved forward, cautiously stepping over Mr. Wilson's body to check for any sign of life. I could hear Colt breathing hard behind me, struggling to keep it together.

But it wasn't the blood, or even the bodies, that worried me the most.

There were scratches on the walls, deep gouges in the drywall that looked like someone, or something, had clawed its way through. And beside Mr. Wilson's body was a trail of blood leading toward the back door, which was hanging open.

Something had come through here. And it had left.

"We need to get out of here," I said, my voice steady but low. I grabbed Colt's arm, pulling him toward the front of the house. "Now."

Colt didn't argue. We moved fast, retracing our steps through the hallway and out the front door, back into the quiet of the street. The moment we were outside, I slammed the door shut behind us, locking it like it would somehow keep whatever had happened inside from spreading.

Colt was shaking, his knuckles white as he gripped the bat. "What... what was that?"

I didn't answer right away. I didn't have an answer to give him. Whatever had come through the Wilsons' house wasn't just sickness. It was something worse. Something violent.

"We need to get home," I said, my voice sharp. "Stay close."

We moved quickly down the sidewalk, the air around us suddenly feeling too thin, too quiet. My mind raced, trying to piece together what we had just seen, but the only thing that made sense was that we were no longer alone in Cane Bay.

By the time we reached our front door, I could feel Annie's eyes on us from the window. I knocked twice, our signal and she opened the door, ushering us inside.

"What happened?" she asked, her voice tight with panic. "What did you see?"

I shook my head, looking over at Colt, who had gone pale and silent. "It's bad," I said simply. "The Wilsons are gone. And something else came through their house. We're not alone here."

Annie's hand flew to her mouth, and Nash looked up from the kitchen, wide-eyed.

"We need to be ready," I said, locking the door behind us. "Because whatever it was, it's out there now. And it's coming."

C.F. HAYES

The walls of our house suddenly felt too thin, the windows too fragile. We had fortified everything, but somehow, it didn't feel like enough anymore.

The world wasn't just closing in. It was here.

Chapter 9: A Visitor at Dusk

The rest of the day passed in a haze. Even though we were back home, the unease from the Wilsons' house followed us like a shadow. Colt didn't say much after we got back. He sat by the window, his bat across his lap, eyes distant. Annie could sense something was wrong but didn't press him. She focused on keeping Nash occupied, though I could tell her mind was running the same race as mine: What was out there? And when would it come knocking on our door?

I kept replaying the scene in my head. Mrs. Wilson's cold, lifeless body on the couch, the scratches on the walls, the blood trail leading out the back door. It didn't fit into any of the neat boxes I'd made for this situation. This wasn't just about people getting sick anymore. This was something else.

The house was silent as the afternoon gave way to evening. The sky had darkened, heavy clouds rolling in from the coast, casting a gray pall over everything. I stood by the back door, staring out into the yard, my eyes scanning the tree line that bordered our property. Every rustle of leaves felt like a warning, every gust of wind a whisper that something was out there, watching.

The sound of footsteps behind me broke my concentration. Annie came up, her face drawn tight with worry. She looked tired, the weight of the last few days bearing down on her shoulders. I felt a pang of guilt. I hadn't said much to reassure her, hadn't really told her what we'd seen at the Wilsons'. It was too much to process, and I didn't want to scare her more than she already was.

"Frank," she said softly, "we can't stay like this much longer. The boys... they're scared. I'm scared." Her eyes searched mine, looking for something, anything, that would make sense of the chaos outside.

"I know," I said, my voice low. "We'll figure it out. But right now, we need to stay alert. It's not safe out there."

She glanced at the backyard, her gaze lingering on the darkening sky. "Do you think... Do you think we should leave? Maybe head toward the mountains or something? Get away from all this?"

I had thought about that. Leaving Cane Bay, getting out of Charleston altogether. But something kept me here, something gnawing at the back of my mind that told me it wouldn't be safer anywhere else. Whatever was happening wasn't just local. It was bigger. And running might not keep us from it.

"We're safer here for now," I said, trying to sound confident. "We've got supplies, we know the area. Leaving would mean exposing ourselves to whatever's out there. We stick it out. At least until we know more."

Annie nodded, though I could tell she wasn't convinced. "And what about what you saw at the Wilsons'? Are we just going to sit here and wait for that to come to us?"

I didn't have an answer for that. The truth was, I didn't know how to prepare for what was coming. Fortifying the house had felt like a good start, but after seeing those claw marks, it felt woefully inadequate. Still, I couldn't let that fear show. I had to be strong for her. For Colt and Nash.

"Let's just stay focused," I said, giving her hand a squeeze. "One step at a time."

Suddenly, Colt's voice cut through the air from the living room. "Dad! Someone's outside."

I spun around, my pulse quickening. Colt was standing by the window, peering through the blinds. I crossed the room in three quick strides, grabbing my pistol from the table. My heart pounded in my chest as I reached him.

"Where?" I asked, leaning over him to get a better look.

Colt pointed toward the street. Sure enough, there was a figure standing at the end of our driveway, barely visible in the fading light. They weren't moving, just standing there, staring at the house.

"I don't like this," Colt muttered, gripping the bat tighter.

I didn't either. The figure wasn't dressed in tattered clothes like the news had shown of the infected. No wild movements or erratic behavior. Just stillness. Watching. Waiting.

"Annie, get the boys upstairs," I said, my voice firm but low. She didn't argue, taking Nash's hand and heading toward the staircase.

"What are you gonna do?" Colt asked, his voice wavering slightly.

"Stay here. Keep an eye on the back door. I'm gonna see what this is."

He looked at me like he wanted to say something, but he nodded instead. His jaw was clenched tight, and I could see the nerves playing out behind his eyes.

I slid the front door open just enough to step outside, keeping the pistol low but ready. The figure was still there, standing in the middle of the street, the faint glow of the streetlight casting long shadows across the ground.

"Hey!" I called out, keeping my voice steady but loud enough to be heard. "What do you want?"

For a moment, there was no response. Then the figure moved, stepping closer, their hands up in what looked like a gesture of peace.

"I'm not infected," a voice called out. A woman's voice, tired and ragged but clear.

I stayed where I was, not lowering the gun. "Who are you?"

The woman stopped about ten feet away, still holding her hands up. I could see her more clearly now. She looked to be in her thirties, wearing a faded green jacket and jeans that were caked with mud. Her face was gaunt, eyes hollowed with exhaustion. She didn't look sick—but she didn't look good, either.

"My name's Sarah," she said, her voice shaking slightly. "I've been walking for days. I don't have anywhere else to go."

"Where are you coming from?" I asked, keeping my voice hard. Trust didn't come easy now, not when we had no idea what was happening beyond our little bubble.

"North Charleston," she replied, her eyes darting between me and the house. "It's bad there. Real bad. I was with a group, but we got separated. I... I don't know if any of them made it."

I glanced back at the house, at Colt watching from the window. A part of me wanted to turn her away, tell her to keep walking. We didn't know her, didn't know what she might bring into our home. But there was another part of me, the part that remembered the Corps and the duty we had to each other, that couldn't just leave her out there.

"Are you alone?" I asked, my grip on the pistol tightening slightly.

She nodded. "Yeah. Just me."

I lowered the gun, but only slightly. "Alright. You can come inside. But if you're lying to me if you try anything"

"I'm not," she interrupted, her voice pleading. "I swear, I'm not. I just need somewhere safe."

I gestured toward the door. "Let's go."

As we stepped inside, Colt tensed, the bat still gripped tightly in his hands. Annie appeared at the top of the stairs, her eyes widening when she saw Sarah.

"Who's that?" Annie's voice was tight.

"A visitor," I said flatly. "She's been out there for days, or so she says. We'll keep watch, just in case."

Annie nodded, though she didn't look thrilled about the idea. Nash peeked out from behind her, his eyes wide with curiosity and fear.

Sarah stood in the entryway, her hands still raised slightly like she was afraid to let them down. She looked at each of us, her expression a mix of relief and dread.

"I'm not here to cause trouble," she said quietly. "I just want to survive, same as you."

"We'll see," I replied, closing the door behind her. "For now, you'll stay here. But don't think for a second we won't be watching you."

Sarah nodded, her shoulders sagging with exhaustion. She looked like she was ready to collapse.

"Colt," I said, "get her some water. We'll figure the rest out as we go."

As he went to the kitchen, I caught Annie's eye. She didn't say anything, but I could tell she had the same doubts I did. We had taken a chance letting this stranger in, and only time would tell if it was the right call.

For now, we had more to worry about than just the infected. We had to decide who we could trust.

Chapter 10: The World Outside Our Door

As the days passed, the fog of uncertainty that had blanketed us in those first hours began to clear, at least when it came to understanding what was happening out there. The radio stations had stopped broadcasting their usual programs and were running emergency updates around the clock. Cable news was no better if you could even get a signal. But the bits and pieces of information we could piece together painted a picture of chaos far larger than we'd imagined.

Across the U.S., cities were falling one by one, each succumbing to a rapid and violent spread of the infection. The virus, whatever it was, had swept through major metropolitan areas first. New York, Chicago, Los Angeles... they had all been hit hard. Quarantine zones had been attempted in the beginning, but as it became clear how quickly the infected could turn and how violent they became, it was impossible to contain. The media started referring to it as the "Collapse."

Federal and state governments scrambled, trying to enforce martial law and restore some kind of order, but the infection spread faster than they could react. Soldiers and law enforcement officers were on the front lines of a war they weren't equipped to fight. Within days, the East Coast had effectively fallen, with only pockets of resistance remaining. Areas where the infection hadn't fully reached or where survivors had banded together and fortified.

South Carolina was no different. Charleston, being a historic and tourism-heavy city, became one of the first areas to experience mass panic. The infection had started slowly rumors of strange outbreaks, and people behaving erratically. Then it exploded, seemingly overnight. Hospitals were overwhelmed. The highways were clogged with people trying to flee to God-knows-where, creating choke points that turned into death traps as the infected overtook the cars stuck in traffic. By the time the National Guard had been fully mobilized, it was too late. Reports came in of neighborhoods being overrun, military checkpoints failing, and the infected spreading out into the Lowcountry.

With the coast in shambles, those who could move inland, trying to escape the carnage, headed to smaller towns and rural areas. Summerville, being a large suburban town just outside of Charleston, quickly became a refuge for the displaced, but it wouldn't stay that way for long.

Summerville had always been a buffer between the chaos of Charleston and the quieter stretches of South Carolina. The town thrived on its mix of small-town charm and suburban sprawl. But that charm started to fade the moment the first reports of the infected in Charleston hit the airwaves.

In the first few days, the Summerville police department and county officials set up checkpoints on the major roads leading in and out of town. There were attempts to block traffic coming from Charleston, but with thousands of panicked people trying to flee, there was only so much they could do. The infection spread not just through bites but through exposure to the blood and bodily fluids of the infected. It was chaotic. For every family that made it out of Charleston and hoped for safety in Summerville, there was someone bringing the infection with them.

The Summerville Medical Center became a hot zone, with injured civilians and infected victims crowding the emergency room. Doctors and nurses worked around the clock, but they weren't prepared for the kind of violence and illness that was breaking down the doors. Eventually, they had to close the hospital entirely.

In town, the grocery stores, gas stations, and pharmacies were picked clean within a matter of days. People looted what they could, taking supplies, weapons, and anything they thought might help them survive. And when the shelves were empty, desperation set in. People began turning on each other. Neighborhoods that had once been safe havens turned into battlegrounds, where survivors fought to protect their homes from raiders and the infected.

The National Guard set up a command post near the Charleston Air Force Base, but even they were spread too thin. Their radio broadcasts were clear: If you were still in Summerville, stay inside, fortify your home, and don't trust anyone you didn't know. The infection was moving too fast for them to keep up, and containment was no longer an option.

Here in Cane Bay, things felt different, quieter, somehow. The development was relatively new, and its sprawling, suburban layout gave it the feel of a gated community. Families had moved here for the peace and quiet, the good schools, and the relative isolation from the hustle and bustle of the city. But that isolation was now both a blessing and a curse.

On the surface, Cane Bay still looked like it had before everything fell apart. The neatly trimmed lawns, the row of mailboxes, the quiet streets. It all gave off a veneer of normalcy. But just beneath the surface, the cracks were starting to show.

With the grocery stores and supplies in Summerville running low, the residents of Cane Bay began to realize that they were cut off. We had stocked up when we could, but it wouldn't last forever. Those of us who had been smart enough to prepare had what we needed for now, but not everyone had. Some houses were already empty, families that had left in a panic, hoping to find safety elsewhere. Others had barricaded themselves inside, hoping that the infection would pass them by.

We weren't hearing as much from our neighbors anymore. The occasional face at the window, the distant sound of a dog barking, but not much else. Even the development's Facebook group, once bustling with posts about block parties and neighborhood events, had gone dark. People were afraid to go outside. And rightly so.

The infection hadn't reached Cane Bay yet, at least not in the way we'd seen it hit other places. But it was coming. We knew that much. The Wilsons' house had been the first real sign, scratches on the walls, blood leading into the woods, and Mrs. Wilson dead on her couch, though not from the infection itself. The questions about what had happened to her husband lingered in the back of my mind.

We still had electricity, for now. But the outages were becoming more frequent. The local power grid couldn't be counted on for long, and when the lights went out for good, it would signal the beginning of a very different kind of survival.

The news from Sarah, the woman we had taken in, wasn't good. She'd come from North Charleston, and what she described painted a grim picture of what was creeping toward us. The infected were violent, yes, but it wasn't just mindless violence. There was a disturbing awareness to their actions, something beyond simple rage. They were hunting. They attacked in groups, moving from neighborhood to neighborhood, wiping out anyone who couldn't defend themselves.

But what was worse, far worse, was that they didn't stop. There was no getting tired, no resting. The infected kept going, day and night until there was nothing left but silence and death.

In the quieter moments, after dark, you could hear it, the faint sound of screams in the distance carried on the wind. Or the occasional crack of gunfire, growing less and less frequent. Whatever was happening in Summerville was coming our way, and we needed to be ready.

Cane Bay Plantation felt like a waiting room, safe for now, but not for long. We had our supplies. We had our weapons. But with each passing day, the tension grew thicker, and the question of when, not if, the infection would reach us weighed heavier on all of us.

Annie and I sat in the living room late that night, listening to the wind rattle the windows. The boys were asleep upstairs, but I could tell neither of us would be getting much rest. There was too much at stake, too much to consider.

"How long do you think we have?" she asked quietly, her voice barely above a whisper.

I didn't answer right away. The truth was, I didn't know. But if Sarah was right, if what we'd seen so far was only the beginning, then we didn't have long at all.

"We'll be ready," I said finally, though the words felt hollow in my mouth. "Whatever happens, we'll be ready."

She nodded, but the fear in her eyes told me she wasn't convinced.

The infection was closing in. And soon, Cane Bay would no longer be the quiet refuge it once was. It would be a battleground. And we were all that stood between our family and the darkness waiting outside.

Chapter 11: Fortifying for the Worst

By the next morning, the tension in Cane Bay was almost palpable. The thin veil of normalcy was slipping away fast. People who had once waved from their driveways or shared polite conversation at the mailbox were now unseen, hiding behind closed doors and curtains. It was like the development had turned into a ghost town overnight.

The radio was still feeding us reports of the collapse. There were fewer updates now, just brief, automated emergency broadcasts from FEMA or the National Guard. The South Carolina governor had declared a state of emergency a week ago, but whatever order they had hoped to maintain had broken down entirely. The military was struggling to hold key locations, and as for law enforcement... Well, there wasn't much of that left anymore.

I sat at the kitchen table, cleaning my rifle as the static-filled radio hummed in the background. Annie stood by the window, nervously watching the street, while Colt and Nash sat quietly on the couch. They had their screens in hand, but I knew they weren't playing games or watching videos anymore. The seriousness of the situation had finally sunk in, and they were just as anxious as the rest of us.

"We're not safe here, are we?" Nash asked, breaking the silence. He didn't look up from his phone, but his voice was small, uncertain.

I exchanged a glance with Annie before answering. "We're as safe as we can be for now. But we need to be ready for whatever comes next."

Colt, ever the skeptic, spoke up. "You think the infected are gonna make it all the way out here? I mean, we're pretty far from the city."

I paused, considering my answer. "We've already seen signs of them getting closer, Colt. The Wilsons' house wasn't an accident.

There's no guarantee we'll be spared just because we're out of the way."

He fell silent at that, his eyes flicking to the front door like he expected something to burst through at any moment.

With the neighborhood growing quieter by the day and fewer people willing to venture outside, I decided it was time to focus on making the house more secure. I'd been thinking about it for days, but now it felt urgent. If the infected made it this far, we needed to be ready to hold them off.

"Colt, Nash," I called, setting the rifle down. "You two are gonna help me board up the windows."

Annie looked over, concern etched in her face. "Do you think that's really necessary?"

I stood up and ran a hand through my hair, feeling the weight of the decision. "We can't wait until it's too late, Annie. If something happens, I want to know we did everything we could to keep the house secure.

She didn't argue, just nodded, and went to check on our supplies while I led the boys to the garage.

The stack of plywood I'd picked up during our last supply run was still sitting there, along with a set of tools I'd kept for weekend projects. I handed Colt the power drill and handed Nash a hammer and some nails. It wasn't going to be pretty, but we'd make it work. I needed the boys to feel like they were part of this—like they had some control in a situation that was spiraling fast.

We worked silently for the next couple of hours, covering the windows on the first floor and reinforcing the doors as best we could. Colt struggled at first, clearly frustrated with the clunky drill, but he caught on quickly. Nash, on the other hand, had that determined look he always got when he was trying to prove himself. He hammered each nail into the plywood like he was fending off the infected already.

Annie kept busy, taking inventory of our food, water, and first-aid supplies. We weren't in bad shape, but we weren't exactly ready for the long haul either. If things continued the way they were, there was no telling when—or if—help would arrive. We had enough to last a couple of weeks, maybe a little more if we stretched it, but after that, things would get desperate.

When we finally finished with the windows, I stepped back, wiping the sweat from my forehead. "That should do it."

Colt looked around, his eyes lingering on the boarded-up windows. "It feels... different now. Like we're trapped."

"We're not trapped," I said, though I understood what he meant. "We're making sure nothing gets in that we don't want in. This is just a precaution."

Nash stepped forward, dropping his hammer on the floor. "So, what's the plan? If they come here, I mean."

I took a breath, glancing over at Annie, who had joined us in the hallway. "If they come, we defend ourselves. We don't let them in, no matter what. And if we need to... we run."

"Run where?" Colt asked, his voice edging on disbelief.

"Out the back, into the woods. It's not ideal, but we can move faster on foot than they can. We'll take what we can carry and find somewhere safe."

With the house as fortified as we could make it, we settled in for what felt like a long wait. The days were growing shorter, and the power outages were becoming more frequent. We'd gone two days without electricity now, the food in the fridge slowly warming up, and the only light at night came from the candles and flashlights we had stockpiled.

The boys had started to ask more questions about the infected. What they were like, how they moved, what would happen if they came across one. I tried to be honest with them without scaring them too much, but the truth was, I wasn't sure myself. All I knew was what I'd seen on those grainy videos—wild, erratic behavior, extreme violence, no hesitation. They weren't human anymore, and there was no reasoning with them. It was either kill or be killed.

Colt spent more time with me now, asking to help with cleaning the guns or checking the boards on the windows. Nash, on the other hand, stayed close to Annie. He wasn't scared, he was too proud to admit that, but he wasn't as eager to be involved in the preparations as his brother. I didn't push him. He'd step up when it counted.

Every now and then, I'd catch Annie staring out the window, her expression distant. I knew she was thinking about the future, about what would happen if this became our life for good. If there was no going back. It was hard to say anything reassuring when I had those same thoughts running through my head.

It wasn't long before the signs of the infection spread through Cane Bay, too. Rumors circulated of strange figures seen wandering in the woods at night, of houses broken into, families that had simply disappeared without a trace. We hadn't heard from the neighbors in days, and when I ventured out onto the street to check the perimeter, the silence was eerie.

The few people who were still here had barricaded themselves inside just like us, waiting, hoping that the infected wouldn't find their way this far out. But deep down, we all knew it was only a matter of time.

One evening, just before dusk, we heard gunshots. Close this time. Too close. I grabbed my rifle and headed to the window, scanning the street. The boys rushed to the living room, both of them wide-eyed.

"What is it?" Colt asked, his voice urgent.

"Get back," I ordered. "Stay out of sight."

I could see movement down the street. Two figures running toward one of the houses near the entrance of the development. They were armed, but I couldn't tell who they were. Just as I was about to call Annie over, there was a crash, the sound of a door being kicked in, and then another shot. Whoever was out there, they weren't the infected. But they were just as dangerous.

Annie stood beside me, her face pale. "What do we do?"

"We stay here," I said, keeping my voice low. "We don't engage unless they come for us."

I wasn't sure who these people were. Looters, survivors, or something worse, but one thing was clear: The world outside our door was growing more dangerous by the day. And Cane Bay was no longer the safe haven it had once seemed.

Chapter 12: The New Reality

The night after the gunshots rang out, I barely slept. The quiet of the house only amplified the noise in my head, the distant memories of firefights, of watching my brothers in arms drop to the ground, and the creeping dread that this time, it wasn't soldiers I'd be facing but infected, or worse, desperate men.

In the early hours, with Annie lying beside me in restless sleep, I slipped out of bed and made my way downstairs. The glow of the few candles we had burning gave the living room an eerie, flickering light. Colt and Nash had both fallen asleep on the couch, despite everything.

I checked my rifle again, my hands moving automatically. The weight of the gun felt reassuring, but also like a burden I hadn't carried in years. A part of me wished I didn't have to again. Another part, the one that had stayed sharp and alert after my years in the Corps, knew better. This was survival now. And I had a family to protect.

The next morning, I gathered everyone around the kitchen table. The sun hadn't fully risen, casting an orange glow over Cane Bay, but we couldn't wait. After last night, it was clear that whatever order had existed was gone. We couldn't afford to stay idle.

"Alright," I started, looking each of them in the eye. "We need a plan, a real plan. Last night was a warning. It's only going to get worse."

Annie sipped her coffee, her face lined with exhaustion. Colt leaned forward, nodding, and Nash played with the edge of his shirt, trying to look strong but clearly feeling the weight of the conversation.

"What's the plan?" Colt asked, a seriousness in his tone I hadn't heard before. He was stepping into his role, slowly, but I could see it happening.

I cleared my throat. "First, we need to secure more supplies. What we have won't last long enough if things keep going the way they are. We also need to figure out an escape route if this place becomes overrun."

"Escape route?" Nash's voice trembled. "But where would we go?"

I rubbed my chin, thinking of the maps I'd seen of the area. "There's forest behind us. If the infected, or whoever else, breaches the neighborhood, we can slip through the woods. From there, we'll figure it out—head toward the nearest river, maybe, or find a rural area where we can stay hidden."

Colt leaned back in his chair. "And supplies? We can't just walk into Publix anymore."

I nodded. "No, we can't. But there's more than one way to get what we need. There are abandoned houses in the development, people who left in a hurry. They might have left food behind, water, medicine."

Annie raised an eyebrow. "You're talking about looting."

I looked at her, the harsh reality settling in. "We're not taking from people who are still here. But anyone who's gone? They're not coming back, Annie. We need to survive."

She didn't argue, just nodded slowly. We were all adjusting to the new rules, or lack thereof.

By noon, I had geared up to scout some of the houses in the neighborhood. Colt insisted on coming with me, his expression set in that determined way that reminded me of my younger self. I gave him one of the smaller handguns, which he took with surprising confidence. Nash stayed with Annie, keeping an eye on the house while we were gone.

The streets of Cane Bay were quiet, too quiet. Not a soul in sight. Most of the houses looked abandoned, windows dark, cars left in driveways. There were signs of struggle in some places, doors kicked in, windows shattered. It was as if the remnants of society were scattered across the pavement, in the form of upturned trash bins and belongings left behind in a hurry.

We moved carefully, sticking close to the tree line. As we approached the first house, I motioned for Colt to stay low. We didn't know who might still be around, and I wasn't taking any chances.

We entered through the back door, which was already hanging ajar. Inside, it was a mess. Furniture overturned, the remnants of a life once lived. It looked like whoever had been here had left in a panic. I could see broken picture frames and clothes strewn across the floor. The air was thick with the musty scent of abandonment.

Colt moved beside me, his gun raised, though his hands shook slightly. "What are we looking for?"

"Anything useful," I replied quietly. "Food, water, batteries, first-aid supplies. If they left in a hurry, there might still be some essentials."

We split up, moving through the house quickly but carefully. I found a few cans of food in the pantry, along with some bottled water. In the bathroom, I grabbed a half-used bottle of ibuprofen and some bandages. It wasn't much, but every little bit helped.

Colt found a flashlight and some extra batteries in the garage, along with a half-empty propane tank that could come in handy. He also discovered an old baseball bat by the door. He picked it up, giving it a test swing, and nodded to himself.

As we left the house, we saw something that made my stomach churn, bloody handprints smeared across the front door. They were old, dried, but still a reminder of how close the danger was. We were lucky this time. But I knew that luck wouldn't last.

When we returned to the house, Annie was waiting by the front door, her face etched with worry. Nash was upstairs, keeping watch from the bedroom window.

"What did you find?" she asked, as Colt and I brought in the supplies.

"A few things," I said, setting the food and water on the counter. "Enough to last us a little longer."

She nodded, though I could tell she wasn't reassured. None of us were.

"We'll do another run tomorrow," I said, trying to sound more confident than I felt. "We'll check the rest of the houses, see what we can find."

Colt sat down at the table, still gripping the baseball bat. "And after that?"

I sighed, glancing out the window. The sun was starting to set, casting long shadows across the yard. "After that... we'll see. If things get worse, we'll move. But for now, we stay here, we fortify, and we stay ready."

Annie came up beside me, resting her hand on my arm. "We'll get through this," she said softly, though I wasn't sure if she was telling me or herself.

I put my arm around her, pulling her close. "We will. But we need to be smart. No mistakes."

That night, as the wind howled outside and the house creaked in the darkness, I lay awake, thinking about the future. This was our life now. Surviving one day at a time, always waiting for the next threat to appear.

I could hear Colt stirring in the other room, probably just as restless as I was. Nash had fallen asleep early, his exhaustion finally overtaking him, but I knew he'd wake with the same fear in his eyes tomorrow.

Annie shifted beside me, her hand reaching for mine in the dark. "What if help never comes?" she whispered. I didn't have an answer for her. So I just squeezed her hand and listened to the night, waiting for the inevitable.

Chapter 13: Descent into Chaos

By the time the sun rose the next day, the atmosphere in Cane Bay Plantation felt suffocating. The few neighbors who were still around had either barricaded themselves inside their homes or packed up and left under the cover of darkness. We hadn't heard from anyone nearby, and the power had been flickering on and off, making it hard to know what was happening outside our small corner of Summerville.

The radio stations were nothing but static, and without cell service, we were cut off from the outside world. All I had to rely on were my instincts. Right now, they were screaming that things were about to get a lot worse.

We had spent the previous day scavenging what we could, and it helped, but there was only so much you could prepare for. Annie had taken to organizing the supplies, trying to stretch out our resources as long as possible. Colt, with his baseball bat now a permanent fixture by his side, had taken over keeping an eye on Nash, who was struggling more as reality began to settle in.

But there was no escaping it now. We were in this for the long haul.

It was just after noon when Colt came downstairs, his face pale. He had been on lookout from the second-floor window, a spot we had designated as the watch post to see if anyone was approaching the house.

"Dad, you need to see this," he said, his voice unusually quiet.

I followed him upstairs, Annie close behind. Nash stayed downstairs, fiddling with a set of old batteries and a flashlight, trying to keep busy. When I reached the window and looked out, I could see what had rattled Colt.

Just beyond our backyard, in the distance where the development met the tree line, a group of people were moving through the woods. At first glance, they seemed like ordinary survivors, families, maybe, trying to find a safe place to stay. But something about the way they moved set off alarm bells. They were too fast, too erratic.

"Dad, they're infected," Colt said, gripping the bat tighter.

I squinted, watching the group as they stumbled and crashed through the brush. They weren't walking like normal people. Their movements were jerky, uncontrolled, like they were driven by pure instinct.

And then I saw it, the unmistakable red stains on their clothes, their mouths hanging open in a grotesque display.

"We need to secure the house, now," I said, turning away from the window.

Annie's face went white, but she didn't hesitate. "What do we do?"

I took a deep breath. "We reinforce the doors and windows. Make sure every entrance is covered. If they get too close, we don't hesitate. We can't afford to let them breach the house."

The next hour was a blur of hammering and barricading. We nailed boards over the windows, secured the back door with extra locks, and moved heavy furniture in front of any weak points. Colt and I worked in tense silence, our eyes constantly darting toward the backyard, where the infected were getting closer, though they hadn't yet reached the edge of the property.

Nash helped as best as he could, though I could see the fear in his eyes. I kept him busy handing us tools and materials, trying to keep his mind off the fact that, at any moment, we might be fighting for our lives.

"We're running out of time," Annie said, her voice strained as she helped me move a bookshelf in front of the front door. "What if they get in?"

I didn't have an answer for her. All I could do was hope we were prepared enough.

Once the last window was covered, I called everyone into the living room. We sat in a tight circle, the tension thick in the air.

"Alright," I said, keeping my voice low but firm. "Here's the plan. We stay quiet, we stay low, and we don't draw any attention to ourselves. If they pass by, we let them go. But if they come for us... we defend the house."

Colt nodded, his jaw set. Nash looked unsure, but he didn't argue. Annie simply took my hand, her eyes full of determination. We had no choice but to be ready.

The hours dragged on, and the weight of the situation pressed down on all of us. I sat by the window, peeking through the cracks in the boards we had nailed up, watching as the infected moved closer, their numbers slowly growing.

They didn't seem to have any direction, wandering aimlessly through the woods and into the streets of the neighborhood. I could hear the distant sounds of gunfire every now and then, other families, other survivors trying to hold on to their homes. The sound was a grim reminder that we were all on our own now.

"Dad," Nash whispered, sitting beside me, his voice barely audible. "What if they don't leave? What if they come for us?"

I put my arm around him, pulling him close. "We'll be ready," I said. "We're going to stay strong. You're doing great, kid. Just keep your head on straight, alright?"

He nodded, but the fear was still there, lurking just beneath the surface.

As the day turned to night, I was starting to think we might make it through without incident. The infected had lingered around the edge of the development but hadn't come any closer. I thought, maybe, just maybe, we'd get lucky.

That's when the banging started.

It was faint at first, barely noticeable over the wind howling outside. But then it grew louder, more insistent, someone was at the front door.

Colt was at my side in an instant, the bat gripped tightly in his hands. "Dad, what do we do?"

I held up my hand, motioning for everyone to stay quiet. The banging turned into a pounding, and I could hear voices outside, desperate, panicked voices.

"Let us in!" someone screamed. "Please, we need help! They're coming! Please!"

I hesitated, torn between the instinct to help and the need to protect my family. Annie stood frozen by the kitchen, her eyes locked on me, silently asking the same question.

But before I could decide, the voices outside changed. Shrieks of terror, followed by the unmistakable sound of bodies crashing to the ground.

I rushed to the window, peeking through the cracks. What I saw made my blood run cold.

The infected had found them. The people who had been banging on our door. They were being torn apart in the street, their screams echoing through the night.

Annie gasped, her hand covering her mouth as Colt stepped back, his face pale.

"Dad..." Nash's voice trembled. "They're coming."

The infected were moving toward the house now, drawn by the noise. The pounding on the door resumed—this time, it wasn't survivors asking for help. It was the infected, slamming their bodies against the wood, desperate to get inside.

"Positions!" I barked, snapping into full Marine mode. Colt raised his bat, Nash grabbed the flashlight, and Annie stood beside me, her hands shaking but ready.

The door rattled on its hinges, the sounds of the infected growing louder and more frenzied. We had only moments before they broke through.

I took a deep breath, gripping the rifle tightly, and prepared for what was coming.

"Hold the line," I said, my voice steady despite the fear gnawing at me. "We fight for this house."

The infected slammed against the door again, and this time, the wood splintered.

Chapter 14: Hold the Line

The door splintered again, louder this time, sending a tremor through the entire house. The pounding from outside was relentless, a grotesque rhythm that grew louder with each desperate slam of the infected bodies against our barricades. I tightened my grip on the rifle, feeling the weight of the moment settle on my shoulders. I'd been in tough spots before, but never one like this—never with my family at stake.

"Stay back," I warned Annie, Colt, and Nash. They stood frozen in place, wide-eyed but ready. Annie clutched a kitchen knife, her knuckles white. Colt had his bat raised, standing between Nash and the door, as if his presence alone would be enough to shield his younger brother from the horror outside.

The door buckled again, the wood cracking under the pressure. I cursed under my breath. We didn't have much time.

"I'm ready, Dad," Colt said, his voice steady but laced with tension. I glanced at him, his face illuminated by the dim light. He looked so much older than his eighteen years in that moment, and it hit me like a gut punch. He wasn't a kid anymore. None of us had the luxury of being kids anymore.

"Just stay behind me," I said, locking eyes with him for a second. "Don't do anything stupid. We hold them here. They do not get in this house."

I turned my focus back to the door. The infected outside had gotten more aggressive, their primal growls now audible over the sound of the wind. They were so close I could hear their ragged, uneven breathing. They weren't human anymore, but the hunger driving them was terrifyingly real.

Another impact. This time, a section of the door splintered completely, leaving a jagged hole large enough to see through. Through the crack, I could see their distorted faces—bloodshot eyes, mouths smeared with blood, teeth gnashing as they tried to push their way in.

Annie let out a muffled gasp, her grip on the knife trembling.

"Frank," she whispered, her voice a mixture of fear and urgency. "We can't hold them off much longer."

I didn't respond, focusing instead on the movement outside. There were at least a dozen of them now, clawing at the broken door, their frenzy escalating with each passing second. I lifted the rifle, aiming through the crack.

"I'll buy us some time," I muttered, taking a deep breath to steady myself. I squeezed the trigger.

The first shot rang out, echoing through the house like a thunderclap. The bullet hit one of the infected square in the head, dropping it instantly. The others barely hesitated, stepping over their fallen comrade with a single-minded focus.

I fired again. Another infected fell. Then another. But for every one I dropped, it seemed like two more took its place. Their numbers were overwhelming.

"They're not stopping!" Colt shouted, panic creeping into his voice as the door continued to give way.

"I know!" I barked back, firing again. I could feel the strain in my muscles, the weight of the rifle starting to wear on me. My shots were slowing, and I knew I couldn't keep this up forever.

The door finally gave out with a sickening crack, and the infected poured in.

"Colt, now!" I yelled.

Colt swung his bat with everything he had, the sound of it connecting with a skull making a sickening thud. One of the infected dropped to the floor, but another was right behind it, lunging forward. I fired off another shot, taking it down just before it reached him.

"Annie, get back!" I shouted as two more infected came through the door. She stumbled backward, her eyes wide with terror, but she held her ground. Nash clung to her side, too scared to move.

I fired again, but I was running out of ammo. One of the infected managed to push through the chaos, charging toward Annie and Nash.

"Mom!" Nash screamed.

Without thinking, I rushed forward, swinging the butt of the rifle with all the strength I had left. The infected staggered, but it didn't fall. It reached for me, its bloody hands clawing at my shirt, and I shoved it back just enough to get another shot off. It collapsed at my feet, lifeless.

But there were still more coming.

Colt swung the bat with a mix of fear and fury, but I could see him slowing down, the exhaustion taking its toll. The infected were relentless, and we were barely holding the line.

"We need to fall back!" I shouted, realizing we couldn't keep this up much longer. "Everyone, upstairs! Now!"

Annie grabbed Nash, pulling him toward the stairs. Colt hesitated for a moment, glancing at me, his chest heaving with exhaustion.

"Go!" I ordered, covering him as he followed the others up the stairs.

I fired off two more shots before retreating, the infected closing in behind me. We slammed the door to the upstairs hallway shut, barricading it with anything we could find—a dresser, chairs, anything that would slow them down.

My heart was pounding, the sound of the infected scratching and banging at the barricade sending chills down my spine. We were trapped, but at least we had bought ourselves a little time.

Annie was shaking, holding Nash close to her. Colt stood by the window, looking out at the darkened street below. His bat was slick with blood, his hands trembling.

"What do we do now?" Nash asked, his voice small and scared.

I didn't have an answer.

We had prepared for this, boarded up the house, gathered supplies, made a plan. But no amount of preparation could have prepared us for the sheer terror of what was happening.

"We wait," I said finally, my voice hoarse. "We wait and we survive."

The banging downstairs grew louder, more desperate, and I knew it was only a matter of time before the infected broke through.

But we weren't going down without a fight.

"Keep your weapons close," I told them, looking each of them in the eye. "Stay together. We'll make it through this. We have to."

As the noise below intensified, I took one last look out the window, hoping for some kind of sign. Anything that would tell me help was on the way. But all I saw was darkness.

In that moment, it hit me. No one was coming. The world outside had gone silent. We were on our own.

And the fight for survival had only just begun.

Chapter 15: It's Everywhere

The banging downstairs had stopped sometime in the night. At first, we thought maybe they'd lost interest, and moved on to another house. But the growling and shuffling sounds just beyond the barricade told a different story. They were still there—just waiting. Waiting for us to make a mistake.

It was just after dawn when I opened my eyes. I hadn't really slept, not since the door downstairs gave way. The adrenaline had worn off, and my body felt like it had been hit by a truck. I sat up, careful not to wake Annie, who was curled up next to me on the floor, her breathing shallow but steady. Nash was still asleep, his head resting in her lap, clutching his tablet like it was the last piece of normalcy he had left.

Colt sat by the window, peering out through the small crack in the blinds. His face was pale, dark circles under his eyes, but his hands were steady. His bat lay across his lap, still stained with the blood of the infected from the night before. He hadn't said much since we barricaded ourselves up here, but I could see the gears turning in his head, just like mine were.

"How we looking?" I asked, my voice low.

Colt didn't turn, his eyes still scanning the street. "Quiet out there. Too quiet."

I nodded, standing and stretching out the stiffness in my legs. "That's usually a bad sign."

He finally looked at me, the weight of everything that had happened in the last few days visible in his expression. "Are we going to make it, Dad?"

I wanted to give him an answer that would make it all go away, tell him everything was going to be fine, that help was on the way. But that would've been a lie, and he deserved better than that.

"I don't know, son," I admitted. "But we're going to do everything we can to survive. That's all we've got right now."

Colt nodded, his jaw tightening as he looked back out the window. "There's still no sign of anyone else. No cars, no people. Just... empty."

That didn't surprise me. From what I'd seen on the news before the power cut out, the government's response was unraveling fast. The infected had spread quicker than anyone could've anticipated. Major cities had fallen first—New York, Chicago, Los Angeles. Then the smaller towns and suburbs, like ours, where the resources were thinner, and people weren't prepared.

South Carolina was no exception. Charleston had been overrun within days. Summerville and Cane Bay were close behind, and the sporadic reports I'd heard made it clear there wasn't much hope for containment. The National Guard had been deployed, but they were stretched too thin. Too many infected, too few soldiers. If there were any official rescue operations, they weren't coming anywhere near us.

Annie stirred next to me, blinking awake. She looked around, disoriented for a moment before the reality of our situation came rushing back.

"Morning," I said softly, brushing her hair out of her face. "You doing okay?"

She gave me a small nod, though the strain was written all over her. "As okay as we can be, I guess. What's the plan?"

I sighed, running a hand over my face. "We can't stay up here forever. Sooner or later, we're going to need more food, water... we need to figure out if there's anyone else still out there. Anyone who might be able to help."

Annie glanced toward Nash, still sleeping, and then to Colt by the window. "You're right," she said quietly. "But how? We're surrounded."

I didn't have an easy answer. The infected downstairs weren't going anywhere, and going out the front door was suicide. We needed a way out that wouldn't draw their attention. Something that would give us a chance to make it to the truck, or at least scope out the neighborhood.

"The attic," I said after a moment of thinking. "If we can get up there, maybe we can get onto the roof, see what's going on outside without exposing ourselves."

Annie looked at me, unsure. "And then what? Even if we get out, where do we go?"

"We'll figure it out," I said, trying to sound more confident than I felt. "We just need to take it one step at a time."

I walked over to Colt and tapped him on the shoulder. "Get ready, we're going to try something."

He turned and raised an eyebrow, clearly skeptical. "What exactly?"

"The attic," I said, nodding toward the ceiling. "If we can get onto the roof, we might be able to get a better look at what's going on out there. See if there's a clear path to the truck or to any of the other houses."

Colt stood, his bat still in hand. "You sure that's a good idea?"

I wasn't sure of anything anymore, but sitting around wasn't going to keep us alive. "It's our best option right now."

Annie gently woke Nash, who groggily sat up, his eyes puffy from a restless night of sleep. "Are we safe, Dad?" he asked, his voice soft.

"We're safe for now," I said, ruffling his hair. "But we're going to check out a way to get out of here, okay? Stay close to your mom and Colt."

I grabbed the flashlight and climbed onto a chair, pushing open the attic door. The ladder creaked as I pulled it down, and for a second, I froze, waiting to see if the noise had attracted any attention from the infected downstairs.

Nothing. At least, not yet.

"Okay, I'm going up," I said, climbing into the attic. The air was stifling up there, filled with the musty smell of insulation and old Christmas decorations. I crawled toward the small window that faced the front of the house, carefully pulling it open. A faint breeze hit my face, bringing with it the scent of smoke and decay.

I poked my head out and scanned the street below. It was just like Colt had said—eerily quiet. No cars, no movement, just the occasional gust of wind rustling the leaves. The infected were still clustered near our front door, mindlessly pacing back and forth, waiting for us to make a move.

Across the street, I saw something that caught my eye. Movement. A shadow in one of the neighbor's houses, barely visible through the broken window.

Someone was alive over there.

I pulled my head back inside and climbed down from the attic, my mind racing. "There's someone across the street," I said as I reached the bottom of the ladder.

Annie's eyes widened. "Are you sure?"

"I saw movement in the house. They're holed up, just like us."

Colt's face lit up with a glimmer of hope. "Maybe they know something. Maybe they've got a plan."

"Maybe," I said. "But first, we need to figure out how to get across without drawing the infected right to us."

Annie looked at me, worry etched in her features. "Frank, you're not thinking about going over there, are you?"

"We don't have a choice, Annie," I said gently. "If we stay here, we're sitting ducks. If they're still alive, maybe we can work together, pool resources. It's the only way we're going to survive this."

She didn't like it, but she knew I was right.

"All right," she whispered, her voice cracking. "Just... be careful."

I nodded, tightening my grip on the rifle. We were about to make a move, and if we played our cards right, it might just be the break we needed.

The world had changed overnight. But survival was in our blood. And today, we'd fight to hold on to it.

Chapter 16: The Gamble

The plan wasn't perfect. Hell, it wasn't even good, but it was all we had. Getting across the street to the house where I'd seen the movement was a gamble—a big one. If I screwed up, I'd bring the whole horde down on us. But if we did nothing, we'd starve in this house.

I stood by the window, watching the infected shuffle outside. They moved like animals, their heads jerking side to side, searching for any sound, any scent. Their numbers had thinned since the night before, but a few still lingered near the broken door, their growls echoing faintly.

Colt joined me, his bat still in his hands. "How do you want to do this?"

I turned to him, thinking through the options. We had to keep it simple. No time for overcomplicated plans.

"We create a distraction first," I said, laying it out. "Something to pull them away from the house. Once they're focused elsewhere, I'll head over to the neighbor's place. You stay here, keep an eye on things from the attic. If anything happens, I need you ready to help your mom and Nash. Understood?"

He frowned, his face tightening. "Why can't I go with you? I can handle it."

I shook my head. "I know you can, but I need you here. We can't risk leaving the house unguarded. I won't be long."

Colt hesitated, clearly torn between wanting to be by my side and following orders. Finally, he nodded. "Okay, but if things go south, I'm coming after you."

I put a hand on his shoulder. "If things go south, you stay with your mom and brother. That's your job."

We locked eyes, and I could see the resolve in him, the same fire that burned inside me when I was his age. I'd raised him to be tough, to think for himself, but I'd also taught him when to follow orders.

I turned back to Annie, who was sitting on the edge of the couch, holding Nash close. "You keep the boys safe, no matter what happens," I said.

Annie's eyes were filled with worry, but she nodded. "Just come back, Frank. Don't do anything stupid."

"I'll be back," I promised, though deep down, I knew that nothing about this situation was guaranteed.

I grabbed the flare gun from my go-bag, checking to make sure it was loaded. "This should get their attention," I muttered, mostly to myself.

I climbed back up to the attic, Colt following close behind. We needed to get a good vantage point to fire the flare, somewhere that would draw the infected far enough from the house to give me a shot at making it across the street. I popped the small window open again and crawled onto the roof. The shingles were still slick with morning dew, and I had to steady myself to keep from slipping.

The street below was deserted, save for the infected milling around in the front yard. I aimed the flare gun toward the trees about two blocks down. If we could lure them far enough away, I might have a clear shot at getting into the neighbor's house.

I took a deep breath and squeezed the trigger.

The flare shot out with a sharp hiss, streaking across the sky in a burst of red light before disappearing into the woods. It exploded with a loud crack, sending a plume of smoke into the air. Instantly, the infected below jerked their heads toward the noise. They growled, their bodies twitching as they began shambling toward the direction of the sound.

"Come on... keep moving..." I whispered under my breath, watching as more of them joined the group, staggering down the street and away from our house.

After a tense few minutes, the front yard was finally clear.

I turned to Colt. "Keep watch from here. I'm going."

He gave me a firm nod. "I'll signal you if anything changes."

I climbed back through the window, grabbed my rifle, and made my way down the stairs. Annie was waiting by the front door, her face pale. "Be careful," she whispered.

"I will," I said, squeezing her hand before stepping outside.

The air was thick with the scent of decay, and the silence was unsettling. Every crunch of gravel under my boots felt like a gunshot in the stillness. I kept low, moving quickly but carefully, scanning the street for any sign of movement. The infected were still heading toward the flare, their backs turned to me.

I reached the edge of the neighbor's yard and ducked behind a bush, checking to make sure the coast was clear. The house looked abandoned from the outside, but I knew I'd seen movement. Someone was in there.

I sprinted across the open lawn, my heart pounding in my chest. When I reached the front door, I pressed my ear against it, listening for any sounds from within. Nothing.

I knocked once, then again, louder this time.

"Hey! I saw you!" I hissed, keeping my voice low. "We're alive over here. Open up!"

For a moment, there was no response. I was about to knock again when the door creaked open just a crack. A man's face appeared, gaunt and shadowed, his eyes wide with fear.

"Who are you?" he whispered, his voice shaky.

"Name's Frank," I said. "My family's holed up across the street. We saw you, figured you might know something about what's going on."

The man hesitated, glancing behind him nervously. "You're alone?"

"For now," I said. "Just trying to find some answers. We're not looking to cause trouble."

He opened the door wider, and I stepped inside, quickly shutting it behind me. The house was dark, with curtains drawn over the windows. The smell of stale air hit me immediately.

"We've been here since it started," the man said, leading me into the living room. "My wife, my son... we didn't know what else to do."

As he spoke, I saw two figures huddled on the couch—his wife, clutching a young boy who couldn't have been more than eight. They both looked terrified.

"I'm sorry about all this," the man said, running a hand through his hair. "It's been... I don't even know how long. Days? Weeks? We've lost track."

"What have you heard?" I asked, keeping my voice low. "Anything on the radio or from anyone else nearby?"

The man shook his head. "Nothing good. We had power for a while, but it cut out yesterday. Last thing we heard was the military pulling out of Charleston. They said the infection's spread faster than they expected. People are turning in hours, not days. No one's coming."

I clenched my jaw, the news confirming what I had feared. We were on our own. No cavalry was coming to save us.

"We've been rationing what little we have left," the man continued, "but it won't last. My wife is sick. Not the infection, but we need medicine. She hasn't been able to keep anything down."

I glanced at the woman on the couch. She was pale, her skin clammy, and I could see the exhaustion in her eyes. They were barely holding on.

"I can't promise anything," I said, "but we have some supplies. We'll help however we can."

The man's eyes filled with relief. "Thank you," he whispered.

But before I could say anything more, a noise from outside made both of us freeze. A low, guttural growl.

They were back.

The infected had returned.

"Shit," I muttered, gripping my rifle. "Stay quiet."

The man's face went pale as we crept toward the front window. I peeked through the curtains and saw them—the horde had returned, and they were more agitated than before.

My heart raced as I looked back at the man and his family. We had to move fast.

The window of opportunity was closing.

And if we didn't act now, none of us would make it out alive.

Chapter 17: No Way Out

The moment I looked out the window, my stomach dropped. The infected had returned, and they weren't just wandering anymore—they were hunting. Their heads jerked in all directions, their snarls growing louder, their movements more erratic. They could smell us. The flare had bought us time, but now it seemed like the noise had drawn in even more.

"Get away from the windows," I whispered to the man, pulling the curtains tight. "Stay low. Stay quiet."

He nodded, ushering his wife and son into the corner of the living room, their backs pressed against the wall. The woman's breathing was shallow, and the boy's eyes were wide with fear. They didn't make a sound, though; they were used to this kind of terror.

My mind raced, trying to figure out the next move. We couldn't stay here. The infected were already circling the house, and it wouldn't take long before one of them tried to break in. I couldn't let that happen—not with these people and my own family still waiting across the street.

I leaned toward the man. "What's your name?"

"Daryl," he whispered back.

"Alright, Daryl. Here's the deal. My family's right across the street in that house. We have food, water, weapons. You come with me, and we can make it there. But we need to move fast."

Daryl swallowed hard, glancing back at his wife and son. "Are you sure? I mean... will we make it?"

I didn't lie to him. "I don't know. But if we stay here, we won't."

He closed his eyes for a second, then opened them with a nod. "We'll go."

I turned to the wife, who was struggling to sit up straight. "Can she walk?"

Daryl's face twisted in worry. "She's weak, but I can carry her."

I looked back out the window. The infected were circling, their heads twitching, their mouths gaping open. There was no telling how long we had before they started banging on the doors and windows. We needed a distraction—something to lure them away long enough for us to slip across the street.

I felt the weight of the flare gun in my pocket and pulled it out. The odds of this working again weren't great, but it was all we had.

"Here's what we're gonna do," I said, formulating a quick plan. "I'm going to fire another flare, further this time. Hopefully, it'll pull them far enough away. We stick together and move fast. No stopping, no noise. Got it?"

Daryl nodded quickly. "Got it."

I looked at the boy, whose wide eyes hadn't left me since I entered the house. "You stick close to your dad, alright? Don't make a sound."

The boy nodded, trembling but determined.

I led them into the hallway, inching toward the back door. The house had a small yard, fenced in. From there, it was just a sprint to the street. But the infected were too close. If they saw us, we'd be done for.

I took a deep breath, slipped the door open a crack, and aimed the flare gun toward the far side of the neighborhood. I fired, the red streak cutting through the sky. The flare exploded with a crack, lighting up the trees in the distance. I could hear the infected grunting and growling, their attention shifting as they started moving toward the noise.

"Now," I whispered, ushering them through the door.

Daryl carried his wife over his shoulder, and his son clung to his side as we slipped out into the yard. I scanned the area—there were still a few infected lingering near the house, but most had started lumbering in the direction of the flare.

I pointed toward the back gate. "We're gonna run straight for the street. Once we're across, my house is the second one. Don't stop, don't look back."

I counted to three, my heart pounding in my chest, and then we ran.

Daryl struggled under the weight of his wife, but he didn't stop. The boy stayed right by his side, silent as a shadow. I kept the rifle close, my eyes darting around, watching for any sign of movement.

We reached the gate and burst out onto the street. For a second, it felt like we might actually make it.

But then, from the corner of my eye, I saw them—three infected, turning toward us, their eyes locking onto our movement.

"Shit," I muttered under my breath. "Keep going!"

They stumbled forward, faster now, their growls rising into screeches as they picked up speed. They were coming straight for us.

"Go! Get inside!" I shouted at Daryl.

He pushed forward, almost at my house now, his wife groaning in his arms. The boy was crying silently, his eyes fixed on the infected closing in on us.

I raised my rifle, aiming at the closest one, and fired.

The shot hit it square in the chest, but it didn't stop. They never stopped.

I fired again, this time hitting its leg, and it stumbled, crashing to the ground. The other two were still coming, but we were almost at the house.

I sprinted after Daryl, reaching the front door just as Colt opened it. His eyes widened when he saw the scene unfolding behind me.

"Get them inside!" I yelled, firing another round at the closest infected.

Colt grabbed the boy and pulled him inside, followed by Daryl and his wife. I backed up toward the door, still firing, the last infected stumbling just feet from me.

I slammed the door shut just as it crashed into the porch, its snarls vibrating through the walls.

Annie rushed forward, helping Daryl lay his wife down on the couch. She was pale and barely conscious, her breathing shallow.

"We made it," Daryl gasped, collapsing into a chair, his whole body trembling. "Oh God, we made it."

But as I leaned against the door, catching my breath, I knew it wasn't over. We'd bought ourselves time, but with each passing minute, the infected were getting more aggressive. They weren't just wandering anymore—they were hunting.

And sooner or later, they'd find a way in.

We had to be ready.

"Colt," I said, standing up straight. "Get the windows boarded up. And double-check the doors."

He nodded, already moving. I turned to Annie, who was tending to Daryl's wife. "How's she doing?"

Annie shook her head. "Not good. She needs medicine. Something for the fever."

"We'll see what we have," I said, though I knew we didn't have much.

Daryl was still shaking, staring at the floor. "Thank you," he whispered, barely audible. "Thank you for getting us out."

I nodded, though I wasn't sure how long we could keep them safe. How long we could keep any of us safe.

The infected were relentless. And every time we went outside, every time we made noise, we risked bringing them closer. We couldn't stay like this forever.

Sooner or later, we'd have to make a move.

And when we did, we'd have to gamble everything.

Chapter 18: The Plan

The house was eerily quiet, despite everything going on outside. Colt finished boarding up the last window, his hands covered in dirt and sweat. Nash sat in the corner, fiddling with the small knife I'd given him for protection, his eyes wide and alert. Annie was sitting next to Daryl's wife, who still hadn't improved. She was barely breathing now, her face slick with sweat as her fever raged on.

We were running out of time. Not just for her, but for all of us.

I paced the living room, my mind racing with possibilities. Every scenario I played out ended in the same way: we were stuck. There was no way out of Cane Bay Plantation without drawing more infected toward us. Supplies were low, and the roads were likely blocked. Worse still, the infected weren't showing any signs of slowing down. Each hour they seemed to grow more aggressive, their numbers swelling as more people turned.

"We can't keep doing this," I muttered under my breath, glancing toward the front door where the boards were nailed down. "We're sitting ducks."

Colt looked up from his work, eyes serious. "So what do we do, Dad?"

I didn't have an easy answer. For days, we'd been trying to figure out the best course of action, but nothing seemed like a good option. Not with the streets crawling with the infected. But the truth was, staying here was only a temporary solution. If we didn't move soon, we'd be trapped for good.

"We need to think long-term," I said, trying to keep my voice steady. "We need supplies, food, and medicine. And we need a plan to get out of here."

Annie looked up from her place by Daryl's wife. "Where would we even go, Frank? Everywhere's overrun. You've seen the news."

"I don't know yet," I admitted. "But we can't just sit here waiting for things to get worse. We've already used up most of what we have. And if this fever gets worse..." I let my words trail off, but everyone knew what I was thinking.

Colt's face tightened as he stood up and wiped his hands on his pants. "You're right. But where do we even start? It's not like we can just waltz into town and raid the stores."

"That's exactly what we need to do," I said. "But smart. There's a Walmart and a couple of pharmacies close by. If we hit them quick, grab what we need, and get out, we might be able to hold out a little longer."

Daryl finally spoke up from the corner of the room. His voice was hoarse, but he was listening. "We tried going into town last week. It's a death trap. Too many of them. You'll be lucky to make it out alive."

I nodded. I'd seen it too. Every time I peeked out, the streets were getting worse. But what choice did we have?

"It's risky, but we don't have much of an option. If we stay here, we die. If we go out, we at least have a chance."

Annie's eyes were filled with worry, but she didn't argue. She knew as well as I did that we were backed into a corner.

"I'll go," Colt said, standing taller than I'd ever seen him. There was a new edge in his voice, a seriousness that wasn't there before. "I'm not a kid anymore, Dad. I can handle this."

For a moment, I wanted to say no. He was only eighteen, and the thought of sending him out into that chaos made my stomach churn. But he was right. Colt had grown up faster in these last few days than I ever thought possible. He'd been stepping up in ways I hadn't expected, showing the kind of grit that reminded me of myself at his age.

"Alright," I said, nodding. "But we go together. We'll scout the area first, figure out the best path, and stay as quiet as possible. The second things get bad, we pull out. Understood?"

Colt nodded, his face set. Nash looked up from his spot on the floor, his voice small but firm. "I want to help too."

I crouched down next to him, putting a hand on his shoulder. "I know you do, but you're staying here with your mom. You need to keep her safe. That's just as important."

Nash's lips pressed into a thin line, but he didn't argue. He understood the weight of what I was asking.

"Alright," I said, standing up. "Let's gear up."

We didn't have much in terms of weapons, but we made do. I strapped the rifle across my back and handed Colt the shotgun, showing him how to load it properly. Daryl, despite his condition, offered his machete for backup, and I took it gratefully. Every tool counted.

Before we left, Annie pulled me aside, her face pale but resolute. "Be careful, Frank. If anything happens..."

"Nothing's gonna happen," I said, though the knot in my chest betrayed my own fears. "We'll be back."

She hugged me tight, and for a second, I allowed myself to relax in the embrace. But only for a second. There wasn't time for anything else.

We moved toward the back door, checking the area before slipping out. The infected were still wandering nearby, but we kept to the shadows, moving as silently as possible. Every noise, every rustle of leaves, sent my heart racing. Colt was right on my heels, his grip steady on the shotgun.

We made our way toward the neighborhood's main road, weaving through backyards and staying low. The closer we got to the main drag, the worse things looked. Cars were abandoned, some crashed into each other, and bodies littered the streets. Not all of them were infected. Some had died trying to escape.

"There," I whispered, pointing toward a pharmacy at the corner. The glass doors were shattered, and from a distance, it looked like the place had already been picked clean. But we had to try.

We crept closer, using the parked cars as cover, until we reached the entrance. The shelves were ransacked, but there were still some supplies—painkillers, bandages, over-the-counter meds. Nothing major, but enough to get us through the next few days.

"Grab what you can," I whispered to Colt. We moved quickly, stuffing our bags with whatever we could find.

Then, from outside, we heard it—the unmistakable sound of a groan. Colt froze, his eyes wide as he looked at me.

"They're coming," I whispered. "We need to move."

I led him toward the back of the store, hoping to find another way out, but the alley behind the pharmacy was blocked. We were trapped.

The infected were getting closer now. Their growls echoed off the walls as they shuffled through the broken doors. Colt's grip tightened on the shotgun, and I could see the fear creeping into his eyes. But he didn't panic. He was ready.

"Stay close," I whispered. "We fight our way out."

The first infected stumbled into view, its eyes wild, its mouth dripping with blood. I raised the rifle and fired. The shot echoed through the store, and the infected dropped to the ground.

But more were coming.

Colt fired the shotgun, the blast tearing through another one. The noise was deafening, but we didn't have a choice now. We had to fight.

They kept coming, their bodies piling up as we fired round after round. My heart raced as I reloaded the rifle, every second feeling like an eternity. We couldn't keep this up.

"We need to run," I shouted over the gunfire. "Now!"

Colt nodded, and we sprinted for the front of the store, dodging between the aisles as the infected swarmed around us. My legs burned, and my lungs ached, but we didn't stop. We couldn't.

We burst through the doors and into the street, the cold air hitting my face like a slap. The infected were still coming, but we had enough of a lead.

"Go! Go!" I shouted, and we ran, pushing ourselves as hard as we could.

By the time we reached the house, we were both gasping for breath, but we'd made it. Colt slammed the door shut behind us, and I collapsed against the wall, my chest heaving.

Annie rushed over, her eyes wide with relief. "Are you alright?"

"We're fine," I said between breaths. "Got some supplies, but it's bad out there. Real bad."

Colt sat down next to me, wiping the sweat from his face. "What now?"

I looked at him, then at the rest of the group. We were safe for now, but it was only a matter of time before the infected found their way here.

"We plan," I said, standing up and pulling myself together. "We figure out our next move. Because we can't stay here much longer."

And deep down, I knew the truth. No matter how prepared we thought we were, there was no way to be ready for what was coming next.

Chapter 19: Unrest

The air was thick, and not just from the humidity that clung to everything like a second skin. It was the tension—the feeling that something was coming, something worse than anything we'd faced so far. Inside the house, everyone was quiet, going about their tasks with a nervous energy that made the walls feel like they were closing in. We were running out of time, and we all knew it.

I sat at the kitchen table, maps spread out in front of me. Colt leaned against the counter, still pale from the raid we'd pulled off yesterday. Nash sat quietly by the window, peeking through the blinds every so often, watching for movement. Annie was in the next room, tending to Daryl's wife, who had been slipping in and out of consciousness for days. She was getting worse, and without real medical supplies, there wasn't much we could do.

Daryl stood by the door, his arms crossed. He was growing more restless by the day, and I could see the frustration building in his eyes. "What's the plan, Frank?" he asked, his voice barely masking his irritation. "We can't stay cooped up in here forever."

He wasn't wrong. The supplies we'd grabbed yesterday would only last us another few days, maybe a week if we stretched them. But leaving the house again felt like walking into a death trap. Every trip outside was a gamble, and sooner or later, our luck was going to run out.

"We need to think bigger," I said, staring down at the map. "Cane Bay isn't going to hold. It's only a matter of time before the infected spread through here completely. We need to find somewhere more secure."

"And where the hell is that?" Daryl snapped. "Every place we've seen is either overrun or stripped bare."

"I don't know yet," I admitted. "But we can't just sit here and wait to die."

Colt spoke up from the counter, his voice steady despite the exhaustion I saw in his eyes. "What about the schools? They've got fences, solid buildings. Maybe we could clear one out and make it defensible."

I nodded slowly, considering it. The schools in Cane Bay were built to be safe, to withstand hurricanes. Strong walls, limited entry points, and they were large enough to house a group like ours. If we could get in and secure the place, it might buy us more time.

"That's not a bad idea," I said, glancing over at Daryl. "It's a risk, but it's better than sitting here waiting for the infected to break through."

Daryl frowned, but he didn't argue. He knew as well as I did that staying put wasn't an option.

"We'll need more than just the four of us," he said, his tone more measured now. "There are still people out there. I've seen them. Families, stragglers. If we can gather a group, we might stand a better chance."

I hesitated. Adding more people to our group meant more mouths to feed, more risks. But it also meant more hands, more defenses. In a situation like this, numbers mattered.

"We'll take it slow," I said. "Scout the area, see who's still around. If they're willing to help, we bring them in. But we need to be careful. Not everyone's going to be trustworthy."

Colt nodded. "What about the infected? If we go out there again, we're going to run into more of them. A lot more."

I glanced toward the window where Nash was sitting. He hadn't said much since we'd come back from the raid, and I could see the fear in his eyes. He was young, but he was no fool. He understood the gravity of what we were facing, and that scared me more than anything.

"We're going to have to be smart about this," I said, my voice low. "We move fast, stay quiet, and we don't take unnecessary risks. If we can secure the school, it'll give us a fighting chance."

Annie walked into the room then, wiping her hands on a towel. Her face was pale, and there was a tightness around her eyes that told me she wasn't about to deliver good news.

"She's not going to make it, Frank," Annie said quietly, her voice thick with exhaustion. "Daryl's wife... it's just a matter of time now."

Daryl's face twisted, the frustration turning into something more raw, more desperate. He looked away, jaw clenched. I could see the battle raging inside him—whether to accept the reality of the situation or hold on to the last shred of hope that his wife would somehow pull through.

"She's still breathing," he said through gritted teeth. "She might—"

"No," Annie interrupted softly. "She won't. You need to prepare yourself, Daryl."

The room went silent. Daryl's shoulders slumped, and he pressed the heel of his hand against his forehead, standing there for a long moment, just breathing.

"I'm sorry," Annie said again, but Daryl didn't respond. He just stood there, as still as the air outside.

We all knew what was coming. Daryl's wife was going to die, and when she did, she would turn. We couldn't afford to let that happen inside these walls. It was the hard reality of the world we were living in now.

"We need to deal with this," I said quietly, stepping toward Daryl. "Before it's too late."

He didn't move, didn't speak. The weight of it all seemed to crash down on him in that moment, and for the first time since I'd met him, Daryl looked utterly defeated.

"I'll do it," he said finally, his voice hollow. "I'll take care of it."

Annie moved to offer comfort, but I stopped her with a look. Daryl needed to handle this on his own, as much as it hurt. There were no easy answers anymore.

"I'll go with you," I offered, but he shook his head.

"No. I need to do this alone."

We watched as he walked into the room where his wife lay, the door closing softly behind him. The silence that followed felt like a lead weight pressing down on all of us.

Colt shifted uncomfortably. "What happens next?" he asked, his voice barely above a whisper.

I looked at him, then at Nash, whose wide eyes were still glued to the window.

"We get ready," I said. "Tomorrow, we're going to scout the school. And we're going to find a way to survive."

But even as I said the words, the weight of what was coming pressed heavy on my chest. Nothing would be easy from here on out, and deep down, I knew we were only just beginning to understand the true scope of what we were up against.

Chapter 20: Gathering Forces

The morning was heavy with a kind of stillness that felt wrong. Even the distant groans of the infected seemed muted, like the calm before the storm. I hadn't slept much—none of us had. Daryl had kept to himself since last night, dealing with the aftermath of his wife's death in his own way. He had buried her, and, mercifully, she hadn't turned before he had the chance to say goodbye.

I watched the sunrise through the blinds, the dull orange glow spreading over the streets of Cane Bay Plantation. It was hard to believe that just a few weeks ago, this place had been filled with life. Kids playing in the yards, neighbors chatting by their mailboxes. Now, it was a ghost town—infected lurking in the shadows, waiting for their next victim.

I felt a presence behind me and turned to see Colt, already dressed in his worn jeans and boots, a rifle slung over his shoulder. He'd grown up fast in these last few weeks, too fast. At 18, he was already taking on responsibilities no kid should ever have to face. But he'd handled it like a soldier. I could see that determined look in his eyes, the same one I'd seen in the Marines. It was a look I recognized in myself.

"You ready?" he asked quietly, glancing at the maps we'd laid out the night before.

I nodded, folding them up and tucking them into my pack. "Yeah, we're going to head out soon. Where's Nash?"

"Still upstairs with Mom. She's trying to keep him busy."

Annie had been incredible through all of this, but I could see the strain on her, too. She was worried about Nash. He wasn't as strong as Colt, not yet. The fear had settled in deep with him, and Annie was doing her best to shield him from it. But we all knew that, sooner or later, he'd have to face it head-on.

Daryl came into the room, his face worn and his eyes bloodshot. He didn't say anything at first, just looked between Colt and me. I could see the weight of his grief hanging on him, but there was something else now—resolve. He wasn't going to let this break him.

"We moving out?" he asked, voice hoarse.

"Yeah," I replied. "We'll take the truck as far as we can. Scout the school. See what we're dealing with."

Daryl nodded, grabbing his shotgun from the table. "Let's get it done."

Annie appeared in the doorway, Nash by her side. His eyes were wide, but he wasn't saying much. He just stared at the weapons we were loading into the truck, the reality of it all sinking in.

"Stay close to your mom," I said, crouching down to his level. "We're going to check things out. We'll be back before dark, alright?"

Nash nodded silently, but I could see the fear in his eyes. He didn't want us to go. Hell, I didn't want to go either, but we had no choice. Staying put wasn't an option anymore.

I stood up and kissed Annie on the forehead. "Keep an eye on the radio. If anything changes, you get Colt's walkie and let us know. Stay inside, no matter what."

She gave me a tired smile, but there was strength in her eyes. "Be careful."

We piled into the truck—me driving, Colt in the passenger seat, Daryl in the back. As we pulled out of the driveway, I glanced at the house in the rearview mirror. I hated leaving them, but we needed to find a new plan. Something more sustainable. And right now, the school seemed like our best bet.

The roads were quiet, eerily so. We passed a few scattered infected, but nothing like what we'd seen near the city. They wandered aimlessly, their bodies deteriorating, some too weak to even chase after us as we sped by. It was like watching the world slowly rot.

When we reached the school, I parked a good distance away and killed the engine. We couldn't risk drawing too much attention. The building loomed in front of us—familiar, yet now alien. The fences were still intact, and from what I could see, the doors were closed. That was a good sign. Maybe this could work.

"We go in quiet," I said, pulling my rifle from behind the seat. "Check for supplies, see if the place is secure."

Colt and Daryl nodded, and we moved out, keeping low as we approached the school. The silence was deafening, each footstep feeling like a shout in the stillness. I scanned the windows, looking for any signs of movement inside. Nothing.

We reached the fence and Colt boosted himself over first, followed by Daryl and then me. The place seemed empty, but I wasn't taking any chances. I signaled for them to follow me as we approached the front doors, rifles raised.

I nudged the door with the barrel of my gun, and it creaked open slowly. The interior was dimly lit, sunlight streaming through the high windows in the hallway. It smelled musty, like a place that had been abandoned for weeks, but there was no sign of recent activity.

"We clear the classrooms first," I whispered, leading them down the hall. Each door we passed, we checked—most were empty, desks and chairs scattered, some overturned. No signs of life, no infected. So far, so good.

We reached the gymnasium, and that's when things changed. The double doors were locked, a chain looped through the handles. I motioned for Colt to stand back, and Daryl and I worked together to pry it open. As soon as the chain gave way, the door swung open with a screech, and the smell hit us—a pungent, rancid odor that made my stomach turn.

Inside the gym, bodies were piled in the center of the floor, some covered in makeshift blankets, others left exposed. It was a gruesome sight, and it told me everything I needed to know. Whoever had been here before us hadn't made it.

"Shit," Daryl muttered, stepping back.

Colt gagged, turning away from the sight. I clenched my jaw, forcing myself to take it in. These people had tried to do the same thing we were doing. They had tried to survive, but something had gone wrong. Maybe they'd let someone in who was infected. Maybe they'd run out of supplies and gotten desperate. Either way, this wasn't going to be our sanctuary.

"We're leaving," I said, my voice firm. "Now."

We turned and headed back down the hallway, faster this time. Every step echoed in the empty space, and my pulse quickened. We needed to get out of here before we ran into any more trouble.

Just as we reached the front doors, a sound stopped us in our tracks—a shuffle, faint but unmistakable, coming from the other end of the hall. I raised my hand, signaling Colt and Daryl to freeze. My heart raced as I listened, straining to pick up any other sounds. The shuffle grew louder, closer.

"Go," I whispered harshly, motioning for them to head for the exit. We moved quickly, stepping through the doors and pulling them shut behind us as quietly as we could. I turned to see the source of the noise—a figure, hunched and staggering, coming around the corner at the far end of the hall. Infected.

We sprinted back to the truck, adrenaline pumping through my veins. Once inside, I fired up the engine and hit the gas. We peeled out of the parking lot, leaving the school behind.

"That was close," Colt muttered, catching his breath. "What now?"

I gripped the steering wheel, my mind racing. The school had been a bust. It wasn't the safe haven we'd hoped for. But we couldn't give up. Not yet.

"We keep looking," I said, determination in my voice. "We'll find something."

As we drove back to Cane Bay, I couldn't help but feel the weight of the situation pressing down on me. Time was running out. We needed a new plan and fast.

Chapter 21: Tensions Rising

The drive back to Cane Bay was suffocatingly quiet. Colt sat in the passenger seat, eyes fixed on the passing trees, but I could tell his mind was miles away. In the back, Daryl's shotgun lay across his lap, his knuckles white as he gripped the barrel, tension rippling through him. The bodies in the school gym had shaken us all, but Daryl looked like he was barely holding it together.

"We're running out of places," Daryl said at last, his voice strained. "That school was supposed to be our best shot."

I stayed quiet for a moment. He wasn't wrong, but I couldn't let that hopelessness take hold. Not now. Not with Annie, Nash, and the others depending on us to keep it together.

"I know," I said eventually, tightening my grip on the wheel. "We'll figure something out. There's gotta be another place."

Colt's voice was sharp, bitter. "Like where? Every spot we've checked is crawling with infected or... something worse."

I glanced at him, catching the frustration in his eyes. I couldn't blame him. We'd been moving from one failed plan to the next, and the weight of it was starting to take its toll. I had to admit, a part of me was starting to feel it too. But I couldn't show that—not to them.

"We'll check some of the smaller neighborhoods next," I said. "Maybe one of them's still intact. Fewer people means fewer infected."

"Maybe," Colt replied, though I could hear the doubt in his voice.

The rest of the drive was heavy with silence, the tension choking the air in the cab. When we finally reached the house, I cut the engine and just sat there, staring at the front door. From the outside, it looked peaceful, normal even. But nothing inside was the same anymore.

Annie was waiting for us at the door, her face lighting up with relief when she saw we were okay. Nash was right behind her, hovering like a shadow. As we stepped inside, I could feel the weight of their expectation—waiting for good news, for some kind of reassurance that things were going to get better.

"We checked the school," I said, my voice flat. "It's not going to work. Too many bodies. It's not safe."

Annie's face fell, but she didn't say anything. I could see the exhaustion in her eyes, the same exhaustion we were all feeling. Nash looked up at me, his face pale and drawn. He didn't ask any questions. He didn't have to.

"What now?" Annie finally asked, her voice soft.

I glanced at Colt and Daryl. We hadn't come up with any solid plans on the drive back, but we didn't have the luxury of time to sit around and think.

"We'll check the smaller developments," I said, trying to keep my voice steady. "There's gotta be one that's still secure."

"And if there isn't?" Nash asked quietly, his voice barely a whisper.

I hesitated for a moment, but I didn't want to lie to him. "Then we stay here and make this work."

Annie nodded slowly, but I could see the worry in her eyes. The supplies we'd gathered wouldn't last forever, and we all knew it. The infected were getting more aggressive, and it was only a matter of time before they started pushing into the less-populated areas like ours. We had to be ready for that, too.

That evening, the group gathered in the living room to discuss what little options we had left. It was a small group now—just us, Daryl, and a few other families who hadn't abandoned Cane Bay yet. Everyone was on edge, tired and hungry, but no one was ready to give up.

"We need to reinforce the perimeter," I said, looking around at the others. "Barricade the windows, set up traps, anything to slow them down if they get in."

"You think they're coming this far?" one of the men, Todd, asked, his voice shaky.

"They're coming," Daryl cut in, his voice grim. "It's just a matter of time."

The room fell silent. We'd all seen it by now—neighborhoods overrun in a matter of days, cities collapsing under the sheer numbers of the infected. The government hadn't been able to stop it, the military was scattered and ineffective. We were on our own.

"We'll take turns on watch," I continued. "Two people at a time, rotating every few hours. If you see anything—anything—don't hesitate. Sound the alarm. We don't have the luxury of waiting."

The group nodded, though I could see the fear in their eyes. They weren't soldiers, and I didn't expect them to be. But we didn't have a choice anymore.

As the meeting broke up, I pulled Annie aside. She'd been quiet the whole time, and I knew something was weighing on her.

"You okay?" I asked softly, brushing a hand through her hair.

She smiled faintly but shook her head. "I'm scared, Frank. For the boys. For us. I don't know how much longer we can keep this up."

"I know," I admitted, pulling her into my arms. "But we have to keep going. One day at a time."

She rested her head on my shoulder, and for a moment, we just stood there, holding on to each other like it was the only thing keeping us grounded.

"We'll get through this," I whispered, though I wasn't entirely sure if I was trying to convince her or myself.

The next few days passed in a blur of preparation. We reinforced the windows with whatever we could find—wooden planks, metal scraps, even old furniture. Colt and Daryl worked tirelessly to set up makeshift barriers around the house, piling up debris in the yard to create obstacles that might slow the infected down.

Todd and the others did their part too, taking turns on watch and helping with the fortifications. We were building something that could hold—at least for a little while.

But the unease never left. Every time I stepped outside to check the perimeter, I felt it—that creeping sense of something coming, something inevitable. The infected were out there, waiting. It was only a matter of time.

One afternoon, as I sat by the window on watch, I heard it. Faint at first, but unmistakable. The low moan of the infected. I froze, listening. The sound was coming from the woods behind the house, growing louder.

I grabbed the radio and clicked it on. "Colt, Daryl. Get ready. We've got movement."

Seconds later, Colt was by my side, rifle in hand. His eyes were wide, but there was no fear in them now. Just determination.

Daryl came in from the back, his shotgun loaded and ready. "Where are they?"

I pointed toward the woods. "There. They're close."

We stepped out onto the porch, weapons at the ready. It was still, the air thick with humidity, but the groans were growing louder now. I could see shapes moving between the trees, stumbling and staggering toward the house.

"Everyone inside!" I shouted over my shoulder. "Get ready!"

Colt and Daryl took up positions beside me as the first infected broke through the tree line, their twisted faces illuminated by the porch light. There were more of them than I'd expected, at least a dozen, maybe more.

"Here we go," I muttered, raising my rifle and taking aim.

The first shot rang out, splitting the night, and the fight for Cane Bay had begun.

Chapter 22: The Siege

They hit just after dusk. Like they knew the exact moment to strike, when the light was gone, and the world felt uncertain. They came in waves, crashing against our barricades like a relentless tide. We'd prepared, but nothing could really brace you for the sight of them. Wild-eyed, hungry, bodies broken but still moving.

The crack of the rifle shot echoed through the night, splitting the oppressive silence that had hung over Cane Bay. I watched as the first infected dropped to the ground, a gaping hole in its skull. The rest of them barely noticed. They just kept coming. Groaning, moaning, moving like one mindless wave of hunger.

"Stay sharp!" I shouted, my voice steady despite the rush of adrenaline flooding my veins.

Colt was already lining up his next shot, his breathing controlled, just like I'd taught him. Daryl crouched beside him, the shotgun at the ready. His finger tapped the trigger restlessly, waiting for the infected to close the gap.

"They're coming fast!" Colt muttered, his voice tight. I could hear the edge of fear creeping in, but he held it together.

I fired again, dropping another one of the infected as it stumbled over the uneven ground. I didn't have time to think about how many there were—whether there'd be more behind this group. Right now, we just had to hold the line.

"They'll hit the barricade in less than a minute," Daryl said, his voice steady. He was calm, but I knew the look in his eyes. He'd seen this before. This was survival mode.

The infected were closing in on the debris we'd piled up, their bodies pressing against the wooden planks and metal scraps we'd hastily thrown together over the past few days. It wasn't much, but it was all we had.

From inside the house, I could hear Annie's voice, trying to calm Nash and the others. I hadn't seen the boys since the attack started, but I trusted her to keep them safe. I had to.

"Colt, take the ones on the left," I ordered, squeezing off another shot. "I'll handle the middle."

Colt nodded, pivoting smoothly to pick off a pair of infected that had veered off toward the side of the house. His aim was good, but there were just too many of them.

"They're gonna breach the barricade!" Daryl yelled, firing a blast from the shotgun that tore through one of the infected, sending it crashing into the others.

The impact barely slowed them down. The barricade shuddered under the weight of the infected as they pushed forward, clawing at the wood, snarling with wild, animalistic desperation. The noise of their growls and moans was unbearable, a constant reminder of what was at stake.

"Fall back to the porch!" I ordered, motioning for Colt and Daryl to pull back.

We retreated a few steps, weapons still raised, as the infected pushed harder. The first plank cracked, and the barricade started to give way. One of them forced its way through, its decayed fingers scraping against the porch railing as it pulled itself toward us.

"Go for the head!" I shouted, snapping my rifle up and firing. The infected jerked, its head snapping back as the bullet hit its mark. It crumpled to the ground, but another one was already squeezing through the gap.

"They're breaking through!" Daryl shouted, firing off another round.

I took another shot, dropping a third infected, but there were too many. More of them shoved their way through the weakened barricade, stumbling over the bodies of their fallen. The wave of undead surged forward, relentless.

"Inside!" I yelled, backing toward the door. "Everyone inside, now!"

We scrambled into the house, slamming the door shut behind us. I could hear the infected pounding against the walls, their snarls and groans growing louder by the second. Colt locked the door, his chest heaving, eyes wide.

"What do we do?" he asked, voice tight with panic.

I took a breath, trying to keep my own fear in check. "We hold them off as long as we can. Keep them out."

Daryl was already moving toward the windows, checking the barricades we'd set up earlier. "These won't hold forever."

"I know," I said quietly, glancing toward Annie, who was standing in the kitchen doorway with Nash and a few of the others. The look on her face said everything. She was terrified, but she was trying to stay strong for the boys.

I walked over to her, placing a hand on her shoulder. "We'll get through this."

She nodded, but I could see the doubt in her eyes. She didn't believe it, not really. I wasn't sure I did either, but I had to keep moving. There was no other option.

Outside, the pounding grew louder. The infected were pressing harder, their weight against the walls causing the wooden planks to creak and groan. We could hear the sharp, angry sounds of them clawing at the windows, desperate to get inside.

"Get ready," I said, moving back toward the door. Colt and Daryl flanked me, both of them tense, waiting for the inevitable breach.

The first window shattered, glass raining down onto the floor. An infected hand reached through, grasping at the air, followed by another.

"They're inside!" someone shouted from the back of the house.

"Colt, cover the windows! Daryl, with me!" I barked, charging toward the back.

We rounded the corner just in time to see one of the infected stumble through the back door, its face twisted into a grotesque snarl. I didn't hesitate—I fired, the bullet tearing through its skull, dropping it instantly.

More were coming. I could hear them outside, clawing at the walls, smashing through the windows. The house wouldn't hold much longer.

"Annie! Get everyone upstairs!" I shouted, my voice barely audible over the chaos. "Now!"

She didn't argue. Grabbing Nash by the arm, she herded him and the others toward the staircase, their footsteps pounding on the wooden steps.

"We need to buy them time!" I called to Daryl as we fell back toward the kitchen.

He nodded grimly, firing off another round as two more infected pushed through the back door. The sound of gunfire echoed through the house, but it barely seemed to make a dent in the horde pressing in from all sides.

I fired again, but I knew we couldn't hold them off forever. We needed a way out, and fast.

"Colt!" I shouted, my mind racing. "Find an exit!"

"I'm on it!" he called back from the front of the house, his voice tight with strain.

We couldn't stay here. The infected were overwhelming us, and it was only a matter of time before they breached every barrier we had.

I took down another one of the infected, my heart pounding in my chest. We were running out of time, and I didn't know if we'd be able to get out in one piece.

"We need to move!" I yelled to Daryl, glancing toward the stairs where Annie and the others had gone.

He fired one last round before turning to me. "Lead the way."

We sprinted toward the stairs, the sound of the infected behind us growing louder with every step. Upstairs, Annie was huddled with the others, her eyes wide as we reached the landing.

"There's a window in the back bedroom," she said breathlessly. "We can jump from there."

I nodded. It wasn't much of a plan, but it was better than staying here and getting torn apart.

"Go!" I shouted, pushing them toward the bedroom. "I'll cover the rear."

Annie hesitated, but she knew better than to argue. She grabbed Nash and the others, and they started moving toward the window.

Colt was already there, prying the window open as quickly as he could. "It's a drop, but we can make it," he said, his voice tight with urgency.

"Get Nash out first," I ordered, glancing back down the stairs. The infected were closing in. We didn't have much time.

Nash went first, his small body slipping through the window and down to the ground below. Annie followed, then the others. Colt was last.

"Hurry!" I shouted, backing toward the window as the first of the infected reached the top of the stairs.

Daryl fired one last shot, then turned and jumped through the window, landing with a grunt below.

I fired two more rounds, then jumped out the window, hitting the ground hard. The infected were right behind us, spilling through the broken windows and doors, but we didn't stop. We ran into the night, hearts pounding, knowing that the siege had only just begun.

Chapter 23: Into the Unknown

The cold night air bit at my skin as we sprinted across the backyard, our feet crunching against the dirt and fallen leaves. Behind us, the house was collapsing into chaos—the moans of the infected spilling out through broken windows, filling the night with their mindless hunger. We didn't have time to look back. The only thing that mattered now was getting as far away from Cane Bay as we could.

"Keep moving!" I shouted, glancing back to make sure everyone was still with us. Colt was next to me, his rifle slung over his shoulder, face pale but determined. Nash ran ahead with Annie, his small figure barely visible in the darkness. Daryl brought up the rear, the shotgun in his hands ready, even though we all knew there was no time to stop and fight.

My heart pounded in my chest, more from fear than exertion. I had trained for this my whole life, but nothing prepares you for running from monsters in your own backyard. Every instinct screamed at me to turn and fight, but I knew better. This wasn't a battle we could win—not yet.

"We've got to find shelter!" Annie called back, her voice tight with panic. "Where do we go?"

I scanned the tree line ahead of us, my mind racing. Cane Bay was mostly houses, neatly manicured lawns, and planned streets. The woods were thin, offering little cover, but it was the only direction that might buy us some time. There was no way we could outrun the infected in open spaces.

"The woods!" I shouted, pointing toward the dark line of trees just beyond the yard. "We can lose them in there!"

We veered toward the trees, the infected still trailing behind, but slower now. I could hear their groans, their heavy footsteps, but they weren't gaining on us as fast as I'd feared. Still, they were relentless. And we were running out of time.

We crashed through the underbrush, branches snapping beneath our feet. The moonlight filtered weakly through the trees, casting eerie shadows on the ground. Every movement in the dark felt like a threat—every rustle of leaves or crack of a branch sent a shiver down my spine.

Once we were deep enough into the woods, I slowed, holding up a hand to signal the others to stop. Everyone was gasping for breath, their faces pale and strained.

"Are we safe here?" Nash asked, his voice trembling.

I crouched down next to him, placing a hand on his shoulder. "For now. But we can't stay here long."

Annie wiped sweat from her brow, her breath coming in short gasps. "Frank, we need a plan. We can't just keep running."

I nodded, knowing she was right. We'd managed to escape the house, but we were in no shape to keep running through the woods all night. The infected would eventually catch up, and we had no idea what other dangers were out here.

"We'll keep moving," I said, keeping my voice calm. "But we need to be smart. We head south, away from the development, and find somewhere we can hunker down for the night."

"Like where?" Colt asked, his voice laced with frustration. "There's nothing but houses and open fields around here."

Daryl stepped forward, wiping the sweat from his brow. "There's an old service road that runs through these woods. Leads to a couple of utility sheds. They're small, but they're solid, and they're off the grid. We might be able to hole up there for the night."

I nodded, grateful for Daryl's knowledge of the area. "That's our best shot. Let's move."

We continued through the woods, the only sound the rustling of leaves underfoot and the distant moans of the infected behind us. My senses were on high alert, every fiber of my being focused on keeping my family safe. I could feel the weight of the rifle in my hands, the metallic taste of fear in my mouth, but I pushed it all down. There was no room for fear now.

After what felt like hours, Daryl finally led us to a small clearing. In the moonlight, I could make out the outline of a squat, weathered utility shed—barely more than a shack, but it was something. The door hung slightly ajar, and the windows were boarded up, but it looked sturdy enough to keep the infected out for the night.

"Stay quiet," I whispered as we approached. "We don't know if anyone else has already taken shelter here."

I edged forward, signaling Daryl to cover me as I slowly pushed the door open with the barrel of my rifle. The shed smelled of damp wood and mildew, but it was empty. I could feel the tension in my body ease slightly. It wasn't much, but it was shelter. It would have to do.

"Get inside," I whispered, motioning for the others to follow me.

Annie and Nash slipped in first, followed by Colt and Daryl. I shut the door behind us and slid the rusty bolt into place. The shed was small and cramped, but it was dry, and the walls felt solid. We were safe—for now.

Nash huddled close to Annie, his eyes wide and scared. Colt sat by the door, his rifle resting on his knees, his face a mask of determination. Daryl leaned against the far wall, shotgun at the ready.

I crouched down beside Annie, wrapping an arm around her. Her face was pale, and I could see the exhaustion in her eyes.

"We'll be okay," I said quietly. "We just need to make it through the night."

She nodded, but I could see the fear she was holding back. The same fear I felt gnawing at the edges of my own resolve. We were in the middle of a nightmare, and there was no waking up from it.

"Frank," Daryl said from across the room, his voice low. "What's our next move?"

I stared at the floor, my mind racing. We couldn't stay here. We'd need food, supplies, and a more defensible location. But there was something else eating at me—something I hadn't wanted to admit to myself until now.

"We can't go back to Cane Bay," I said quietly. "It's lost."

Colt looked up, his brow furrowed. "What do you mean? We can't just leave—what if there are others still out there? What if we can still save people?"

I met his eyes, trying to keep my voice steady. "Colt, you saw what happened. Cane Bay is overrun. There's nothing left to save."

He stared at me, his jaw clenched, but he didn't argue. He knew I was right, even if he didn't want to accept it.

"We regroup tomorrow," I said, my voice firmer now. "We find somewhere safer—somewhere we can hold out for longer. But for tonight, we rest. We'll need our strength."

Everyone settled in, the small space filling with a heavy, oppressive silence. I took the first watch, sitting by the door with my rifle in hand, listening to the sounds of the night. Every creak of the wind through the trees, every distant rustle, sent a jolt of tension through my body.

I glanced over at my family, huddled together in the corner. Annie's eyes were closed, though I knew she wasn't asleep. Nash was curled up next to her, his small frame trembling with exhaustion and fear. Colt sat nearby, his back against the wall, his hands resting on his rifle. He wasn't sleeping either.

As I sat there in the darkness, my mind wandered to what lay ahead. The world we knew was gone, replaced by something brutal and unforgiving. Every step forward felt like walking into the unknown. But I knew one thing for certain: I would do whatever it took to keep my family alive, no matter what waited for us in the days to come.

The infected might have taken Cane Bay, but they hadn't taken us. Not yet.

And as long as I was still breathing, they never would.

Chapter 24: Hard Choices

Morning came slowly, the first light creeping through the cracks in the boarded-up windows of the shed. I had barely slept, my body running on the last reserves of adrenaline and sheer willpower. The others were stirring. Annie woke first, carefully extricating herself from Nash, who was curled up beside her. Colt's eyes were already open, dark with worry and fatigue, but he didn't say anything as we shared a brief look.

The world outside was still, the calm deceptive after the chaos we had left behind in Cane Bay. The infected were out there somewhere, but they hadn't found us. Not yet. That thought offered little comfort, though. They would come eventually. They always did.

"We need to move," I said, breaking the silence. "We can't stay here."

Annie nodded, brushing the hair from her face. She looked exhausted, and I knew she was scared, but she kept it together, like always. "Where do we go, Frank?"

That was the question that had been gnawing at me all night. We couldn't go back to the house—it was overrun. Staying in the shed wasn't an option either. We needed a plan, something more concrete than just running.

"There's a high school south of here," Daryl said, speaking for the first time since last night. "Summerville High. Big place, lots of rooms, defensible if we can clear it out."

I nodded slowly. The school could work, but it wasn't without risks. Schools were sprawling, hard to secure entirely, but they were built to handle large numbers of people. The gym could serve as a shelter if we fortified it, and there might be supplies left in the cafeteria.

"It's a start," I said. "We'll head there, see what we're working with."

Nash stirred, rubbing his eyes and looking up at us. "Are we leaving now?"

"Soon," I replied, trying to sound reassuring. "We need to pack up and get ready to move."

Colt stood, slinging his rifle over his shoulder. "I'll scout ahead, make sure the path is clear."

"No," I said firmly. "We stay together. We don't split up unless there's no other choice. Too many variables out there."

Colt frowned but didn't argue. He knew better. In times like these, separation meant death.

We gathered what little we had—a couple of bottles of water, some canned food we had scavenged from the house, and our weapons. It wasn't much, but it would have to do. The infected were slow, but there were a lot of them, and getting cornered was a real danger.

The trek through the woods was quiet, the oppressive silence making every step feel heavier. The trees cast long shadows as the morning sun crept higher, and my senses were on high alert for any sign of movement. The air smelled damp, and the ground was soft from the previous night's rain, making our progress slow.

As we neared the edge of the woods, I held up a hand, signaling everyone to stop. Ahead, I could see the rooftops of houses, part of a small subdivision just outside the high school grounds. There was no movement, but that didn't mean it was safe.

"I'll go first," I whispered, crouching low and moving toward the tree line. I scanned the area, listening for any sounds, watching for any movement. Nothing. I motioned for the others to follow, and we quickly made our way across the street and through the empty neighborhood. The stillness was unnerving. No birds, no cars, no people. Just silence.

The school loomed ahead, its brick walls and tall windows imposing in the bright morning light. The gates were open, but the parking lot was empty. I didn't like it. Something felt wrong.

We moved carefully toward the entrance, sticking close to the walls for cover. I checked the door—it was unlocked. Pushing it open slowly, I stepped inside, my rifle raised. The interior was dark, the long hallways stretching out into shadow.

"Stay close," I whispered, leading the way inside.

The school smelled of stale air and mildew, the kind of smell that comes from a place left untouched for too long. Our footsteps echoed down the hallway, each step amplifying the sense of abandonment that filled the place.

"Check the classrooms," I said, nodding toward the doors on either side of the hall. "We need to clear this place before we settle in."

Colt and Daryl moved quickly, checking each room while I kept watch with Annie and Nash. The school was huge, much larger than I had expected, and clearing it would take time.

After a few minutes, Colt reappeared. "It's clear, but the doors in the back are busted. It looks like someone forced their way in."

I felt a knot tighten in my gut. "Any sign of the infected?"

"Not yet," he replied. "But there's blood in one of the classrooms. Dried. It's been there a while."

I cursed under my breath. We weren't alone. Maybe whoever had been here was long gone, but the blood meant something had happened, and we couldn't afford to be caught off guard.

"We clear the gym next," I said. "If it's secure, we can fortify it. It'll give us a base to work from while we figure out our next move."

The gym was large, the basketball court gleaming under the harsh fluorescent lights. Rows of bleachers lined the walls, and a set of double doors at the far end led to what I assumed was a locker room or storage area.

"Lock those doors," I told Colt and Daryl, pointing to the entrance. "Annie, see if you can find anything useful in the storage rooms—first aid kits, blankets, whatever we can use."

As they moved to their tasks, I stood in the center of the gym, listening to the silence. It felt wrong to be here, like we were intruding on a place that had once been filled with life but was now nothing more than a tomb.

Nash came up beside me, his small face serious. "Are we going to stay here, Dad?"

"For now," I said, resting a hand on his shoulder. "Just until we find somewhere better."

He nodded, but I could see the fear in his eyes. He was young, but not so young that he didn't understand what was happening. None of us were the same people we had been when this started. The world had forced us to change.

"We'll make it through this," I said, though the words felt hollow. "We're survivors."

Nash nodded again, but he didn't say anything. He didn't need to. We both knew the truth—we were alive, but survival came with a price. Every day brought new dangers, new choices. And every choice carried consequences.

Annie returned with a small stash of supplies—mostly old sports equipment and a couple of first-aid kits, but it was better than nothing. We set up camp in one corner of the gym, barricading the doors as best we could with the bleachers and any furniture we could find.

As the day wore on, the reality of our situation settled in. We were safe for the moment, but the world outside was crumbling. Cane Bay was lost, and there was no telling how far the infection had spread. The government had fallen silent, the military was overwhelmed, and the roads were no longer safe. But we had each other. And for now, that was enough.

As the sun began to set, I sat by the doors, keeping watch. Colt sat beside me, his rifle resting in his lap. Neither of us spoke, but the silence between us was heavy with unspoken questions. Questions we didn't have the answers to.

"What now?" he finally asked, his voice barely more than a whisper.

I didn't look at him. "We survive. One day at a time."

He nodded, but I could see the doubt in his eyes. He was young, but not so young that he didn't understand the weight of those words. Survival wasn't just about staying alive—it was about finding a reason to keep going. And in this world, that was the hardest thing of all.

Chapter 25: Routine and Tension

The next few days passed in a blur of routine and tension. In the gym of Summerville High, we set up a makeshift home. It wasn't much, but it felt more secure than any place we'd been in since the outbreak started. The walls were high, the doors solid. It wasn't perfect, but it gave us breathing room.

The boys were adjusting. Colt kept to himself mostly, sitting by the door with his rifle, watching the hallways like a hawk. He was growing into his role fast—too fast, maybe. Nash, on the other hand, tried to keep a semblance of normalcy, kicking around an old soccer ball we'd found in the storage closet. I couldn't help but think of how this would have been just another day at school for him a few months ago, another practice, another game. Now, the ball was a reminder of what had been lost.

Annie busied herself, organizing what little supplies we had and checking in on everyone. I could tell she was struggling too, but like always, she kept it together for the boys. That was Annie—she had the strength of ten people, even when things were crumbling around her.

We rationed our food and water carefully. Daryl and I took turns patrolling the school's perimeter, making sure no one—or nothing—was coming our way. It was quiet for the most part, eerily so. The streets around the school were abandoned, littered with debris and broken-down cars, but no sign of the infected. That didn't mean they weren't there, waiting, but for now, we had a little time to think and plan.

Every evening, we'd sit together in the corner of the gym, talking about our next steps. Colt was always the first to push for more action, more scouting, more scavenging. He wanted to be out there, doing something, anything to keep moving forward. But I wasn't willing to take any unnecessary risks. Not yet.

"We need more supplies, Dad," Colt said one night, his voice edged with frustration. "We can't keep sitting here, hoping things will magically get better. We're running out of food, and the water isn't going to last much longer."

"I know that," I replied calmly, looking him in the eye. "But we're not going to rush into something without a plan. We'll do a supply run when we're ready."

Colt shook his head, his jaw clenched. "We don't have time. Every day we wait, things get worse. People are getting more desperate out there."

He wasn't wrong, but I couldn't afford to let him think this was just a matter of taking action for the sake of it. There were too many unknowns—too many ways things could go sideways.

"We'll go," I said finally, my voice firm. "But not until we're prepared. And not alone. We do this as a team, or not at all."

Colt stared at me for a moment, then nodded, his frustration simmering down. He was young, but he understood the stakes. He just needed to be reminded sometimes that this wasn't like the games he used to play—this was life and death.

Daryl cleared his throat. "There's a grocery store about three miles from here. Small, but it might have some supplies left. It's risky, but worth checking out."

I glanced at Annie, who sat quietly beside Nash, her face tight with worry. She didn't say anything, but I knew what she was thinking. Another run meant more danger. But staying here with dwindling resources was just as dangerous.

"Alright," I said after a long pause. "We'll go in the morning. Colt, Daryl, and I. Annie, you stay here with Nash."

Annie looked like she wanted to protest, but she held back. She trusted me. Always had. But I could see the fear in her eyes.

"Be careful," she said softly, her hand brushing mine.

"I will," I promised.

Morning came quickly, and by dawn, we were ready. Colt, Daryl, and I packed our gear—rifles, knives, flashlights, and what little food we had left. The plan was simple: get in, grab what we could, and get out. No heroics. No unnecessary risks.

The grocery store Daryl mentioned was a small mom-and-pop shop on the edge of Summerville, one of those places that probably hadn't been touched yet because it wasn't a big chain. It was risky, but it was our best shot at finding food and maybe even some medical supplies.

We moved carefully through the streets, sticking to the shadows and avoiding main roads. It was clear that the town was in bad shape. Cars were abandoned everywhere, windows smashed, doors left wide open. Occasionally, we'd see a body lying in the street, the victim of either the infected or looters. It was hard to tell anymore.

The infected themselves were few and far between, but we couldn't be too careful. One wrong move and we'd be overwhelmed. Every corner we turned felt like it could be our last, every sound setting my nerves on edge.

When we finally reached the store, I motioned for Colt and Daryl to stop. The front door was ajar, and there were no signs of movement inside. But that didn't mean it was empty.

"Stay close," I whispered, leading the way in.

The interior of the store was dim, the lights long since dead. Shelves were overturned, and most of the perishable food was already rotten, but there were still some cans of vegetables and soups, a few bottles of water. It wasn't much, but it was something.

Colt and Daryl quickly went to work, filling their bags while I kept watch. My heart pounded in my chest, the silence making every noise sound louder than it should have been.

Then I heard it—a low, guttural groan coming from the back of the store.

"Frank," Daryl whispered, his eyes wide. He had heard it too.

I raised my hand, signaling them to stay still. Slowly, I moved toward the sound, my rifle ready. The groan came again, louder this time, followed by the unmistakable sound of shuffling feet.

I rounded the corner of one of the aisles and froze.

Two infected stood there, their faces pale and gaunt, their eyes wild with hunger. One of them had a chunk of flesh missing from its neck, the wound still oozing dark blood. The other looked worse—its arm was broken, hanging at an unnatural angle, but it didn't seem to care.

They hadn't seen me yet, but it was only a matter of time.

I took a deep breath, steadying my aim. I had to be quick, precise.

The first shot rang out, echoing through the store. The infected with the broken arm went down immediately, a clean hit to the head. The second one turned, its mouth opening in a twisted snarl, but before it could lunge, I fired again.

It collapsed to the floor with a thud, the silence returning just as quickly as it had been broken.

"Let's move," I called to Colt and Daryl, my voice low but urgent. "We've got what we need."

They didn't argue, quickly gathering the last of the supplies before we headed for the exit. We moved fast, not daring to linger. The sound of gunfire would attract more of them, and we needed to be long gone before that happened.

By the time we made it back to the school, the sun was high in the sky, casting long shadows across the empty parking lot. Annie and Nash were waiting for us, their faces lighting up with relief as we approached.

"We got some stuff," Colt said, his voice tired but triumphant as he dropped the bags at Annie's feet. "It's not a lot, but it'll last us a few more days."

Annie hugged him tightly, her eyes glassy with unshed tears. "I'm just glad you're back."

I watched them for a moment, a sense of weariness settling into my bones. Every day was a battle now. Every decision felt like it could be our last. But we were still here. Still standing.

For now, that was enough.

Tomorrow, we'd face the same dangers. Tomorrow, we'd keep fighting.

Because that's what survivors did.

Chapter 26: The Broken Grid

By the time we got back from the supply run, I could feel the strain in my muscles. The constant tension of being on alert had taken its toll, but as I looked at the bags of canned goods, bottles of water, and the few meager medical supplies we had managed to gather, I knew it had been worth it. For a moment, it felt like we had won a small battle. But deep down, I knew the war wasn't over.

Colt was pacing again, restless as always. He had that same fire in his eyes, the one that told me he wasn't going to sit still for long. I caught Annie's eye as she tended to Nash, who was hunched over, still kicking around that deflated soccer ball. They both seemed different now, as if the realities of the world were settling into them in a way that couldn't be undone. The boys had grown up fast, too fast.

"We need to think longer-term," I said, breaking the silence as I sat down beside Annie. "These supply runs are going to dry up. We can't depend on finding what we need forever. It's going to get worse out there."

Annie didn't say anything for a minute, just nodded as she packed the last of the cans into a corner. "We've got to start thinking about how we can sustain ourselves," she finally replied. "Maybe even reach out to other survivors."

"Reaching out means exposing ourselves," I said. "We don't know who we can trust. I've seen too much—people will do anything when they're desperate."

"But staying isolated isn't a long-term plan, either," she pressed. "We can't do this alone, Frank."

She was right. But the thought of depending on others was hard to stomach, especially when every day brought new horrors. The world had fractured. Communication was down, the grid barely hanging on by a thread. The radio stations we had picked up before were silent now. No more government updates. No more rescue plans.

The only sounds we heard at night were the distant echoes of screams and gunfire, growing fainter with each passing day. Society was unraveling faster than any of us could have imagined.

That evening, as the sun dipped low behind the trees, Colt joined me at the perimeter fence. His eyes scanned the horizon, his hands gripping his rifle with the kind of focus that reminded me of myself at his age. Too young to carry so much weight, but determined, nonetheless.

"Dad, we need to start building defenses," he said, not looking away from the tree line. "If people find out we're here, if they come looking for what we have, we'll be sitting ducks."

I nodded, but his words sparked a worry I'd been avoiding. It wasn't just the infected we had to fear anymore—it was other survivors. Desperation did terrible things to people. And with each passing day, the chances of someone discovering us increased.

"You're right," I said, my voice low. "We'll start reinforcing tomorrow. We need to make this place impenetrable."

"I can help," Colt said quickly. "I'll take the night watch too."

I turned to him, seeing the determination in his face. He wanted to be part of this, to shoulder the responsibility. Part of me wanted to say no, to shield him from the harsh realities that were coming. But I knew better. Colt had already seen too much. The innocence was gone.

"Alright," I said, placing a hand on his shoulder. "But take shifts. We'll all pull our weight."

The next day, we set to work. Using materials scavenged from the surrounding buildings, we began reinforcing the entrances to the school—barricading the gym doors, fortifying the windows with anything sturdy we could find. Daryl had some experience with carpentry, and he took the lead in constructing makeshift barriers that could slow down intruders, whether they were infected or otherwise.

Colt, true to his word, worked tirelessly alongside Daryl. His movements were sharp, his focus unbreakable. Every piece of wood hammered into place, every bolt tightened, was done with a fierce dedication.

Nash tried to help where he could, though he spent more time at Annie's side. She had taken on the role of caretaker, keeping everyone fed and looking after those who had grown sick or injured. We had found a few survivors from other areas—people who had wandered in, some of them barely alive. It was hard, but Annie didn't turn anyone away. That was who she was. Even in this new world, her heart remained unbroken.

As we worked, the wind carried strange sounds—rustling in the trees, faint howls in the distance. It was hard to tell if it was the infected, animals, or something worse. We couldn't afford to be complacent.

By late afternoon, the first of the solar panels Daryl had salvaged from a nearby house started to work, giving us a trickle of power. It wasn't much, but it was a start. Enough to keep the radios charged, enough to run a few lights at night.

We sat together in the gym that evening, the dim glow of a single bulb casting long shadows across the room. The silence between us was heavy, each of us lost in our own thoughts. Nash was the first to speak.

"Do you think it's ever going to go back to normal?" he asked, his voice small, almost a whisper.

I looked at him, his young face still full of questions that I didn't have answers to. He wasn't just asking about the infected, the violence. He was asking if we'd ever have the life we had before—school, friends, a future.

"I don't know," I said honestly, meeting his gaze. "But we're going to do everything we can to survive. That's all we can do right now."

Nash nodded, his expression thoughtful as he stared at the flickering light. He was quiet for the rest of the night, and I could see the weight of this new world starting to settle on his shoulders too.

As the days wore on, the defenses strengthened. We had barricades, solar power, and a schedule for guard shifts. But with every passing moment, the unease grew. It was only a matter of time before someone—or something—found us.

It was early morning when it happened.

Colt was on watch at the south end of the building when he heard it—a rustling in the bushes, followed by the unmistakable sound of footsteps. Slow, deliberate. He gripped his rifle tighter, his heart racing.

Through the trees, figures began to emerge—ragged, limping, their clothes torn and filthy. But these weren't the infected. They were survivors.

"Dad," Colt whispered over the radio, his voice tight. "We've got company."

And just like that, the delicate balance of our new normal teetered on the edge, ready to shatter at any moment.

Chapter 27: Unwelcome Guests

The radio crackled with Colt's voice, low but urgent.

"There's people. About a dozen. They're moving in slow, Dad. What do we do?"

I grabbed my rifle from where it was leaning against the wall and glanced at Annie, who had overheard. Her face tightened, worry etched deep into her features, but she didn't say a word. She knew the stakes. Nash, sensing the shift in mood, paused from where he was tinkering with an old radio. He looked at me, wide-eyed.

"Stay with your mom," I told him, my voice firm. "No matter what happens, don't come outside."

"Frank, be careful," Annie said quietly, her hand resting lightly on my arm for just a moment. It was more of a plea than a statement.

I nodded, then made my way through the narrow hallways toward the gym entrance where Colt was stationed. As I reached the lookout point, he was crouched low, peering through a crack between the boards we'd nailed over the windows. His eyes met mine for a brief second before returning to the figures that now hovered just outside the tree line, half in the shadows.

The group looked ragged, weary. Clothes torn and covered in dirt, faces gaunt. They weren't the infected, but they weren't far from the edge either. Desperation clung to them like a second skin.

"I counted twelve," Colt whispered, his breath fogging up the glass. "But I don't know if there's more hiding further back. They're just standing there."

I knelt beside him, heart pounding in my chest as I sized up the situation. They hadn't rushed in, which meant they either didn't know we were here—or worse, they did, and they were trying to gauge how strong we were.

A figure stepped forward from the group—a tall man, older than most of the others, with wild eyes and hair matted against his head.

He looked thin, like he hadn't eaten in days. His movements were slow, calculated. He raised his hands up, palms out, in what was probably supposed to be a non-threatening gesture.

"Hey!" His voice cracked through the air, hoarse but loud enough to carry. "We don't want any trouble! Just need food, maybe some shelter!"

Colt shifted beside me, his grip tightening on the rifle. He glanced at me, waiting for the call.

I stood up, my legs stiff, and stepped toward the door, careful not to open it too far. The barricades we'd set up would hold for now, but I wasn't about to risk anything.

"What do you want?" I called out, keeping my voice firm but neutral. I didn't want to provoke them, but I needed to make it clear we weren't easy pickings.

The man took a few steps closer, and as he did, I could see the faces of the others more clearly—women, children, and a few younger men, all looking equally worn out and terrified. It was hard to tell whether they were dangerous or just desperate. At this point, there wasn't much difference.

"We've been out here for days," the man said. "Ran into some of those... things back in Ridgeville. We lost most of our group. We've got no food, no water. We're not looking for trouble, just a place to lay low for a while."

I scanned the group again. They were huddled together, clinging to each other like they had nowhere else to go. The man's eyes met mine, pleading.

But I couldn't trust them. Desperation made people dangerous.

"How many are you?" I asked.

"Twelve," he replied quickly. "Just twelve. The rest... didn't make it."

Colt shifted beside me, glancing at the door. He didn't need to say anything; I could feel his unease. He wanted to trust them, but he was still a kid. He didn't understand what people were capable of when they had nothing left.

"We've got our own people to look after," I said. "Supplies are tight. I can't offer you shelter."

The man's face fell, the hope draining from his eyes. His hands dropped to his sides, and for a moment, I thought he might just walk away. But then, something shifted in his expression—something darker.

"I get it," he said, his voice lower now. "But see, the thing is... we don't have anywhere else to go. And we've got women and kids here. You don't want their blood on your hands, do you?"

There it was. The shift from desperation to threat.

Colt tensed beside me, his finger inching toward the trigger, but I raised a hand to keep him still.

"I'm not responsible for you," I said, keeping my voice calm but cold. "This is our place, and we'll defend it if we have to."

The man's lips curled into a twisted grin, like he'd been expecting this. "I don't think you understand. We're not asking."

I felt the weight of the rifle in my hands, the cool metal grounding me as I prepared for what I knew was coming next. Behind him, the rest of the group started to shift, some of the younger men stepping forward, weapons appearing in their hands—makeshift knives, pipes, one even had a handgun. They'd come prepared for this.

"Dad," Colt whispered, his voice tight. "What do we do?"

I took a deep breath, keeping my eyes on the man in front of me. "You aim for the ones closest to us. Don't hesitate. If they make a move, we defend ourselves."

Colt nodded, his jaw set. He was ready.

The man in front of us took one more step, his hand reaching behind him. I didn't need to see what he was pulling out. I could feel the shift in the air, the tension snapping into action.

"Get ready," I muttered to Colt.

And then, in a flash, the man lunged.

Colt fired first, the crack of the rifle echoing through the trees. The man dropped to the ground, his body crumpling in a heap. Chaos erupted as the rest of the group charged toward us, their shouts mixing with the gunfire.

I didn't think. I just reacted. Years of training kicked in as I pulled the trigger, again and again, aiming for the closest threats. Colt was beside me, his shots precise, but there were too many of them.

From inside the school, I heard Annie shout for Nash. I glanced back for a split second, my heart racing as I realized the door wasn't fully barricaded. If they got through...

Another gunshot rang out, this time from behind me. Daryl appeared at the other end of the gym, his shotgun blasting through the air. The force of it knocked two of the attackers off their feet, sending the rest scattering back into the woods.

"Fall back!" I shouted to Colt, grabbing his arm as we pulled away from the doorway.

The fight wasn't over, but we'd bought ourselves some time. The survivors who'd attacked us retreated into the woods, dragging their wounded with them. But they wouldn't be gone for long.

We had won the battle, but the war for our survival was far from over.

Chapter 28: Thin Line Between Trust and Survival

The aftermath of the skirmish lingered in the air like smoke from a burned-out fire. Colt and I stood in the gym, breathing hard, both of us scanning the tree line for any sign of movement. The sun had dropped lower, casting long shadows across the clearing. Daryl had disappeared back into the school building after the fight, no doubt checking on his wife and son.

Colt broke the silence first, his voice shaking slightly. "Do you think they'll come back?"

I didn't have a clear answer, but I knew one thing for sure. Desperate people don't give up easily.

"They might," I said, my gaze still fixed on the trees. "But next time, we'll be ready."

I placed a hand on Colt's shoulder, squeezing it lightly. He had done well. Better than I could've hoped, but I could see the toll it had taken on him. His face was pale, and his hands trembled slightly, still clutching the rifle. I remembered what it felt like after your first real firefight—the rush of adrenaline, the shock, the way your hands felt like they were vibrating long after the danger had passed.

"You did good, son," I said, my voice firm. "Real good."

Colt nodded, but his eyes were distant. "They looked... like us. Just normal people."

I couldn't argue with that. The people we'd just fought weren't monsters—they were just trying to survive like we were. That was the terrifying part. The infected were easier to deal with; you knew what to expect. But people? People were unpredictable.

"You saved us," I said, meeting his eyes. "You did what you had to do."

He didn't respond, but I could tell he was still wrestling with it, still trying to come to terms with the fact that he had taken a life. I let it sit. There was no easy answer for that, no words that could erase what he was feeling.

"We need to check on your mom and Nash," I said, steering him back toward the school.

The hallway felt eerily quiet as we made our way to the main area where Annie and Nash had been staying. My stomach tightened as we approached, but the tension eased slightly when I heard voices coming from inside.

Annie was there, standing by the window, rifle in hand. She turned when she saw us, her face a mixture of relief and concern. Nash was beside her, his eyes wide, clutching a hammer he had grabbed during the chaos.

"Are you okay?" Annie asked, crossing the room toward us. Her eyes flickered over Colt, checking for any sign of injury.

"We're fine," I said. "They didn't get through, but we need to stay on alert. I don't think they'll come back tonight, but we can't take any chances."

Nash looked up at me, his voice barely a whisper. "Did you kill them?"

I exchanged a glance with Annie before answering. "We did what we had to. They were coming for us."

He nodded, but I could see the weight of my words settle on him. He wasn't old enough to fully grasp it yet, but he wasn't a kid anymore either. None of us were.

"We're safe for now," I said, trying to ease the tension. "But we're going to need to make some decisions soon. We can't stay here forever."

Annie's face tightened. "What do you mean?"

I sighed, rubbing the back of my neck. "Those people are going to come back, or others like them. And the longer we stay in one place, the more of a target we become."

"We've fortified this place," Annie argued. "We've got supplies, walls, a plan."

"Yeah, but we're not the only ones who know that," I replied. "Word's going to spread. We're too visible here."

Colt, who had been silent, spoke up. "Where would we go?"

I didn't have an answer, but I knew we couldn't keep doing this. We couldn't keep waiting for the next attack, hoping we'd be able to fend off every group that came our way. The world had changed, and we had to change with it.

"We'll figure it out," I said, more to reassure them than anything else. "But for now, we need to get some rest. We'll talk in the morning."

Annie didn't look convinced, but she nodded, pulling Nash closer to her. I could see the exhaustion in her eyes, the strain of trying to hold it all together for the boys.

I took one last look out the window, scanning the tree line for any sign of movement. The sun had fully set now, casting the world into darkness. The air was still, but I could feel the tension building, like the quiet before a storm.

We were safe for now, but I knew it was only a matter of time before something—or someone—came knocking again.

That night, sleep didn't come easily. I lay on the cot, staring up at the ceiling, listening to the creaks of the old building and the occasional rustle of leaves outside. Every sound made my muscles tense, every shadow outside the window looked like a threat.

But beyond the immediate dangers, my mind kept drifting to the bigger picture. How long could we survive like this? Moving from one place to another, always looking over our shoulders, never knowing if the next person we met would be a friend or an enemy.

And then there was the question I hadn't dared ask myself yet: What if there was no getting back to normal? What if this was it? What if the world we knew was already gone, and we were just hanging on to the edges of something that had already crumbled?

As the night wore on, the weight of it all pressed down on me. I had my family, and that was what mattered most. But out here, surrounded by uncertainty and danger, I didn't know how long I could keep them safe. And the thought of losing them... that was a fear I couldn't even begin to face.

Morning came slowly, the first rays of sunlight creeping through the cracks in the windows. I sat up, feeling the ache in my muscles from the tension of the night before. Colt was already awake, sitting by the door with his rifle across his lap. He hadn't slept either.

"Get some rest," I told him. "I'll take over."

He nodded and stood, but before he left, he looked back at me. "Dad?"

"Yeah?"

"Are we going to be okay?"

I met his eyes, the weight of his question heavy in the air. I wanted to tell him yes. I wanted to tell him that everything would be fine, that we'd find a way through this. But I couldn't lie to him, not anymore.

"We'll do what we have to," I said. "Whatever it takes."

He nodded, his expression grim, and walked away.

As I sat by the door, rifle in hand, I knew one thing for sure: Whatever was coming next, we'd face it together. And I'd do whatever it took to keep my family alive. No matter the cost.

Chapter 29: The Hardest Decisions

The morning was heavy with silence. Annie, Colt, Nash, and I sat around the table in the school's cafeteria, the weight of last night's fight still lingering in the air. Outside, the early morning sunbathed the parking lot in pale light, but the sense of dread was growing stronger.

I rubbed my eyes and looked at each of them. We needed to have the conversation I had been avoiding—how long could we stay here, and what was next?

"We can't stay here much longer," I finally said, breaking the silence. "It's only a matter of time before those people come back. Or someone else like them."

Annie was the first to speak up. "Where would we go? We don't even know what's out there, Frank. There's no guarantee it's any safer than here."

I nodded. "I know. But sitting here makes us a target. We're vulnerable, and we can't keep fighting off every group that comes through. We need a plan to get somewhere safer, more sustainable."

Colt, who had been listening intently, spoke next. "What about the coast? We could try to get to one of the smaller islands, maybe Sullivan's Island or somewhere near the marshes. It's isolated."

I considered it for a moment. "That's an option, but we'd need to scout it out first. We don't know how bad things have gotten near the coast. Plus, we'd need supplies to make a move like that."

"We've got enough to last a few days," Annie said. "But beyond that, we're running low. Even if we leave here, we'll need to find more supplies on the way."

Nash looked between us, his young face pale. "But what if we run into more people like those last night? They had guns, Dad. They were organized."

I exhaled slowly, trying to steady myself. He was right. We couldn't just wander out into the world without knowing what was waiting for us. But staying here any longer wasn't an option either.

"We have to assume that everywhere we go, we're going to run into other people," I said. "Some will be like us, just trying to survive. But others... well, we saw what desperate people are willing to do. We need to move carefully."

Annie crossed her arms, staring at the floor. "I hate this. I hate that we're being forced to leave behind everything we've worked for. It's not right."

"I know," I said quietly. "But we've got to adapt. The world isn't what it was."

A silence fell over the room as we all processed what was ahead of us. Leaving Cane Bay, our home for the past few years, wasn't just a physical move—it was accepting that nothing would ever be the same again. The neighborhood we knew, the routine, the sense of community—it was all gone.

"We'll need to gather whatever supplies we can from here before we go," I said. "Weapons, food, water. Anything that will help us survive."

Colt leaned forward. "I can help with that. I'll check the gym, see if there's any more equipment we can use for protection."

Nash, always eager to help in any way he could, raised his hand slightly. "I can come too."

"No," I said firmly. "You stay here with your mom. It's not safe for you to go out there right now."

Nash's face fell, but he didn't argue. He knew, as much as it frustrated him, that he wasn't ready to face the danger out there just yet.

Annie stood up, her eyes meeting mine. "I'll help you pack. We'll gather as much food and water as we can carry."

We all rose from the table, the reality of our situation pressing down on us. There wasn't much time. Every second we stayed put was a gamble, and the odds were getting worse.

As we moved through the school's hallways, I couldn't help but feel a deep sense of loss. This place had given us shelter when we needed it most, but now it felt like a prison. The walls that had protected us were now closing in.

I led Colt into the gym, the air heavy with the smell of sweat and dust. We went through the storage rooms, gathering anything that could be of use—a few more baseball bats, rope, some flashlights, and a couple of old fire axes. It wasn't much, but it was better than nothing.

Colt found a stack of old duffel bags, and we packed them with what we could. He worked quickly, his movements steady but tense. I could tell last night's events were still weighing on him.

"You did good last night," I said, trying to offer some reassurance. "I know it wasn't easy."

Colt nodded but didn't meet my eyes. "I didn't think it'd be like this. Fighting other people. I thought it'd be the infected we'd have to worry about."

"So did I," I admitted. "But sometimes, it's the living who are more dangerous."

He zipped up the last bag, his face grim. "I guess so."

I placed a hand on his shoulder. "We're going to get through this. As long as we stick together, we've got a chance."

He nodded again, more determined this time. "Yeah. We'll make it."

Back in the cafeteria, Annie and Nash had gathered as much food and water as they could find. It wasn't much, but it would get us through a few more days.

"Are we ready?" Annie asked as we loaded up the bags.

I looked at the small pile of supplies we had gathered. It wasn't nearly enough for what lay ahead, but it was all we had.

"We're ready," I said, though the weight of uncertainty pressed down on me.

We stood by the doors, the outside world waiting for us like an open wound. The wind rustled the trees, and in the distance, I could hear faint sounds—the signs of a world still collapsing.

"Let's move," I said.

And with that, we stepped out into the unknown, leaving behind the last remnants of the life we once knew.

Chapter 30: Beaufort and the Marines

The drive south was quiet, the tension thick in the truck. Colt sat next to me, his gaze fixed on the road ahead. Annie and Nash were in the backseat, Nash clutching a map of South Carolina as if it might tell him something new. We'd left Cane Bay behind, a place that had been home but now felt like a memory, a ghost of the normal life we had once known.

The plan was simple enough: get to Beaufort. The Marine Corps Air Station down there might still be operational, and if it was, we'd stand a chance at finding some order, some structure. I had spent years in the Corps, and if there was one thing I trusted, it was the way the Marines handled a crisis. If any branch of the military could hold out against this, it was them.

"I thought the Marines would already be here," Nash said, breaking the silence.

"They're probably focused on the bigger cities," I replied. "Charleston, Columbia, even Savannah. Summerville's too small to be a priority."

Colt leaned back in his seat, his eyes still scanning the horizon. "What if Beaufort's like everywhere else? What if there's no one left?"

His question hung in the air for a moment. It was a fear I had been pushing down since we'd decided to make the trip. Every place we had passed so far—abandoned, overrun, or worse—had reinforced the possibility that the military was just as crippled as the rest of the country.

"Then we'll adapt," I finally said, gripping the steering wheel tighter. "We always do."

The roads were eerily empty as we passed through rural areas, occasional wrecked cars and debris marking signs of chaos that had hit weeks ago. But the deeper we went into the Lowcountry, the more things changed. Military presence had thinned out around Charleston and the Midlands, but Beaufort was a Marine town. Even before we saw the base, I had a feeling the landscape would shift.

As we approached the outskirts of Beaufort, it became clear we were getting closer to something more organized. Roadblocks had been set up along the main highway, military vehicles scattered along the side. The wreckage of a transport truck lay overturned in a ditch, a brutal reminder that things had spiraled out of control fast. A few of the corpses lying by the roadside had military gear on. Marines, or at least they had been once.

We rolled slowly through what had once been a checkpoint. The barricades were knocked down, but signs of a recent firefight littered the area—spent casings, bloodstains, and the unmistakable stench of death in the summer heat. Whoever had fought here had either won and moved on or lost and was long gone.

Nash scrunched up his face at the sight. "Do you think the base is still standing?"

"I hope so," I said, though I was starting to doubt it.

Another mile or two and the town itself came into view. Beaufort, nestled along the waterfront, had always been a peaceful place, a spot where old oak trees draped in Spanish moss lined the streets. Now, it was different. Smoke rose from several buildings in the distance, and the once-bustling marina looked like it had been abandoned in a hurry. But the one thing that stood out—the one thing that gave me hope—was the sound of helicopters in the distance.

"They're still here," Colt said, sitting up straighter.

The sound of military choppers cutting through the air was unmistakable. It wasn't just a relief; it was a reminder that the world wasn't completely lost. There was still some fight left.

We followed the road leading toward the Marine Corps Air Station, driving through the ghost of a town that had clearly been evacuated. Signs of the panic were everywhere—abandoned cars, broken storefronts, shattered windows. But there were no bodies, no signs of infected roaming the streets. That was different from everywhere else we'd been.

As we neared the base, we hit another checkpoint. This one was manned.

Two Marines stepped forward, rifles in hand, signaling for us to stop. They looked rough—dirty, tired, but alive.

I rolled down the window, and the Marine on the left came up, his eyes scanning the inside of the truck. "What's your business here?"

"I'm Frank Keller," I said, keeping my tone steady. "Former Marine. We're looking for safety, some stability."

The Marine studied me for a moment before nodding. "It's chaos out there, but you've made it to the right place. You'll need to be cleared before entering the base, but we're still operational."

"Is the command still intact?" I asked.

He nodded again, though there was a hint of uncertainty in his eyes. "Most of it. We're doing what we can to keep things under control. It's bad out there, but the Corps is holding."

I glanced over at Annie, who looked relieved, and then back to Colt and Nash. For the first time in a while, there was a glimmer of hope.

"Follow the road," the Marine continued. "You'll get screened inside, and then we'll see what can be done for you."

We drove past the checkpoint and onto the base. The sight of military order was like a breath of fresh air. Helicopters buzzed overhead, and soldiers were moving with purpose. Makeshift tents had been set up near the entrance, and a field hospital was visible in the distance.

The base wasn't untouched by the chaos—far from it. There were wounded being treated, and the lines of civilians waiting to be processed were long. But it was clear the Marines were doing everything they could to keep some semblance of order.

We pulled up near the screening tents, where another group of Marines directed us to park. A few minutes later, we were sitting under the shade of a tent while a corpsman checked us for signs of infection or injury. I could feel the weight of the last few weeks bearing down on me—exhaustion, fear, the constant state of readiness.

"How bad is it?" I asked the corpsman as he finished checking Colt's vitals.

He sighed, shaking his head. "Worse than we thought it could get. The infection spread faster than anyone anticipated. Cities have fallen, even some military bases. But we're holding the line here."

"Any word from higher command? The Pentagon?"

"They're still operational, but barely. Communications are down across most of the country, but we're getting fragments. It's a mess. Right now, all we can do is keep the infected away and hold this position."

I glanced at Annie, who was listening intently. "Is it just us? South Carolina?"

"No," the corpsman said. "This is happening everywhere. It's global."

That hit me like a punch to the gut. I had known things were bad. Hearing that this wasn't just an American problem, this was everywhere, made it feel more hopeless.

"How long can you hold out?" Annie asked quietly.

"As long as we need to," the corpsman replied. "We've got supplies for now. We're focusing on evacuation efforts. They're pulling people from coastal areas and trying to get them inland."

"Evacuation?" Colt asked. "Where are they sending people?"

The corpsman paused, his face grim. "They're trying to set up safe zones. Military bases, fortified towns. Right now, it's trial and error. Some places hold, others... don't."

I looked at my family, then back at the base around us. For the first time in weeks, we weren't fighting for our lives. But how long would that last?

"We'll stay here for now," I said, making the decision. "But we're not relying on anyone to save us. We stay sharp. We keep moving forward."

The fight wasn't over yet, but for now, we had a moment to breathe. And that was enough.

For now.

Chapter 31: Sergeant Frank Makes a Comeback

The days on the base blurred together, a routine of check-ins, security sweeps, and staying alert. Even as a civilian, I couldn't ignore the rhythm of military life—it was something ingrained in me. I'd spent the last 25 years out of the Corps, but being here, among Marines again, the old habits kicked in faster than I'd expected.

Beaufort wasn't a safe haven, not in the way I'd hoped. The Marines were holding their ground, sure, but every day we heard more reports of infected breaching other bases, collapsing towns that had once been marked as evacuation zones. The "safe zones" were shrinking, and even though the base hadn't been hit yet, everyone knew it was only a matter of time.

Colt and Nash had been spending time with other teenagers, some of them survivors like us, others Marine brats whose parents were stationed here. I watched them from the tent, hoping they'd adapt to this life, learn to survive in a world that didn't make sense anymore. Annie, meanwhile, had found her place with a group of women helping to organize medical supplies, keeping busy in a way that made her feel useful. But I... I hadn't found my place yet.

I was restless. Watching, waiting, feeling the itch of needing to do something. I wasn't used to being idle.

One afternoon, after a morning spent helping secure some of the outer perimeters, I was walking back to the family tent when I spotted an old face.

Sergeant Major Baker. He had been one of the men I looked up to when I was in. Seeing him now, older, a little more grizzled, but still carrying that same commanding presence, took me back. I wasn't the fresh-faced recruit I used to be, but there was a mutual recognition in his eyes as I approached.

"Keller," he said, his voice rough but steady. "Didn't expect to see you here."

"Didn't expect to be here, Sergeant Major," I replied, giving him a nod. It felt strange, the pull of old habits. "How are things looking?"

He snorted, glancing around. "Could be worse. Could be better. The Marines are holding, but we're stretched thin. Supply chains are hit or miss, and the infected are getting smarter—or at least, more relentless."

I nodded. I'd seen it myself. "What's the plan?"

He eyed me carefully, as if gauging whether I was still the man he remembered. "We're gearing up for a major operation. Recon missions, resupply runs, and securing the civilian areas around here. The infected are pushing from the north, coming down from Savannah. We need to keep them back, or we'll be overrun."

"What do you need?" I asked, knowing where this conversation was heading.

He smirked, crossing his arms. "You tell me, Sergeant. You're not exactly enlisted anymore, but we could use men who know how to handle themselves. You've still got that fight in you?"

It had been so long since anyone had called me "Sergeant," but the title fit like an old jacket, worn but familiar. I hadn't realized how much I missed it until now.

"You think I'm too rusty?" I asked, half-joking, half-challenging him.

Baker chuckled. "We'll see. Got a recon team going out tomorrow. We're heading north toward some old supply depots. See what we can scavenge before the infected hit those areas. You up for it?"

I didn't need to think about it. "I'm in."

He clapped me on the shoulder, the old camaraderie settling in like no time had passed. "Good to have you back, Keller. We move at 0600."

That night, I told Annie. She was sitting on the edge of the cot, folding some spare blankets, when I sat down next to her. The worry was already in her eyes before I even opened my mouth.

"You're going out with them, aren't you?" she asked, not looking up from her task.

"I have to," I said softly, knowing she understood why. "They need all the help they can get, and I can't sit around here while they're out there fighting."

Annie stopped folding, her hands resting in her lap. "I knew this was coming. You're not the kind of man to stay behind the lines."

I reached for her hand, squeezing it gently. "I'll be careful. I promise."

"I don't want you to just be careful, Frank," she said, finally looking at me. "I want you to come back. Every time."

I pulled her close, the weight of the moment hanging between us. I had faced combat before, but this... this was different. The enemy wasn't human, but the stakes were higher than ever.

"I'll come back," I whispered. "I swear."

At 0600 the next morning, I found myself standing among a group of Marines, gear strapped on like old times, ready for the mission. The recon team was small—four of us total. Sergeant Major Baker, Corporal Harris, a young kid who couldn't have been more than 23, and Sergeant Gomez, a woman built like a tank who looked like she could handle anything thrown her way.

"Simple job," Baker said, briefing us before we headed out. "We're sweeping the northern perimeter, heading toward an old supply depot that's been marked as abandoned. Intel suggests there's still usable equipment there—ammo, medical supplies, rations. We get in, grab what we can, and get out before the infected catch on."

The hum of the military vehicle beneath us was a reminder of just how much things had changed. This wasn't a mission in Iraq or Afghanistan. This was home. We weren't fighting insurgents or militants. We were fighting for survival.

The drive was quiet at first, the kind of tense silence that comes when you know something's waiting for you on the other side. We passed through the remnants of small towns, areas that had once thrived but now lay in ruins—overgrown with vines, abandoned cars left to rust, and the occasional wandering infected too far gone to pose a threat.

When we reached the supply depot, the sight was eerily calm. The gates were still intact, though the chain-link fence had been bent in places where the infected had likely tried to force their way in. We moved with precision, scanning the area for any signs of movement. The Marines knew their job, and the rhythm of clearing buildings came back to me with ease.

Inside the depot, we found more than we expected. Crates of MREs, a stockpile of medical kits, and enough ammunition to arm a small platoon. But the real prize was an armored vehicle parked in the back—one that hadn't been touched.

"This could be a game-changer," Gomez said, running her hand along the side of the vehicle. "If we can get it running."

As Harris started working on getting the vehicle operational, I moved to check the perimeter with Baker. That's when we heard it—a low, guttural sound carried by the wind. We turned, eyes scanning the tree line beyond the fence.

"They're coming," Baker muttered, already signaling to the others.

I could see them now, stumbling out of the woods—slow at first, but picking up speed when they spotted us. A horde of infected, more than I could count, pouring out like a tide of death.

"We need to move!" I shouted, running back to the depot.

Harris had managed to get the vehicle started, and we piled in just as the first infected reached the fence. The metal rattled violently as they slammed into it, their rotting hands clawing at the barrier, eyes wild with hunger. As we sped away, the depot fading in the distance, the reality of the situation hit me hard. This wasn't just a fight for survival anymore. This was war. And I was back in it, whether I wanted to be or not. Sergeant Frank Keller was back in the fight. And this time, it was personal.

Chapter 32: Fight, Sleep, Rinse, Repeat

The days in Beaufort had blurred into a rhythm—fight, sleep, rinse, repeat. Each morning, we'd wake up before the sun broke the horizon, clean our gear, and load up for the next operation. It felt like I was back in a war zone, but this enemy wasn't carrying rifles or firing back. It wasn't a battle over territory, resources, or even freedom—it was a battle for survival, plain and simple.

The Marines' main focus had shifted to clearing out the infected from around Beaufort. Every day, they sent out squads to push the hordes back, creating as much of a buffer as they could between the base and the relentless waves of the undead. It wasn't about winning; it was about buying time. Every block we cleared, every group of infected we took out, bought us another day.

But no matter how many we put down, it didn't feel like progress. More kept coming. They always kept coming.

I lay awake in my cot, staring at the canvas ceiling of the tent, the silence pressing down on me like a weight. I could hear the distant drone of helicopters on patrol and the low murmur of voices from outside, but it was the quiet inside that was the worst. That's when my mind raced.

Fight, sleep, rinse, repeat.

I could still feel the grit of dirt under my nails, the sore ache in my muscles from swinging my rifle like a club when the ammo ran out. I'd seen more of the dead in the past week than I had in my entire life. I was used to death—combat teaches you that—but there was something different about this. The enemy wasn't supposed to get back up.

Every mission left me drained, both physically and mentally. The Marines fought hard, but I could see it in their eyes too. Even the toughest among them had started to show signs of wear. It wasn't just the physical toll—it was the endless nature of it all. The knowledge that no matter how many infected we put down, there were always more. Always.

I sat up in bed, running a hand over my face, trying to shake the fog from my mind. Annie and the boys were asleep in the next tent over. I hadn't seen much of them lately, not with the constant ops. We'd had a few moments together—quiet dinners, the occasional conversation between missions—but I knew it wasn't enough. I could see the worry in Annie's eyes every time I left, the way Colt and Nash watched me like they weren't sure if I'd come back. They'd seen enough to know how dangerous it was out there.

I stood up, the stiffness in my joints reminding me of how long it had been since I'd gotten a decent night's sleep. But sleep wasn't something I could afford right now. Not with the Marines depending on every able body to keep the base safe.

As I stepped out of the tent, the cool night air hit me, refreshing in a way. The base was still buzzing with activity—patrols returning from the outskirts, trucks being loaded with supplies for the next day's operation, medics tending to the wounded. It was a well-oiled machine, but even machines break down if they're pushed too hard.

I made my way to the command tent, where Sergeant Major Baker was hunched over a map of the area, marking out the next target zones. He looked up as I entered, giving me a nod.

"Keller," he greeted, his voice gravelly from years of shouting over gunfire. "How're you holding up?"

I shrugged, trying to shake off the exhaustion that clung to me like a second skin. "Same as everyone else, I guess. Tired."

Baker grunted, tracing a line on the map with his finger. "Aren't we all? But we've got to keep going. Can't let up, not with those things out there."

"What's the plan for tomorrow?" I asked, moving to stand beside him.

He pointed to an area just outside the base. "We've cleared most of the inner perimeter, but the infected are pushing back harder to the north. There's an old hospital that's been overrun. We need to clear it and set up a secondary supply post. It's risky, but we need the medical supplies, and the location would give us another stronghold."

I nodded, feeling the weight of the mission settle on my shoulders. Another day, another fight. "How bad is it?"

"Bad," Baker said bluntly. "Intel says it's crawling with infected, but we don't have a choice. If we don't push back, they'll overrun the entire area."

I sighed, rubbing the back of my neck. "Fight, sleep, rinse, repeat," I muttered.

Baker glanced at me, a flicker of sympathy in his eyes. "Yeah. It's the way of things now."

The next day, we headed out before dawn, the convoy moving in tight formation as we approached the hospital. The place looked like it had been ripped straight from a nightmare—windows shattered, doors hanging off their hinges, the once pristine white walls now smeared with blood and grime.

The closer we got, the more I could feel that old instinct kicking in—the awareness of danger, the constant scanning for threats. It was like my brain had switched back into Marine mode, the years since I'd left the service melting away with each step.

We moved in silently, rifles at the ready, the tension so thick you could cut it with a knife. The infected were inside, that much was clear. We could hear them—a low, guttural groan that echoed through the halls.

The Marines worked like clockwork, clearing each room methodically, taking out the infected with precision. I stuck close to Baker, my heart pounding in my chest as we entered the main wing of the hospital. The infected here weren't as fast as some we'd seen, but they were just as deadly, their sheer numbers making up for their lack of speed.

We fought our way through the corridors, room by room, clearing out the infected as we went. The sound of gunfire echoed through the building, mixing with the screams of the undead as they fell under our assault.

It was brutal, exhausting work, but by the time the sun was starting to set, we'd cleared the hospital. The Marines were setting up barricades, securing the area for the night.

As I stood outside, watching the last of the infected fall, I couldn't help but feel a strange sense of emptiness. We'd won the battle, sure, but the war was far from over.

Fight, sleep, rinse, repeat.

It was the new normal, and no matter how many we killed, the fight would never end.

I leaned against a wall, staring out at the horizon as the sun dipped below the trees, casting long shadows across the wreckage of the world. My body ached, my mind was numb, but there was still a fire burning in my chest—the need to keep fighting, to protect my family, to survive.

But how long could we keep this up?

"How're you holding up?" Baker's voice pulled me from my thoughts. He walked up beside me, his expression as tired as I felt.

I glanced at him, then back at the horizon. "Same as yesterday. Same as tomorrow."

He nodded, a grim smile tugging at the corner of his mouth. "Yeah. That's how it goes now."

We stood there in silence for a while, watching as the night crept in, the sky turning dark. The fight would start again tomorrow, just like it always did.

Chapter 33: Beautifying Beaufort

Beaufort was a town of history, charm, and southern grace, but those things had long since faded under the weight of the apocalypse. What used to be a quiet coastal town was now a battleground—a place where the dead roamed the streets, and the living fought to reclaim what had been lost. But there was a plan. A crazy one, maybe, but a plan, nonetheless.

We were going to take Beaufort back.

The idea had started as a small seed in Sergeant Major Baker's head. He'd been stationed here years ago, and he knew the layout of the town like the back of his hand. In the early days of the outbreak, Beaufort had been overwhelmed by the infected, but now that we had a foothold in the area, Baker was determined to take it one step further. He wanted to build a barrier, encircle the town, and create a safe haven for survivors.

It wasn't just about survival anymore. It was about living.

The first step in this mission was simple enough on paper: clear the town of infected. But, like most things in this new world, it was easier said than done. Beaufort was still crawling with the undead, but at least we had the Marines, and they knew how to get the job done. Day after day, we pushed further into the heart of the town, clearing neighborhoods, shops, and historic landmarks. Each step we took was a small victory, but we knew that if we wanted to turn Beaufort into something more than just another warzone, we needed more than just guns and grit.

We needed a vision.

The plan wasn't just about killing zombies. It was about reclaiming Beaufort—making it livable again, safe for families, for kids like Colt and Nash. The town had everything we needed: access to the water for fishing, plenty of land for farming, and structures that could be fortified. We weren't just trying to survive—we were trying to build something. A future.

"Frank, get over here," Baker called out one morning as we stood in what had once been the town square. It was hard to imagine now, but I could picture this place in its prime. Tourists milling about, locals chatting under the shade of the live oaks draped in Spanish moss. Now, the only sounds were the wind and the occasional groan of the undead in the distance.

I walked over to Baker, who was standing with a small group of Marines and engineers. They had a map spread out on the hood of a Humvee, and Baker was pointing to different areas of town.

"We're going to start here," he said, tapping his finger on a section of the map that bordered the waterfront. "The idea is to build a barrier around the town, using the natural geography where we can. The water on the east side will help, but we need to fortify the north and west. We're going to clear a perimeter and start setting up barriers—fences, barricades, whatever we can find. We'll reinforce it over time, but the first step is making sure no more infected can get in."

It was ambitious, no doubt about it. But I could see the logic. If we could enclose the town and keep the dead out, we could create something real—something sustainable. A place where people didn't just hide, but lived. Thrived.

"You really think we can pull this off?" I asked, crossing my arms as I studied the map.

Baker looked up at me, his expression hard but determined. "We have to. There's no other option. If we don't create safe zones like this, we'll be fighting a losing battle forever. This isn't just about Beaufort. It's about showing people that we can take our world back."

I nodded, the weight of his words sinking in. He was right. We couldn't keep running forever. We had to start somewhere, and Beaufort was as good a place as any.

The next few weeks were a blur of sweat, hard work, and constant vigilance. We cleared more of the town, street by street, block by block. It wasn't easy. Every time we thought we had an area cleared, a new group of infected would stumble in from the outskirts, drawn by the noise or the scent of the living. But we kept at it, working through the heat and the exhaustion because we knew what was at stake.

It wasn't just about the present anymore. It was about the future.

The Marines worked like a well-oiled machine, setting up checkpoints, securing buildings, and organizing scavenging runs for supplies. They brought in anything they could find—metal sheets, concrete barriers, even old cars—to start building the perimeter. It wasn't pretty at first, but it was effective. Every day, the barrier grew, inching its way around the town like a protective wall.

And it wasn't just the Marines. We had civilians helping too, people from the base, survivors we'd rescued from nearby areas, and even some locals who'd managed to hide out during the worst of the outbreak. They all pitched in, working alongside the soldiers to rebuild their home.

I found myself working side by side with Colt and Nash more often than not. They were strong kids, tougher than they had any right to be at their ages, but this world had forced them to grow up fast. Colt took to the work with quiet determination, helping haul supplies and reinforce the barricades. Nash, always the more energetic of the two, was constantly running back and forth, helping wherever he could and trying to keep the mood light.

"This place is starting to look like something," Colt said one afternoon as we took a break, sitting on the tailgate of a truck and sipping from our canteens. We were looking out at the perimeter wall, which had started to take shape in the distance.

I nodded, wiping the sweat from my brow. "It's getting there. Still a lot of work to do, but we're making progress."

Nash, ever the optimist, grinned. "Think we'll have a real town again, Dad? Like... you know, normal?"

I looked at him, at his hopeful expression, and I wanted to say yes. I wanted to tell him that everything would be back to normal, that we'd rebuild and life would go back to the way it was before. But that wasn't the truth.

"Maybe not the way it was before," I said carefully. "But we're going to make it better. Safer. A place where people can live again. That's what matters."

By the end of the month, the barrier around Beaufort was nearly complete. The town was still a long way from being fully secured, but we had something now—something tangible. The infected couldn't just wander in anymore, and that gave us a fighting chance. Inside the perimeter, we'd started organizing—clearing buildings, setting up supply lines, even talking about farming and fishing to keep everyone fed.

It wasn't perfect. It wasn't even close. But it was a start.

And for the first time since this whole nightmare began, it felt like we were doing more than just surviving. We were building something, something real.

Chapter 34: Search and Rescue

Beaufort was starting to resemble a town again. Fortified, organized, and alive with the hum of activity as Marines, survivors, and civilians worked together to keep it running. The barrier surrounding the town was holding strong, and for the first time in months, we weren't constantly looking over our shoulders for the undead.

But Beaufort wasn't enough. Not by a long shot.

We knew there were more survivors out there—people holed up in homes, hiding in basements, or trapped in crumbling cities. They were living on scraps, avoiding the infected, and waiting for a miracle. And if we were going to turn this little corner of South Carolina into something real, we needed more people, more supplies, and more resources.

That's where the search and rescue missions came in.

The plan was simple in theory: send out teams to comb through the areas outside of Beaufort. We'd look for survivors, food, medical supplies, and anything else we could use to strengthen our position. It would be a risk, no doubt about it, but we couldn't sit behind our walls and hope the world came to us. If we wanted to thrive, we had to go out there and get it.

I was sitting in a briefing room with Baker and a small group of Marines, engineers, and civilian volunteers. The map of the surrounding areas was laid out on a table, marking key locations where we knew there had been large populations before the outbreak—small towns, hospitals, grocery stores, and supply depots. These were the places we'd be searching.

Baker stood at the head of the table, his face as hard as ever but with a spark of determination in his eyes. "We're splitting into three teams," he said, pointing at the map. "Team One will head east along the coast. We know there are survivors in some of the smaller beach towns. If they're still out there, we'll bring them back."

He turned to the rest of us. "Team Two, you'll be heading north, toward the outskirts of Charleston. It's risky, but there could still be useful supplies in the suburbs. Stay away from the city center—Charleston's overrun. Focus on smaller pockets."

Then he pointed at me and a few others. "Team Three will head west. You'll be covering the rural areas and farmland. There could be survivors holed up in those isolated places, and we'll need the food and equipment."

I nodded, glancing over at Colt and Nash, who were sitting next to me, listening intently. The boys had been eager to do more, and though I was reluctant to let them go too far from the safety of Beaufort, I knew they were capable. Colt especially had proven himself to be a steady hand under pressure, and Nash—well, Nash had the heart of a fighter, even if he still had a lot to learn.

"Frank, you and your boys are on Team Three," Baker said, locking eyes with me. "You'll be out there for a few days. Bring back whatever you can find."

I nodded. "We'll make it count."

Two days later, we were on the move.

The Marines had rounded up a mix of military vehicles and whatever civilian cars we could scavenge. Humvees led the convoy, their engines growling as they cut through the overgrown roads, while beat-up trucks, old sedans, and even a few motorcycles followed close behind. We had a couple of helicopters on standby, but those were reserved for extraction or emergency cases—fuel was still too precious to waste on routine scouting.

I was in one of the lead Humvees, Colt riding shotgun, his eyes scanning the tree line for any signs of movement. Nash was in the back, his rifle slung across his lap, nervously tapping his foot. The boy was excited to be out in the field, but I could see the tension in his eyes. He knew as well as I did that these trips could turn deadly in an instant.

We drove in silence for a while, the only sounds being the rumble of the engine and the occasional crackle of static over the radio. The roads were rough—overgrown with weeds, cracked from months of neglect, and littered with debris from abandoned cars. It was a reminder of how quickly the world had fallen apart.

"Looks quiet," Colt said after a while, his eyes still fixed on the horizon.

"Too quiet," I replied. "Stay sharp."

Our first stop was a small farmhouse about 10 miles west of Beaufort. It had been marked on the map as a potential survivor location—isolated, with plenty of land around it for farming. We pulled up the long dirt driveway, the tires crunching on gravel, and parked in front of the house. It looked abandoned at first glance, but the front door was closed, and there were no signs of a struggle.

"Let's check it out," I said, grabbing my rifle and stepping out of the Humvee. Colt and Nash followed, along with a couple of Marines who were part of our team.

We approached the house cautiously, rifles at the ready, scanning the windows for any movement. I knocked on the door, the sound echoing through the quiet countryside.

"Anyone in there?" I called out.

For a moment, there was nothing but silence. Then, from inside, we heard the faint sound of footsteps. Someone was in there.

"Open the door," I said, stepping back slightly. "We're not here to hurt you. We're with the Marines, out of Beaufort."

The door creaked open slowly, and an older man stepped out, his face lined with exhaustion and fear. He looked at us with wary eyes, gripping a shotgun in one hand.

"Marines?" he asked, his voice rough. "I thought the world was gone."

"Not all of it," I said. "We're clearing the town. We've got a safe zone set up in Beaufort. You alone here?"

The man shook his head. "No. My wife and daughter are inside. We've been here since it all started. Thought about leaving, but... it didn't seem safe anywhere else."

"Well, you're in luck," I said. "We're taking people back with us. Got food, shelter, and protection. You want to come with us?"

The man hesitated, glancing back at the house. "You really think it's safe?"

"It's safer than staying out here," I replied.

After a moment, he nodded. "Alright. Let me get my family."

The rest of the day followed the same pattern. We stopped at every farm, every isolated house, and every small pocket of civilization we could find. Some places were empty—long since abandoned, the occupants either dead or gone. Others, like the farmhouse, were still occupied by survivors who had been too afraid to leave. By nightfall, we had a small group of civilians with us, men, women, even a couple of kids. They were scared, but they were alive.

The convoy turned back toward Beaufort as the sun dipped low on the horizon. We hadn't found much in the way of supplies. Just a few cans of food, some tools, and a bit of ammunition, but we'd found people. And that was just as important.

As we rolled back into the safety of the barrier, I glanced over at Colt and Nash. They were exhausted, but I could see the satisfaction in their faces. We were doing more than just surviving now. We were helping others survive too.

And that, more than anything, gave me hope.

Chapter 35: Contact Front

The horizon was a wash of golden light as the sun dipped toward the marshes. From the rooftop of the makeshift command center, I could see the entire stretch of Beaufort's newly erected defenses. The town was becoming a fortress, but we all knew that no wall would stand forever. Not against what was coming.

It started with a call from the aerial recon team, the ones flying regular sweeps along the coastline and surrounding towns. Our resources were spread thin, but we'd made it a priority to keep eyes in the sky. And now, as we gathered in the command center, the reports had come in—something big was heading our way.

"They're coming from the north," Baker said, his voice tight as he pointed to a map spread out on the table. "Approximately one thousand of them. Maybe more."

One thousand. My heart sank. This wasn't just a random group of shamblers we could pick off. It was a horde—an unstoppable, rotting mass that would overwhelm everything in its path.

"How much time?" I asked, keeping my voice steady.

"They'll reach us by tomorrow afternoon," the recon Marine replied, sweat visible on his brow. "Maybe sooner if they don't get slowed down."

I stared at the map. The zombies were about ten miles out, moving along the same road we had used for search-and-rescue just days before. There was no real cover along the way, nothing to funnel them into. They'd come at us like a flood, smashing against the walls of Beaufort like a tidal wave of death.

Baker's voice cut through my thoughts. "Alright, we don't have time to sit on our hands. Here's the plan."

He motioned for everyone to gather around. I leaned in with the rest of the team—Marines, engineers, and a few of the civilian leaders who had stepped up to help organize the survivors.

"The walls are holding, but we can't let them get that close," Baker said, tracing his finger along the road leading into Beaufort. "We'll intercept them five miles out, right here." He tapped a spot on the map where the road cut through a patch of open farmland. "We set up barricades, force them into a bottleneck. Air support will soften them up with strafing runs, but it's on us to finish the job. We'll dig in here and hit them hard with everything we've got."

There were murmurs around the table, some confident, others uncertain. A thousand was more than any of us had faced at once, and we all knew what happened when a horde hit critical mass. Once the infected smelled human flesh, it didn't matter how much firepower you had—the sheer numbers could overwhelm you.

I took a deep breath. "What about fallback positions? If we get overrun, we need a second line."

Baker nodded. "Agreed. We'll set up secondary defenses two miles out from the walls. If they break through the first barricade, we retreat there. But the goal is to stop them before they reach that point."

I nodded, glancing at the map again. It was a solid plan, but it depended on timing and precision. If the barricades weren't strong enough, or if the air support couldn't thin them out, we'd be in serious trouble.

"How much air support are we talking?" I asked.

"Two birds, fully armed," Baker replied. "They'll make their runs as soon as the horde hits the bottleneck. It's not much, but it's all we've got."

Two helicopters against a thousand zombies. It wasn't exactly reassuring, but it was better than nothing. We'd have to make every shot count.

By the time the sun had set, the plan was in motion.

I stood with Colt and Nash as we loaded supplies into the Humvees. Both of them were quiet, the gravity of the situation sinking in. Colt's face was a mask of determination, while Nash looked more anxious than usual. I put a hand on his shoulder, feeling the tension in his muscles.

"You okay?" I asked.

Nash nodded, though his eyes didn't meet mine. "Yeah. Just... a thousand, Dad. That's a lot."

"It is," I agreed. "But we're ready for it. We've got a good plan. We're not going to let them get through."

Colt finished loading his gear and stepped over, looking at his brother. "We'll be fine, Nash. Stick close to me and Dad, and don't do anything stupid."

Nash smiled faintly. "You mean like you?"

"Exactly like me," Colt replied with a grin.

I chuckled, though the weight of what we were about to face was still pressing down on my shoulders. I wasn't just leading my boys into this fight—I was leading everyone. And if we failed, Beaufort would fall.

The next morning, we were in position.

The barricades had been hastily constructed out of cars, rubble, and any scrap metal we could find. It wasn't perfect, but it would funnel the horde into a narrow path, giving us a chance to concentrate our fire. We had set up heavy machine guns along the sides, and the Humvees were parked strategically, their mounted .50-cals aimed directly at the choke point.

Marines were positioned behind cover, weapons at the ready, while civilians who had volunteered for the fight manned the makeshift barricades. It wasn't just about holding the line. It was about survival.

I stood with Colt and Nash behind one of the Humvees, checking my rifle one last time. The air was thick with tension, the quiet before the storm. In the distance, we could hear the faint moans of the approaching horde.

"Here they come," Colt muttered, his eyes narrowing as he scanned the horizon.

I raised my binoculars and spotted them. A mass of shambling bodies, dragging themselves toward us, slow but relentless. They moved like a living carpet, hundreds of feet shuffling in unison. It was the stuff of nightmares, a wall of death marching toward us without hesitation.

Over the radio, Baker's voice crackled. "Air support is in position. Hold your fire until they reach the barricade."

We waited. The minutes stretched out, each one heavier than the last as the horde drew closer. My pulse quickened, but I forced myself to breathe slowly, steadily. We'd face worse than this, I told myself. But a thousand... damn, it was a lot.

Finally, the first wave hit the barricade.

"Now!" Baker's voice barked over the radio.

The helicopters roared overhead, the sound of their rotors cutting through the air like a saw blade. Within seconds, they were unleashing their payloads—rockets and machine-gun fire tearing through the front ranks of the horde. Bodies exploded in showers of gore, limbs flying through the air as the zombies fell in droves.

But still, they kept coming.

"Open fire!" I shouted.

The roar of gunfire erupted all around us, the heavy machine guns spitting lead into the mass of infected. I squeezed the trigger of my rifle, picking off targets as fast as I could. Each shot dropped a zombie, but it felt like trying to empty an ocean with a spoon.

Colt and Nash were firing beside me, their faces set with grim determination. The .50-cals tore through the horde, but the sheer number of zombies pressing against the barricades was overwhelming.

"They're breaking through!" someone shouted.

Sure enough, parts of the barricade were beginning to buckle under the weight of the undead. The infected were piling up on top of each other, crawling over the bodies of the fallen to reach us.

"Fall back!" Baker ordered over the radio.

We retreated to the secondary position, firing as we moved. The horde was relentless, but we weren't giving up ground easily. As we reached the second line of defense, the helicopters swooped down for another run, tearing through the zombies with a final barrage.

By the time the dust settled, the battlefield was littered with bodies. Hundreds of zombies lay dead, their rotting corpses piled up against the barricades. But the line had held.

We had survived.

For now...

Chapter 36: Interlocking Fields of Fire

The sun was beginning to set by the time the last of the horde was dealt with. I stood on the edge of the battlefield, rifle slung over my shoulder, my boots sticking in the blood-soaked mud. The once open stretch of farmland now looked like a scene out of hell—heaps of decaying bodies piled against the makeshift barricades, the ground littered with spent casings and broken debris.

We had survived, but it was far from a clean victory.

Around me, Marines and civilians alike were catching their breath, some sitting down hard in the dirt, others trying to regroup and salvage what equipment they could. The fight had been brutal. The barricades had barely held, and if it weren't for the heavy machine guns and air support, that horde would have breached our lines without a doubt.

But we had made it. Beaufort was still standing.

I glanced at Colt and Nash, who were sitting next to each other on the hood of one of the Humvees, both of them looking more exhausted than I'd ever seen them. They had fought like hell today—no complaints, no hesitation, just raw determination. Colt had that same fire in his eyes that I'd seen in myself when I was his age, and Nash—he was still young, still scared, but he had risen to the occasion.

"Good job, boys," I said, walking over to them. "We did it."

Colt nodded, wiping sweat and dirt from his brow. "Yeah, but it was close. Too close."

Nash looked out at the sea of bodies with a mix of relief and horror. "Are there gonna be more like this?"

I didn't want to lie to him, but I couldn't sugarcoat it either. "There might be. But we're gonna be ready for the next one."

That's what today had taught us—this wasn't going to be the last horde, not by a long shot. We had managed to scrape by, but if we didn't improve our defenses, the next one could break us.

Back at the command center, the debriefing was somber. Baker stood at the head of the table, going over the events of the day while everyone else listened quietly. The mood wasn't exactly celebratory. We knew that surviving one battle didn't mean we'd win the war.

"We did well today," Baker began, though his expression was grim. "But we got lucky. The barricades barely held. Communications between the teams were spotty, and we weren't able to coordinate our fallback as well as we should've. If this horde had been any larger—or if it hit us at night—it could've been a disaster."

He was right. The comms had been a mess. We were relying on short-range radios, and when the horde started to push through the barricades, the confusion almost got us killed. Units were firing into the same clusters, wasting ammo, while other parts of the line nearly collapsed because they weren't getting enough support. It wasn't sustainable.

"What we need," I said, stepping up to the table, "is interlocking fields of fire. We can't just dump rounds into the horde and hope for the best. If we set up our defenses properly, we can maximize our firepower and make sure we're covering every angle. No gaps. No weak points."

Baker nodded, motioning for me to continue. I walked over to the map on the wall and started laying it out.

"We need to reinforce the barricades, make them higher and more stable. But beyond that, we need to set up fire zones along the defensive line. Heavy weapons like the .50-cals and machine guns should be positioned to cover the widest areas, overlapping with each other so nothing gets through without being hit from multiple directions. And each rifle team needs to know exactly where they're supposed to be aiming. We focus on specific sectors and don't waste ammo doubling up on targets."

I tapped the map, drawing a rough outline of how it could look. "If we can set up better communication between the teams, we'll know where the threat is strongest and adjust our fire accordingly. We'll also need designated fallback zones with pre-established fire positions. That way, if we do need to retreat again, we won't lose our coordination."

One of the engineers, a civilian who had been helping with the barricades, spoke up. "What about the walls? They're not going to hold if we face another horde this size. We need something stronger."

"We'll reinforce them," Baker said. "Double-layered barricades, maybe even some concrete barriers if we can find the materials. But you're right—this won't be enough on its own. We need to improve our early warning systems. Scouts, drones, anything that gives us more time to prepare."

I nodded. "We got lucky today with the aerial recon, but we can't always count on that. We need a dedicated team to patrol outside the walls, watching for movement, reporting back before anything gets too close."

Baker agreed, and we spent the next hour hammering out the details. We were going to need more manpower, more materials, and a hell of a lot more coordination. But we had a plan, and that was more than we'd had before.

Later that night, I found myself back on the wall, staring out into the darkness. The wind was picking up, carrying the smell of death from the battlefield below. The fires from the bodies we had burned earlier were still smoldering, sending thin columns of smoke into the sky.

Colt and Nash were back at the barracks, catching some much-needed rest, but I couldn't sleep. Not yet. Not after what we had just been through.

I leaned against the cold steel of the barricade and let out a breath. My body ached, every muscle sore from the fight. But more than that, my mind was racing. We had won this battle, but the cost had been high—too high. Marines were dead. Civilians too. And if we didn't adapt, if we didn't learn from today, the next fight could be our last.

As I stood there, I thought about the interlocking fields of fire, about the new comms system we needed to set up. We'd survived this time, but survival wasn't enough anymore. We had to get smarter, faster, more disciplined. Because the undead weren't going to stop coming.

Behind me, the town of Beaufort was quiet. The people were resting, recovering from the battle, but I knew they were counting on us—on me—to keep them safe.

"Get some sleep, Sergeant," Baker's voice came from behind me. I turned to see him approaching, his face tired but determined. "We'll need you sharp tomorrow. The hard work's just beginning."

I nodded, though I wasn't sure I could sleep if I tried. "We're gonna need better gear, better comms," I said. "We'll be ready next time."

Baker clapped me on the shoulder. "Damn right we will."

As he walked away, I took one last look out over the field of battle. We had survived the horde, but the next one would come. Maybe it would be bigger. Maybe it would be stronger. But this time, we'd be ready.

We had to be.

Chapter 37: Annie and Frank's Day Off

The air felt lighter today, almost as if the world had taken a deep breath after the chaos of the past few weeks. For once, the sky wasn't filled with smoke or the drone of helicopters. Instead, it was blue—clear and calm, with the sun shining warmly down on Beaufort. It was the kind of day you'd never expect in the middle of a zombie apocalypse.

Annie had made sure of that.

"Frank, we need a break. The boys need a break. Hell, we *all* need one," she had insisted the night before, her voice steady but gentle. "You've been going non-stop. We've lost track of what normal feels like, and I'm not losing you to this fight."

I'd tried to argue. There was always something to do. Defenses to shore up, patrols to organize, weapons to clean. But looking at her, at the worry in her eyes, I knew she was right. The battle never ended, but if I didn't take a step back, I might not be able to keep going at all. Annie had always been my compass, and if she was telling me I needed this, I'd listen.

That morning, she'd rounded up not just Colt and Nash, but eight more kids from around town—orphans and children of other Marines who were too busy or too shell-shocked to care for them right now. Our makeshift family had grown in the strangest of ways, but Annie had taken them all in, giving them a semblance of normal life amidst the chaos. Today, she wanted to give them more than just survival. She wanted them to have fun.

I watched from the kitchen window as they all scattered across the field just outside the town's perimeter. Annie was in the center, a smile bright on her face as she handed out baseball gloves and a beat-up old ball she'd found somewhere.

"You're up first, Nash," she called, tossing him the ball.

Nash grinned, shaking off the stress of the past days as he took his position. Colt was nearby, standing ready at shortstop, his eyes darting between his little brother and the kids spread out in the field. The rest of them, ranging in age from eight to sixteen, were laughing, running around, their voices filling the air with something that had been absent for too long: joy.

I stepped outside, my boots crunching against the gravel as I walked toward them, feeling the weight of my rifle absent from my shoulder. I didn't bring it today. I wasn't Sgt. Frank today. I was just Dad.

"Hey, you're gonna let me in on this game or what?" I asked, walking over to Colt with a grin.

"Dad, you're too slow for this," Colt teased, but there was a glint of excitement in his eyes.

"I might be slow, but I've still got better reflexes than you," I shot back, giving him a playful nudge.

"Let's see about that, old man," he said with a laugh as he tossed me the glove.

I took up my spot at first base, and for a moment, it felt like everything was right in the world. Annie gave me a wave from the pitcher's mound, her hair tied up in a ponytail, her face glowing. She looked younger, happier, like the Annie from years ago when the biggest worry we had was paying bills or dealing with teenage attitude.

She pitched the ball, and Nash swung, the crack of the bat echoing through the air. The ball sailed toward center field, and one of the younger kids scrambled after it, his small legs pumping as fast as they could go. He missed it, of course, but the laughter that followed was infectious.

"Go, Nash!" one of the girls cheered as Nash made it to second base, panting and grinning like he'd just hit a home run.

For the next couple of hours, the game went on. We laughed. We teased each other. The kids forgot, if only for a little while, about the walls and the barricades, the undead just beyond the safe zone. Annie had made sure of it—she was the heart of this family, keeping us grounded, reminding us what we were fighting for.

I even caught myself relaxing, something I hadn't done in what felt like years. Every time I looked at Annie, my heart swelled. She had always been the glue holding us together, but now, in this world we found ourselves in, she was so much more. She was hope.

As the game started to wind down, we gathered the kids together in the shade of a giant oak tree, passing out sandwiches and water. The kids were all sweaty and out of breath, but the smiles on their faces said it all. For today, they weren't just surviving. They were living.

Nash sat beside me, leaning against the tree trunk, his face flushed with excitement. "This was awesome, Dad. I didn't know we could still have days like this."

I ruffled his hair, feeling a rare moment of peace settle over me. "Your mom made sure of it. She's good at reminding me what's important."

Colt, sitting nearby, nodded in agreement. "Yeah, we needed this. Thanks, Dad."

I looked over at Annie, who was sitting in the grass with two of the younger girls curled up next to her, already half-asleep. She caught my eye and smiled, that soft, knowing smile that told me she understood everything I was feeling without needing to say a word.

After the game, we spent the rest of the day lounging around, just being a family. Annie had planned it perfectly. There was no agenda, no structure, just freedom to do whatever felt right. The kids played tag, climbed trees, and even helped Annie build a makeshift swing from an old rope they found in the supply shed.

As the sun dipped lower in the sky, casting long shadows across the field, I found myself sitting beside Annie, watching the kids laugh and run around. The air was warm, the kind of warmth that settles into your bones and makes everything feel just a little bit better.

"You were right," I said quietly, reaching over to take her hand. "We needed this."

She squeezed my hand gently, her eyes softening. "I know you, Frank. You'll run yourself into the ground if you don't take a break. The boys needed you today. I needed you."

I kissed the top of her head, feeling the weight of the world lift just a little. "I needed this too," I admitted.

For a moment, it felt like the world had stopped turning. There was no apocalypse, no zombies, no battle to prepare for. There was just us—a family, sitting under a tree on a beautiful day, holding on to the moments that mattered.

As the stars began to peek out from the darkening sky, I watched the kids settle down, their laughter fading into the night. Tomorrow would bring more challenges, more danger, but tonight, we had this. We had each other.

And for now, that was enough.

Chapter 38: The Boys Are Growing Up

It had been months since the day off Annie and I had spent with the kids. A rare pocket of peace, one we hadn't seen much of since. Life moved on, the same rhythm of survival—always preparing, always watching. But even in a world gone mad, time didn't stop for anyone, and the boys were growing up.

Colt was turning 19 soon. He wasn't the lanky kid I used to tower over anymore. He'd filled out, his frame sturdy from the long hours spent building and training with the other young men in our community. His eyes were sharper now, more focused, like he was already carrying the weight of the world on his shoulders.

Nash, though still younger, was catching up quickly. But today, it wasn't Nash who had my attention. It was Colt.

I had noticed something different about him lately. He'd been sneaking glances across the town square, distracted, and disappearing more often than usual. At first, I thought maybe he was just tired of following the same routine. Then, I caught him talking to a girl after one of the patrol drills.

Her name was Cecilia, a 18-year-old girl from one of the other survivor families in Beaufort. She had come in a few months after we did, quiet but strong, with deep brown eyes and dark, curly hair. She was one of the kids who had taken well to the new reality, tough as nails on the outside but with a softer side I could see coming out around Colt.

I couldn't help but feel a pang of something I hadn't expected... protectiveness. Not just for Colt, but for Cecilia, too. The world wasn't what it used to be, and I wasn't sure how to feel about my son having a love interest in the middle of all this. It was hard enough just keeping them safe.

But when I saw Colt's eyes light up every time he talked about her, I knew this wasn't just a fleeting crush. He was smitten. And to be honest, I could see why. She was a good kid. Smart, brave, and had already proven herself a dozen times over in helping secure supplies and looking after some of the younger survivors. She wasn't just a pretty face; she was capable. And that probably drew Colt in even more.

It was over dinner one night that Annie brought it up.

"I think Colt's got a girlfriend," she said, her voice light but amused as we sat at the small table in our makeshift kitchen.

I raised an eyebrow, pretending to act clueless. "Girlfriend?"

Annie shot me a knowing look. "Come on, Frank. Don't tell me you haven't noticed. Cecilia?"

I sighed, leaning back in my chair. "I've noticed. He's been sneaking off more than usual."

"He's not sneaking off, he's spending time with her," Annie corrected gently. "It's different. Remember when we were their age?"

I chuckled. "Yeah, but we weren't in the middle of the apocalypse."

"No," she agreed, smiling softly, "but love's still love. Even now. They're growing up, Frank. You can't stop it."

I rubbed the back of my neck. Annie was right, but that didn't make it easier. "I just want him to be safe."

"He is safe. And Cecilia's a good kid, you know that. He's not getting distracted—he's growing up. And we should be happy for him. It means he's still finding things worth living for." Her hand reached across the table, squeezing mine. "We've taught him everything we could. Now, we have to trust him."

That was the hardest part. Letting go, even just a little. But seeing how much Colt had matured over these past months, I knew he was capable of handling himself. Still, part of me wanted to sit him down, give him a talk about responsibility, about what it meant to have someone else to protect. About how this world didn't leave much room for mistakes.

Later that evening, I found Colt sitting on the porch, staring out at the quiet streets of Beaufort. He didn't say anything when I sat down beside him, but I knew he knew why I was there.

"Cecilia," I said after a few moments of silence.

He nodded, glancing at me out of the corner of his eye. "Yeah."

"Seems like a good kid."

"She is," he said quickly, his voice almost defensive. "She's smart, tough. She's... different."

I smirked. "Different how?"

Colt shrugged, trying to find the right words. "I don't know. She makes everything... better. Even with all the stuff going on. It's like when I'm around her, it's not as bad."

I nodded, recognizing that feeling all too well. That's how it was with Annie. No matter what the world threw at me, she made it better just by being there. And I could see now that Colt was finding that with Cecilia.

"I get it," I said, leaning forward and resting my elbows on my knees. "But you know it's not like it used to be. The world's different now. You've got to be smart. You've got to protect each other. This... this thing between you two, it's serious."

"I know, Dad," Colt said, meeting my eyes. There was no teenage rebellion in his tone, no rolling of the eyes. He was dead serious. "I know what's at stake. But I'm not just going to push her away because it's dangerous out there. I care about her."

I studied him for a long moment, my heart swelling with both pride and worry. Colt wasn't a boy anymore. He was standing on the edge of manhood, making choices that would shape the rest of his life—choices I couldn't make for him.

"I'm proud of you," I finally said, my voice low but firm. "You've grown up faster than I ever wanted you to, but you're handling it. Just... be careful, alright? Watch out for each other."

He nodded, his jaw set with determination. "We will."

As I stood to go back inside, Colt stopped me. "Dad?"

"Yeah?"

"Thanks. For trusting me."

I smiled, clapping him on the shoulder. "Always, kid."

As I walked back into the house, I couldn't help but feel a bittersweet mix of emotions. My boy was growing up, and there wasn't a damn thing I could do to slow it down. But if this new world had taught me anything, it was that life didn't stop, not even for a second. And maybe, just maybe, love was one of the few things left that could make this place feel human again.

Annie was waiting for me in the kitchen, a knowing look in her eyes. "How'd it go?"

I shrugged, trying to act nonchalant. "He's got a good head on his shoulders."

She smiled, wrapping her arms around me. "Told you. He's going to be just fine."

I held her close, feeling the weight of the world lift just a little, knowing that even in the darkest of times, life went on. And maybe, just maybe, that was enough.

Chapter 39: The Work Continues

Beaufort was starting to feel like something I hadn't experienced in a long time. Safe. It was strange, after all the months of chaos and survival, to wake up and hear nothing but the wind and the occasional murmur of voices in the distance. No more constant gunfire. No more howling or groaning from the undead. The town was transforming, and so were we.

The Marines, with some help from the remaining civilians, had turned this place into something more than just a refuge. It was a stronghold now. The barrier we'd built around the town was fortified with concrete, steel, and barbed wire. Watchtowers rose along the perimeter, each manned by sharpshooters with night-vision scopes, keeping an eye out for any sign of a horde.

But it wasn't just the defenses that were taking shape. The search and rescue missions had paid off in more ways than we expected. Every time we went out, combing through the desolate neighborhoods and overgrown roads outside of Beaufort, we found more survivors. Some were holed up in their homes, too terrified to venture out. Others had been living rough for weeks, wandering like ghosts until we found them.

They came to us in trucks, Humvees, and sometimes in civilian cars we'd commandeered along the way. At first, the newcomers were hesitant, wide-eyed and suspicious. But after a few days inside the walls, they relaxed. They realized that this wasn't just another temporary camp. This was home.

Our population was growing steadily. What had once been a handful of Marines, a few dozen civilians, and a couple of wandering souls was now turning into a community. Families, single survivors, even a few kids who had somehow managed to outlive their parents and found their way to us. We were all here now, in this bubble of relative calm in a world still overrun by the undead.

People were starting to smile again. That was the strangest part. I would walk through the streets, past the rows of barricaded houses and makeshift gardens, and see folks sitting on porches, talking, laughing. Kids were playing with old soccer balls in the open fields between houses, their laughter echoing through the air. It felt surreal, like I had stepped into a dream where everything was still right with the world.

Colt had been spending more time with Cecilia, and while I still kept an eye on them, I knew better than to hover. He was growing into his own, taking on more responsibilities with the patrols, and proving himself as a leader among the younger group of Marines-in-training. Nash had found his place, too, working with the scavenging teams, always eager to bring something useful back to help the cause.

Annie and I, well, we were settling into a routine. We worked in the mornings, helping with whatever needed doing—fortifications, gardening, logistics. By afternoon, we took shifts on the perimeter or helped organize the ever-growing stockpile of food, water, and supplies. It wasn't the life we had imagined for ourselves when we first moved to South Carolina, but it was a life, and it was ours.

The mood in Beaufort had shifted. Where once there had been constant tension, now there was hope. You could see it in the faces of the people around us. The way they walked taller, talked more freely. They weren't looking over their shoulders every five seconds, expecting the worst.

Of course, the danger wasn't gone, not by a long shot. The hordes were still out there. Every once in a while, a group of zombies would stumble toward the walls, drawn by the distant sounds of life. They were always dealt with swiftly. Picked off from the watchtowers before they could get close enough to cause any real threat.

But those instances were becoming less frequent. It seemed like we had cleared out most of the immediate area, and the zombies were losing their hold on the land. Maybe they were just thinning out, wandering aimlessly without enough fresh humans to keep them animated. Either way, Beaufort felt more secure than it ever had.

Our search and rescue efforts had become more organized, too. The Marines were leading missions almost every day now, sending out teams in waves—scouting parties on foot, Humvees packed with supplies, and even helicopters when we had the fuel to spare. Every time they brought back survivors, the gates would open, and I'd watch as people stepped through, looking dazed but relieved. Some cried. Some just stared, still in shock that they had made it out alive.

I remember one family in particular—a mother and father with two kids, no older than Nash. They'd been living out of a car for weeks, barely surviving on canned goods they'd scavenged from abandoned grocery stores. When they stepped through the gates, the mother broke down in tears, clutching her kids like they were the only thing anchoring her to the world. It was moments like that when I realized just how important this place had become.

Beaufort wasn't just a town anymore. It was a symbol of survival, a beacon of hope in a world that had long since lost its mind. People were drawn to it. Survivors out there, still fighting to live, heard about us through word of mouth, radio chatter, or rumors passed along by scavengers. They came because they believed Beaufort could offer something no other place could—safety.

And they weren't wrong.

With every passing day, our community grew stronger. More people meant more hands to work the fields, reinforce the walls, patrol the outskirts. We had doctors now, teachers, mechanics, even a small council that met to discuss the long-term plans for the town. The Marines were still in charge of security, but the civilians were taking on more roles, shaping the future of what Beaufort could be.

Annie had even started a small garden behind our house, working with some of the other women to grow vegetables and herbs. It was a small thing, but it felt like a step toward something bigger. Toward rebuilding. Toward living, not just surviving.

As the sun dipped below the horizon one evening, casting a warm glow over the town, I stood on the porch, watching Colt and Nash kick a soccer ball around with some of the other kids. Annie came up behind me, slipping her arm around my waist.

"You see that?" she asked, nodding toward the kids. "That's what it's all about."

I smiled, pulling her close. "Yeah, I see it."

For the first time in a long while, I let myself believe that maybe—just maybe—we had a future here. Beaufort was becoming more than just a safe zone. It was becoming home. And as long as we kept working, kept fighting, we could hold onto that.

The world outside the walls might still be lost, but here, inside the barrier, we had a chance. A chance to rebuild. A chance to be human again. And that was more than any of us had hoped for.

Chapter 40: Next Steps

The morning air was crisp, a rare cool breeze drifting off the water, bringing a brief relief from the heat. The steady hum of Beaufort waking up filled the air as I stood outside the community hall, sipping on what was left of the coffee we'd scrounged up. Inside, people were starting to gather—Marines, civilians, families—all of us preparing for a meeting that could determine the next steps for our little stronghold.

Annie, Colt, and Nash were with me, standing quietly as the crowd thickened. Colt looked distracted, probably thinking about Cecilia, who was seated with her family a few rows ahead. Nash, on the other hand, seemed focused, ready to hear what the meeting was about. For once, his usual pre-teen energy was subdued, like he knew that today's discussion was important.

"We need to figure out a plan," I said, speaking quietly to Annie. "Food's going to be a problem soon. We've scavenged what we can, but if we don't start thinking long-term, we'll run out."

Annie nodded, concern furrowing her brow. "You're right. We can't keep relying on the scraps we find out there. And we need to make sure everyone's on the same page."

Colt looked over at us, pulling himself out of his thoughts. "What do you think they're gonna say, Dad?"

"I'm not sure, son," I replied. "But it's about more than just us now. It's about the entire community."

The doors to the hall swung open, and the marine commander, Captain Reyes, walked in. He was a solid man—mid-40s, graying at the temples, with a calm but commanding presence. The kind of man people naturally followed. Behind him were a few other Marines, including Sergeant Davis, one of the best tacticians we had. They took their place at the front, the room gradually falling silent as people settled in.

"All right, everyone," Reyes began, his voice steady. "We've made it this far because we've worked together. We've fortified Beaufort, cleared out the immediate threat, and created a place where we can survive. But now, we need to think about more than just surviving. We need to plan for the future. And that starts today."

He paused, scanning the room. People listened intently. This wasn't like the early days of panic and desperation. We had structure now, and this meeting was about solidifying that structure into something sustainable.

"We've got a few key concerns," Reyes continued. "First, and most important, is food. Our supplies are dwindling, and scavenging can only take us so far. We need to start farming in a more organized way and possibly explore other options, like hunting and fishing."

"Second," he said, his voice deepening, "is expanding our safe zone. We've done well securing Beaufort, but the area outside our walls is still a threat. We need to start thinking about pushing out, clearing more ground, and bringing more people in. The more we control, the better our chances of long-term survival."

Reyes paused again, this time letting the weight of his words sink in.

"The third issue is leadership," he said. "While the Marines have been handling security, we need more civilians stepping up to help with organizing the rest. There are too many responsibilities for one group to handle alone."

Sergeant Davis stepped forward and unfurled a map of the area on the table behind them. "Here's the deal," Davis said. "The surrounding neighborhoods are still overrun. We've cleared out some sections, but there's more work to do. We can secure more land if we're smart about it—set up checkpoints, create interlocking fields of fire, and clear out the stragglers before they become a horde again. We can also start using more natural barriers—rivers, forests—to our advantage."

Colt leaned in toward me. "You think we can really push out that far, Dad?"

I shrugged. "We've got the numbers and the skill. But it's going to take time. And people. We'll need the whole community working together."

Reyes continued, "We want to hear from everyone. We'll break into groups after this to figure out who's willing to take on what. Farmers, hunters, builders, medics, scavengers—we need everyone to step up. We're not just fighting to stay alive anymore. We're building something."

Annie glanced over at me. "I can help organize the garden efforts, expand them beyond the small plots we've been working on. We'll need more space, more hands."

I nodded. "I'll keep working with the Marines, but I'll also help organize more scavenging parties. There's still useful stuff out there if we're smart about how we search."

Reyes called the meeting to order again, listing out the responsibilities that needed volunteers. "First things first—food. We need more people working on farming. Annie here's been doing a great job, but we need to expand. Who's willing to help get that going?"

Several hands shot up around the room, including Annie's. A few of the older folks, who'd been farmers before the outbreak, stood up, volunteering to teach others what they knew.

"Good," Reyes said, satisfied. "Next, we need to think about expanding the safe zone. We're looking for people willing to clear out the outer areas—work with the Marines, set up new fortifications, and help secure any usable buildings. Who's in?"

I raised my hand, followed by Colt and a group of others. I noticed some of the Marines nodding in approval. They'd need all the help they could get to push out our boundaries.

"Last," Reyes said, "we need leaders. People who can step up and take responsibility for different areas. Civilians who can organize the day-to-day operations. We'll still be here for security, but this community has to run itself."

An older woman named Sarah, who had been a nurse before everything went to hell, stood up. "I can help organize the medics, make sure the injured and sick are taken care of."

Others followed her lead, offering to take charge of different areas—cooking, maintenance, childcare. People were stepping up. It wasn't just about surviving anymore. It was about building a new life.

When the meeting finally ended, we walked out into the sunlight, feeling a sense of purpose.

Colt broke the silence. "So, we're really doing this? Expanding, farming...building something real?"

I nodded, feeling a mix of pride and apprehension. "Yeah, we are. And it's going to be hard work. But we don't have a choice."

Nash looked up at me, a flicker of excitement in his eyes. "I want to help, too, Dad."

I ruffled his hair. "You will, son. We all will."

As we walked back toward our home, I realized that this wasn't just about defending a small town anymore. It was about growing, evolving, and rebuilding what was left of the world. For the first time in a long time, I felt hope.

Beaufort was just the beginning. Now it was time to see how far we could.

Chapter 41: The Price of Progress

The morning sun crept over the horizon, casting a warm, golden light on the fortified walls of Beaufort. It was early, but already the town was buzzing with life. People were in the fields, tending to the crops we'd managed to plant. The hum of power tools echoed in the air as teams worked on reinforcing the barriers and expanding the safe zone. There was a sense of purpose here now, a focus on building something that could last. But with that progress came a cost—a weight I could feel settling on my shoulders more each day.

Annie was up before me, already busy with the other gardeners in the community plots. Her hands were covered in dirt, but there was a smile on her face as she instructed a group of newcomers on how to plant properly. Seeing her like that—focused, strong—reminded me of why we were doing all this. It was for her, for Colt and Nash, and for the future we were all trying to carve out from this mess of a world.

But today wasn't going to be easy.

"Frank," Captain Reyes called from the gate as I walked toward the town center. He stood there with Sergeant Davis and a few other Marines, their expressions grim. "We need to talk."

I felt the tension in the air, and my gut told me it wasn't good news. "What's going on?"

Reyes gestured for me to follow him. We walked a short distance from the gate, where a small group of civilians and Marines had gathered around a hastily set-up tent. Inside, maps were spread across a table, alongside radios and other bits of scavenged military equipment. At the center of it all was a report.

"The scouting parties came back late last night," Reyes said, his voice low. "We've got movement to the north."

"Zombies?"

He nodded. "Not a horde like the one we dealt with before, but it's growing. Could be a few hundred at least, heading straight toward us. Davis spotted them on one of the night runs, but we didn't have enough light to get an accurate count."

I rubbed a hand over my face, feeling the exhaustion creeping in. "How long do we have?"

"Two, maybe three days, tops," Reyes said. "We're going to have to prepare. Again."

I looked around at the maps, my mind racing through what needed to be done. We'd fortified Beaufort as much as we could, but the walls weren't invincible. And with so many new people coming in from the rescue missions, we had more mouths to feed, more people to protect, and fewer resources to stretch.

"We'll need to organize the defense teams," I said, thinking out loud. "Set up extra patrols along the perimeter. Get the civilians inside and ready for lockdown."

Reyes nodded. "That's what we were thinking. We'll run drills today, make sure everyone knows what to do if things go south."

I glanced at Davis, who was already gathering the Marines. "I'll talk to the civilians," I said. "Let them know what's coming. We don't want panic, but they need to be prepared."

Reyes clapped me on the shoulder. "Thanks, Frank. We're lucky to have you here."

As I walked away, my mind was already shifting into battle mode. This was the price of progress—every step forward was met with a new threat, a new challenge. And while we were growing stronger as a community, it also meant we had more to lose.

I found Colt and Nash near the outer wall, helping some of the other teens with reinforcing a section of the barricade. Colt looked up when he saw me, his face serious.

"Dad, we heard. There's more of them coming, isn't there?"

I nodded. "Yeah, but we've got time to prepare. You're doing good work here. Just keep it up."

Nash looked up from his hammering, sweat dripping down his brow. "I can help with the patrols, too. I'm fast, and I know the area."

I smiled, proud of his determination. "We'll see. Right now, just focus on staying safe. We're going to need you both when this is all over."

Colt wiped his hands on his jeans, looking out at the horizon beyond the walls. "You think we'll ever get ahead of this, Dad? Or is it always going to be like this... fighting, surviving?"

I sighed, not wanting to give him a false answer. "I don't know, son. But we're building something here. Something better than what's out there. That's all we can do—take it one day at a time."

He nodded, though I could see the uncertainty in his eyes. He was growing up fast, too fast, and it weighed on me knowing he didn't get to be a carefree teenager like I'd once hoped.

As the day wore on, the entire town shifted into preparation mode. Teams of civilians and Marines worked side by side, reinforcing walls, setting up lookout points, and stockpiling what little ammunition we had left. The younger kids, including Nash, were sent to the safer areas near the center of town, tasked with keeping the gardens going and preparing meals for the workers.

By the time the sun dipped below the horizon, we were as ready as we could be.

I found Annie sitting on the steps of our house, her hands still dirty from a long day in the fields. She looked up at me, her eyes tired but resolute.

"They're coming, aren't they?" she asked.

"Yeah," I said, sitting down next to her. "But we're ready. Or as ready as we'll ever be."

She leaned her head on my shoulder, and for a moment, we just sat there in the fading light, the sounds of the town slowly winding down around us.

"We've built something here, Frank," she said softly. "No matter what happens, I'm proud of what we've done. Of what you've done."

I wrapped my arm around her, holding her close. "We'll get through this, Annie. We always do."

As darkness fell, I couldn't help but feel the weight of what was coming. The zombies were on their way, and once again, we'd be tested. But this time, we weren't just surviving. We were protecting something worth fighting for—a future, a community, a life. And for that, I'd fight as long as it took.

Chapter 42: Dawn of the Fight

The morning was heavy with anticipation. Every person in Beaufort seemed to move with a sense of purpose, an unspoken understanding that today could be the difference between life and death. We'd prepared as best we could, but it was hard to shake the fear that always lurked just beneath the surface.

I stood at the edge of the town wall, looking out into the distance where the zombies were expected to approach. The quiet before a battle never felt natural. Even after all these years—after all the chaos I'd lived through—the stillness of the moments before contact was unnerving.

Captain Reyes joined me at the lookout, his face as hard as stone, but his eyes told a different story. "They're coming," he said. It wasn't a question, just a fact that we both knew to be true. The scouts had confirmed the horde was only a few hours out, moving slowly but steadily in our direction.

I nodded, feeling the weight of the day settle into my chest. "Everyone ready?"

"As ready as they'll ever be," he replied. "We've got Marines at each checkpoint, armed civilians manning the walls, and runners in place to keep communication going between the sectors."

I glanced down at the group of civilians below—mostly farmers, carpenters, and mechanics, now turned into defenders. Their makeshift weapons and basic training wouldn't hold up long in a sustained fight, but they had heart. And in the end, that was what mattered most.

"Colt and Nash?" Reyes asked, shifting his gaze to the western wall where I'd stationed them.

"They're ready," I said, though my stomach knotted at the thought of my boys being in harm's way. "Colt's with the patrols. Nash is helping with the communication lines."

Reyes nodded, understanding the unspoken worry. "They'll be fine. You trained them well."

I wanted to believe that, but there was always that nagging fear in the back of my mind. It wasn't the zombies that scared me most—it was the thought of losing them, losing Annie, losing everything we'd fought so hard to protect.

As the first signs of the approaching horde came into view—a line of shambling figures on the horizon—Reyes gave the order to alert the rest of the town. The signal was simple: three long blasts from an air horn that echoed through the town, cutting through the tension and setting everything into motion.

"Let's go," Reyes said, heading for the central command post where the radios and maps were set up.

I followed him, my thoughts already running through the battle plan. We'd set up fallback points within the town itself—barriers and choke points where we could hold them off if they managed to breach the outer walls. The hope was that we could thin out their numbers enough before they got too close.

"Frank," a voice called out as we entered the command tent. It was Annie, her face pale but determined. She stood beside Colt, who had his rifle slung over his shoulder, ready for whatever was coming.

"Everything okay?" I asked, scanning their faces for any sign of trouble.

Annie nodded. "We're ready. The kids are all in the shelters, and the food stores are locked down. We'll be fine."

I looked at Colt, who gave me a firm nod. "I've got the west side covered, Dad. Nash is already in position, and I'll be running with the patrols if anything goes wrong."

I gripped his shoulder. "Just be smart, Colt. We've done this before, but it's different now. We've got people to protect."

"I know," he said, his voice steady but laced with the seriousness of what lay ahead.

The air felt thicker as the minutes passed, the sound of groaning and shuffling feet growing louder with each passing second. From the lookout towers, we could see them clearly now—a horde of the undead, hundreds of them, moving in a slow, terrifying wave toward Beaufort's walls.

"Weapons ready!" Reyes shouted, his voice cutting through the rising tension.

The sound of rifles being cocked, arrows drawn, and improvised weapons raised filled the air. Everyone was ready, but no one truly knew what to expect. We'd fought off smaller groups before, but nothing on this scale.

The first of the zombies hit the outer barricades, their bodies crashing against the walls in a gruesome wave. They clawed and moaned, pushing mindlessly forward as the defenders opened fire. Gunshots cracked in the morning air, followed by the sickening sound of metal meeting flesh.

I stood on the western wall with Colt and a group of Marines, our rifles aimed and ready. We picked off the zombies one by one, but for every one that fell, two more seemed to take its place.

"Keep firing!" I shouted. My voice hoarse as I reloaded.

The horde was relentless, their sheer numbers overwhelming. But the wall held—for now.

Suddenly, a shout went up from the eastern side. "Breach!"

I turned, my heart racing. The zombies had found a weak point in the barricade, and they were pouring through in a mass of writhing bodies.

"Colt, stay here!" I ordered as I sprinted toward the breach, knowing I had to help plug the gap.

As I reached the breach, chaos reigned. Civilians were fighting off the zombies with everything they had—baseball bats, pipes, and garden tools—while Marines struggled to keep the line from collapsing completely. I grabbed a fallen rifle and joined the fray, the weight of the weapon familiar in my hands as I fired into the mass of undead.

"Push them back!" Reyes shouted from somewhere nearby, his voice barely audible over the cacophony of the battle.

Slowly, inch by inch, we managed to push them back, plugging the breach with makeshift barriers as more Marines and civilians joined the fight. But the cost was heavy. Bodies littered the ground, both human and undead, and the air was thick with the smell of blood and gunpowder.

After what felt like an eternity, the last of the zombies fell, and the town fell eerily silent once again.

I stood in the aftermath, panting and covered in sweat, my hands shaking as I looked around at the devastation. We'd won—for now—but the cost had been steep.

Reyes approached, his face grim. "We held them off, but we lost too many. We need to regroup."

I nodded, too exhausted to speak. My mind was already racing with thoughts of what needed to be done—reinforcing the barricades, tending to the wounded, burying the dead. But for now, all I could do was stand there, the weight of the day pressing down on me like a lead blanket.

As the sun set on Beaufort, the reality of what we were up against settled in. This fight was far from over, and if we were going to survive, we had to be stronger, smarter, and more united than ever before.

The price of progress was steep, but there was no turning back.

Chapter 43: Actual... Engaged

The morning was alive with activity. After weeks of fighting off hordes, the Marines, along with the townspeople, decided it was time to change tactics. Waiting behind walls while the dead gathered outside wasn't sustainable. We were actually going to take the fight to them.

I stood at the newly reinforced wall, the sharp scent of salt air mixing with the smell of fresh timber and steel. The town of Beaufort was becoming a fortress, but even fortresses could fall. The time had come to push out beyond our safety, clear the areas that were breeding grounds for the undead, and establish control.

"Frank!" Captain Reyes called as he approached, his footsteps heavy against the wooden walkways. "We're almost ready to move. We'll split into three units—one heads west toward Port Royal, one south along the river, and the third takes the northern route."

I nodded, already knowing which direction I'd be leading. I hadn't planned on taking Colt along for this mission, but in the days since the last big fight, something had shifted in him. He was eager, maybe too eager.

"I'll take the river route with my team," I said. "Shouldn't be too much resistance there, but I've seen surprises in places like this before."

"Roger that," Reyes replied. "We'll meet up again at the river crossing. Let's make this clean."

As Reyes headed off, I spotted Colt down below, pacing back and forth. He wasn't preparing for the mission, though—I could tell from the way he kept glancing over his shoulder toward Cecilia. She was standing by the water pump, her auburn hair catching the sunlight, a calmness about her that contrasted sharply with Colt's restless energy.

It didn't take much to figure out what was on his mind. Colt wasn't just distracted—he was preoccupied.

I made my way down to him, each step more deliberate than the last. "Something on your mind, Colt?" I asked, not breaking my stride.

He looked up, surprised that I had come over. "Uh, yeah, Dad. There's something I need to talk to you about."

I crossed my arms, waiting. He'd always been one to speak his mind, but I could see him hesitating, which was unusual. He was different these days—stronger, more capable—but this wasn't the look of a soldier about to face the enemy. It was something else.

"Go ahead," I said, keeping my tone steady.

Colt rubbed the back of his neck, glancing over at Cecilia, who had spotted us and was watching from a distance. "It's about Cecilia. I... I think I'm ready. Ready to take the next step with her."

I raised an eyebrow. "Next step?"

"Yeah." He swallowed hard. "I want to propose. I know things aren't exactly normal right now, and it's not the world you and Mom grew up in, but... I love her, Dad. And I don't want to wait anymore."

The words hit me like a punch to the gut, not because I didn't expect it, but because of how real they were. My son was thinking about a future, a future in the middle of this hellscape, no less. A future that, in any other world, I would have celebrated without hesitation.

I glanced at Cecilia, and then back at Colt. He wasn't a kid anymore. He hadn't been for some time. He was a man now, standing on his own two feet, making choices that carried weight. I just wasn't sure I was ready to let him make *this* choice.

"Does your mother know?" I asked, buying myself time to think.

Colt shifted nervously. "Not yet. I wanted to talk to you first. I mean, I know it's not the best time, but... there's never going to be a perfect time. And it feels right."

I took a deep breath, thinking back to my own days of young love with Annie. We hadn't faced anything like this, a world collapsing. The dead walking. But I remembered that fire. The certainty. And here it was in front of me, staring me down in the form of my own son.

"Look, Colt," I said, trying to gather my thoughts, "I'm not going to lie to you. Things are tough right now, and they might get worse before they get better. This isn't the world I wanted for you or for anyone, really. But if you're sure about this, about her, you need to think long and hard about what it means."

Colt's face grew serious. "I have thought about it, Dad. I know what's out there, and I know what kind of world we're living in. But if I'm going to survive this, I don't want to do it without her. She's it for me."

His words were simple, but they carried a truth I couldn't deny. It wasn't just about love—it was about hope. The future. What little of it we had left.

"Alright," I said after a long pause. "Talk to your mom. I know she's going to have questions. And we'll have to figure some things out. But if this is what you both want..." I trailed off, shaking my head slightly. "Then I won't stand in your way."

Colt's eyes lit up with a mix of relief and excitement. "Thanks, Dad. Really."

I clapped him on the shoulder, the weight of this new reality settling in. The world was falling apart, but here he was, trying to build something out of the ruins.

Annie found us a little while later, her sharp eyes picking up on the vibe immediately. She crossed her arms, leaning slightly to the side, waiting for Colt to spill whatever it was he was holding back.

Colt didn't make her wait long. "Mom, I want to ask Cecilia to marry me."

Annie blinked, her expression unreadable at first. Then, slowly, she exhaled, her arms dropping to her sides. "Marry? Colt, honey... are you sure? I mean, I love her too, but this is—"

"I'm sure, Mom," Colt interrupted, his voice firm but not unkind. "I know it's crazy. But nothing's guaranteed. And I want this. We both do."

Annie glanced at me, searching for my thoughts. I gave her a small nod, letting her know I wasn't against it, but I could see the concern in her eyes.

"I'm not against it," she finally said, her voice soft. "But... there's a lot to think about. What kind of life you'll be able to have. What comes next." She hesitated, then added, "And kids. Are you even thinking about children in a world like this?"

Colt looked between the two of us, his jaw tightening. "Maybe we'll have kids. Maybe we won't. But we want a future, Mom. And kids... kids mean hope. They mean survival."

I exchanged a glance with Annie, and something shifted in her expression. It was subtle, but it was there. She wasn't just thinking about our survival anymore. She was thinking about the long game. About humanity's survival.

"You're right," she finally said, her voice resigned but not defeated. "Kids do mean hope. They mean there's a future worth fighting for."

Colt nodded, a small smile forming on his lips as the weight of our hesitation seemed to lift. "Thanks, Mom. Dad."

As he walked away to find Cecilia, Annie turned to me, her arms crossed again, this time more out of habit than stress. "I wasn't expecting this," she said softly.

"Neither was I," I replied, watching as Colt disappeared into the crowd. "But maybe he's right. Maybe we need to stop thinking about just surviving."

Annie gave a small, thoughtful nod. "Maybe."

As we stood there, the fight to push out the zombies was just beginning. But amidst all that chaos, amidst the uncertainty and fear, something else was growing—something that reminded us there was more to life than just fighting the dead. There was love. There was hope. And sometimes, that was enough.

Chapter 44: Building Something New

The morning sun cut through the mist rising from the river, casting a soft golden light over the town of Beaufort. It was a strange sight—half ruins, half refuge. But for the first time in what felt like years, the town was starting to feel like more than just a shelter. It was starting to feel like something real. Something sustainable.

I leaned on the railing of the makeshift watchtower, looking out at the work being done below. The sound of hammers echoed across the streets as more people joined the effort to reinforce the walls. What was once a loose collection of survivors had become something more organized. Marines had turned into planners and builders, civilians into key players in our effort to reclaim and rebuild. Beaufort was becoming more than just a stronghold—it was becoming a home.

"Frank," Captain Reyes called as he climbed the ladder to join me. He looked out over the town, his face a mask of determination. "Looks like we're making progress."

"Yeah," I replied, nodding toward the teams working to clear debris from the main road. "But we've still got a long way to go."

Reyes grunted in agreement. "We've managed to clear out the majority of the dead in the immediate area, but the search and rescue teams are bringing in more people every day. That means more mouths to feed, more people to protect."

I sighed, knowing he was right. Every survivor we brought in was a potential asset, but they were also another burden. Food was already running low, and while the barrier we built around the town was holding, we couldn't keep expanding without better resources.

"We've got to find a way to start producing food locally," I said. "Raiding stores and scrounging for canned goods isn't going to cut it much longer."

Reyes nodded. "I've been thinking the same thing. We need to figure out how to farm—set up something sustainable. There's plenty of land around here, but we're going to need to secure it."

I rubbed my hand over my chin, considering the challenge. "We'll have to push the perimeter out. Make sure it's clear of any undead before we can even think about planting anything."

"Yeah, and we'll need to protect it once we do. Fencing, watchtowers, patrols... The more we expand, the harder it gets to defend."

I nodded slowly, the weight of responsibility pressing down on my shoulders. We were safe for now, but survival wasn't just about keeping the dead out. It was about building something that could last.

Reyes continued, "There's also the issue of leadership. We can't keep running everything through the Marines. We've got civilians with different skill sets, and we're going to need more structure if we want this to work long-term."

I glanced over at Reyes. "You suggesting we start a government or something?"

He shrugged. "Not exactly. But we need a council—something to bring everyone together. Get input from the civilians, make sure they feel like they're part of this. If we try to run this like a military operation forever, it's going to break down."

I took a deep breath, knowing he was right. "Alright. We'll gather everyone tonight and hold a meeting. Get some voices in the room, start making decisions together."

Reyes clapped me on the back. "Good. It's time."

That evening, the town square was packed. People gathered around the fire pits, the flickering light casting long shadows across the cracked pavement. It felt like a scene out of the old world—a community coming together, sharing warmth and stories. But the stakes were higher now. This wasn't just about survival. It was about what kind of life we were going to build.

Annie stood by my side, her hand resting lightly on my arm. Colt and Nash were nearby, talking with Cecilia and a few of the other teenagers who had formed a small group of their own. They were all growing up faster than we could've ever expected. But in a way, that wasn't a bad thing. They were strong, resilient, and maybe, just maybe, they would build a better world than we did.

Captain Reyes stepped forward, raising his voice over the murmurs of the crowd. "Alright, listen up, everyone. We've been through hell, but we're still standing. Beaufort is secure, and we've started making real progress. But we've got a lot of work ahead of us."

The crowd quieted, all eyes on Reyes.

"We need to start thinking long-term," he continued. "This town can't just be a safe zone anymore. It needs to become a real community, with leadership, resources, and a plan for the future. That's why we're forming a council tonight—so we can start making decisions as a group."

A few heads nodded, and I could hear murmurs of agreement ripple through the crowd.

Reyes gestured toward me, and I stepped forward. "We need volunteers," I said, my voice steady. "People who are willing to step up, take on responsibilities. We need farmers, engineers, medics, scouts, and more. We can't rely on the Marines for everything. This is going to be our town—all of ours."

For a moment, there was silence. Then, one by one, people started raising their hands. A farmer. A nurse. A mechanic. Slowly, the roles began to fill. It wasn't perfect, but it was a start.

As the meeting continued, I couldn't help but feel a flicker of hope. We were taking control of our future, building something new out of the ashes of the old world.

After the meeting, Annie and I walked back toward our house, the boys trailing behind us, deep in conversation. She looked up at me, her eyes reflecting the firelight.

"You think we can really pull this off?" she asked quietly.

I paused, looking around at the people who had come together, the town that was slowly coming back to life. "I think we have to try. If we don't, then what's the point of all this?"

She nodded, her grip tightening on my arm. "I just want the boys to have something to look forward to. A future."

I wrapped an arm around her shoulders, pulling her close. "We're building that future. One step at a time."

As we walked back toward the house, I felt something I hadn't felt in a long time: hope. Not just for survival, but for something more. For a real life.

Chapter 45: Love in the Time of Chaos

The sun was beginning to set over the marshlands, casting a warm golden light over Beaufort's new walls. The barriers we'd built gave us safety, but inside, life was slowly starting to blossom. Even in the midst of chaos, with the constant threat of zombies looming outside our fortified perimeter, love had somehow found a way to bloom.

I watched from a distance as Colt and Cecilia sat by the water's edge, their silhouettes framed by the fading light. They were deep in conversation, the way they had been so many times over the past few weeks. In a world torn apart, their bond had only grown stronger.

Annie joined me on the porch, wiping her hands on her apron after helping with dinner preparations. She followed my gaze and smiled softly. "Those two have something special," she said, her voice tinged with a mixture of nostalgia and hope.

I nodded, watching as Colt reached out to brush a strand of hair away from Cecilia's face. There was a gentleness in his actions, a care that went beyond the usual teenage infatuation. "It's strange, isn't it? Even with everything going on, they've found this... connection."

Annie leaned against the railing, her eyes focused on the young couple. "Love has a way of thriving, even in the darkest of times. Maybe because of the dark times. It's a way to hold onto something real, something good."

I could feel the weight of her words. We'd all been through hell these past months, but seeing Colt and Cecilia together, laughing and talking like any normal teenagers, reminded me that life wasn't entirely lost. There were still pieces of it worth holding onto.

"They're talking about their future," Annie said quietly, surprising me.

"What do you mean?"

She hesitated, then smiled softly. "Colt came to me earlier today. He asked me how you and I knew we wanted to be together. He's thinking about proposing, Frank."

I blinked, the realization hitting me like a ton of bricks. "Proposing?" I echoed, glancing back at Colt. He was only 18. A kid still, in my eyes. But then again, the world had forced him to grow up fast. They all had to. "He's just a boy."

Annie placed a hand on my arm, her eyes full of understanding. "He's not just a boy anymore, Frank. None of them are. This world doesn't allow for that. They've had to grow up faster than we ever did."

I sighed, running a hand through my hair. "I know. But... marriage? He's still so young."

"Age doesn't mean the same thing anymore," she said gently. "They've found love in the middle of all this. And maybe they're thinking about it because they know how fragile life is now."

I couldn't argue with that. Every day was uncertain. We'd lost good people, and the reality was, none of us knew how long we had left. But still, it was hard for me to reconcile the idea that my son, my 18-year-old son, was thinking about marriage.

"I'm just not sure he understands what he's getting into," I admitted, glancing at Annie. "We know how hard it can be, even in normal times. Now? It's a whole different ballgame."

Annie smiled, her gaze soft. "You're right, it won't be easy. But who are we to stand in the way of love? You and I found each other, and we've made it work, even through the hardest times."

She was right, as usual. Colt and Cecilia had found something special, something pure in a world that had been anything but. Who was I to deny them the chance to hold onto that?

As the sun dipped lower, Colt and Cecilia stood and began walking back toward the town. I could see the way Colt looked at her—the way I used to look at Annie when we were young. Hell, the way I still did. It was that mix of admiration, awe, and an overwhelming sense of protection. He would do anything for her, just like I would for Annie.

When Colt finally reached us, he cleared his throat, clearly nervous. "Dad, can I talk to you for a minute?"

I nodded, trying to hide the smirk I could feel tugging at my lips. "Sure, son. Let's take a walk."

We headed down the path along the river, and after a few moments of silence, Colt finally spoke. "I know things are crazy right now, Dad. But... I love Cecilia. I've never felt this way before. I want to ask her to marry me."

Hearing it from his mouth made it real. I looked at him, really looked at him. He was taller than me now, stronger than I ever thought he'd be. The boy I used to teach to fish and throw a ball had become a man in front of my eyes. I wasn't ready for that, but it didn't matter. Life didn't wait for us to be ready anymore.

"You sure about this, Colt?" I asked, my voice low. "Marriage is a big step. It's not something you take lightly."

He nodded, his expression serious. "I know, Dad. But I also know I don't want to waste time. Not with everything going on. I love her, and I want to be with her, no matter what."

I felt a surge of pride. He had grown up, whether I was ready for it or not. "Alright," I said after a long pause. "If you're sure, then I won't stand in your way. Just know that it's not always going to be easy. But if she's the one you want by your side through all of this, then you have my blessing."

The relief on his face was immediate. "Thanks, Dad. That means a lot."

I clapped a hand on his shoulder. "You're a good man, Colt. And Cecilia's lucky to have you."

We walked back to the house in comfortable silence, the weight of the conversation settling between us. Love had a funny way of showing up when you least expected it, even in the middle of chaos. But maybe that was exactly when it was needed the most.

As we reached the house, I saw Annie standing on the porch, her arms crossed and a soft smile on her face. Colt looked over at Cecilia, who was waiting for him near the fire pit, and I could see the determination in his eyes. He was going to ask her. He was going to take that step.

And in that moment, watching my son find something to hold onto in this broken world, I realized something important: Love wasn't just surviving. It was thriving. Even in the darkest times, it had the power to light the way forward.

The sun dipped low on the horizon, casting long shadows across Beaufort's fortified walls. A soft breeze rustled the trees, the only sound besides the distant hum of the town's activity. Colt and Cecilia sat together on the weathered bench by the docks, a place they had made their own in these strange, uncertain times.

In a world ravaged by chaos, where survival was the only constant, their love was an anchor. It wasn't just the affection of teenagers, swept up in the whirlwind of young romance. No, this was something deeper. More grounded. Something that had grown in the cracks of a world falling apart. Something real.

Colt's hand rested gently on Cecilia's, his thumb tracing small circles across her skin. He looked out across the water, the marshlands stretching far beyond the eye could see. The world beyond Beaufort was wild, dangerous. But here, in this small pocket of safety they had carved out, he felt...hopeful. Maybe for the first time in months.

"You ever think about what life would've been like if none of this happened?" Colt asked, his voice soft but steady. He didn't look at her, just kept his gaze fixed on the horizon, but he could feel her eyes on him.

Cecilia leaned back, resting her head on his shoulder. "All the time," she whispered. "But I don't think we'd have met, not like this. I think about that too."

It was true. Before the world had crumbled, their paths might never have crossed. Cecilia had been from another part of the state, her family relocating to a nearby town after things began spiraling out of control. In the chaos that followed, they'd lost nearly everything. Everything except each other.

But here they were. And in this strange, fractured existence, they had found a connection that somehow made sense. It was the only thing that made sense anymore.

"I don't know what the future's supposed to look like," Colt admitted after a long pause. "But I know I want you in it. That's the only thing I'm sure of."

Cecilia shifted to look at him, her eyes soft, the corners of her mouth lifting into a small smile. "We've been through hell and back, Colt. And I've never doubted us, not once." She reached up, brushing a strand of hair from his face. "We've survived everything else. We'll survive whatever comes next. Together."

That word, together, was what it all came down to. They had seen death, destruction, and the constant threat of losing each other, but somehow, they'd clung to this bond. It wasn't just about love anymore. It was about survival, yes, but also about living, truly living, in the moments they could steal from the madness outside the walls.

"I want to marry you," Colt said suddenly, the words escaping him in a rush. He hadn't planned to say it, not here, not like this. But it had been on his mind every day since he'd talked to his dad. "I don't want to wait. Not with everything going on. I want to make sure that no matter what happens, we're in this together."

Cecilia blinked, her lips parting in surprise. For a moment, the world around them seemed to stop. The sounds of Beaufort in the distance, the ever-present fear of the outside world. It all faded. It was just them, sitting by the water, with nothing but their future hanging in the balance.

"You mean that?" Cecilia asked, her voice soft but filled with emotion. "You really want to get married... now?"

Colt turned to face her, his heart racing but his voice calm. "Yeah. I do. I don't know how long we've got, Cece. But I know I want to spend it with you, however long that is."

Tears filled her eyes, but they weren't from sadness. She smiled, a smile that lit up her face even in the dimming light. "Colt, I love you. More than anything. And I'd marry you in a heartbeat."

They sat there for a while longer, in silence, letting the weight of what they'd just decided sink in. They both knew the world wasn't going to get better overnight. There would still be dangers, still battles to fight, and losses to endure. But for once, they had something to look forward to.

That night, Colt told his parents that Ceclia said yes. He didn't expect them to be thrilled at first. He was still their son, their teenage son, and the idea of him getting married in the middle of a zombie apocalypse wasn't exactly what any parent imagined for their child.

Frank's brow furrowed as Colt explained, but he wasn't angry. There was something about the way Colt spoke, the determination in his voice, that reminded Frank of himself at that age. Young love had a way of being reckless, but it was also powerful. And in this world, it was one of the only things keeping people grounded.

"You sure about this?" Frank asked, his voice gruff but not unkind. Even though they had discussed it earlier, Frank wanted to make sure.

Colt nodded. "Yeah, Dad. I'm sure. I love her."

Frank exchanged a look with Annie. They were both quiet for a moment, clearly weighing their feelings. Annie smiled softly and reached out to touch Frank's hand. "They've already been through more than most couples ever do," she said quietly. "If this is what they want, maybe it's not such a bad idea. They need something good. We all do."

Frank sighed, then gave Colt a nod. "Alright, kid. You've got our blessing."

Colt smiled, relief flooding his features. "Thanks, Dad. I won't let you down."

Later that night, Colt and Cecilia walked through the quiet streets of Beaufort, hand in hand. It wasn't the world they had imagined growing up, and their future wasn't guaranteed. But in each other, they had found something worth fighting for, something to believe in when everything else seemed to fall apart.

The stars twinkled above them, and for the first time in what felt like forever, the future didn't seem so bleak. They had each other, and that was more than enough.

In a world full of ruins, love had somehow found a way to prevail.

Chapter 46: We Will Survive

Frank stood at the edge of the newly expanded perimeter, watching as Marines and civilians worked side by side, reinforcing the barrier. Beyond the fence, the marshes stretched for miles. Quiet now, but always harboring hidden threats. The sounds of hammers, drills, and the occasional shout echoed across the landscape. A symphony of survival turned into progress.

Beaufort wasn't just growing in numbers; it was growing in strength. What had started as a small, desperate haven had become a stronghold. Frank, Annie, Colt, Nash, and the others had poured everything into this place. Each day, they fought not just for Beaufort's survival, but for the survival of what remained of humanity.

He could see Colt working alongside some other young men, shoveling dirt and reinforcing the trench that surrounded the outer barrier. Cecilia was nearby, helping to sort supplies, her laugh reaching Frank's ears even from across the field. It warmed him to see them like that, building a future in a world that had tried to tear everything apart.

Annie was inside the newly established medical center, helping treat a few minor injuries and keeping the records straight. She had found her niche in the new order of things, working alongside the few doctors and nurses who had survived. For her, it wasn't just about keeping the community healthy. It was about giving people hope, showing them that even in the darkest times, they could still rely on one another.

The expansion of Beaufort had been hard-won. It wasn't just about clearing more land or building more walls. Every inch of territory was taken back from the dead, slowly, methodically. The Marines, led by Sergeant Reynolds, had become experts in clearing out small pockets of undead, using everything from close-quarters combat to sniper overwatch. Each operation felt like a battle, a victory with a purpose.

Frank took a deep breath, watching the men and women around him work together with a sense of urgency, but also purpose. There was something powerful about the way everyone had come together. Beaufort had become more than just a place of safety, it had become a beacon. People were beginning to hear about it, trickling in from the outskirts, survivors who had managed to outlast the worst of the outbreak.

They weren't just surviving anymore. They were rebuilding.

"We've come a long way," Frank said quietly, feeling the presence of Reynolds beside him.

The Marine sergeant nodded, his arms crossed as he surveyed the work. "Damn right we have. Not sure I would've believed it back when this all started."

Frank chuckled. "Yeah, I don't think any of us did. But here we are."

"Here we are," Reynolds echoed, then gave Frank a sideways glance. "You know, I think we've got a real shot at making this work. Beaufort could be the start of something bigger."

Frank didn't respond right away. He had thought the same thing many times. He knew the importance of what they were doing here, not just for themselves but for the future. If they could secure this town, keep it safe, and expand outward, they could offer hope to other survivors. Maybe even start to reclaim parts of the country that had fallen into chaos.

"We have to," Frank said finally. "There's no other option. We've got to keep pushing."

Reynolds gave him a nod. "That's the plan. We keep pushing, keep building. Make this place strong enough that no one can take it from us."

Frank nodded. "And we teach the next generation to do the same."

He looked out again toward Colt and Cecilia. They were young, but they had adapted to this world faster than he would have thought possible. Colt had stepped up, shouldering responsibilities that most teenagers wouldn't have known how to handle. And Cecilia, she had become a part of their family, her bond with Colt only growing stronger each day. It wasn't just about love anymore. It was about building something that could last, even when the world around them seemed determined to fall apart.

"Colt's going to be leading these efforts one day," Frank said quietly, almost to himself. "He's going to take what we've done here and build something even bigger."

Reynolds glanced over at the young man, his expression softening for a moment. "Good kid. He's got his head on straight, just like his old man."

Frank smirked. "I hope he does better than I did."

"You've done alright, Frank. Don't sell yourself short."

The two men stood in silence, watching as Beaufort expanded, inch by inch, person by person. More survivors had arrived in recent weeks, bringing with them the skills and energy the town needed. Farmers, mechanics, engineers, people with the knowledge to keep everything running. They had even started growing their own crops, with small fields of vegetables and grains beginning to sprout on the outskirts. It wasn't much, but it was a start.

Food would always be a concern, but with careful planning and rationing, they had managed to stay ahead of the problem. Frank and the others knew that as they expanded, they would need to find more sustainable sources. That meant scouting further out, finding old farms, warehouses, anything that could help them stockpile for the future.

But there was another challenge they couldn't ignore: the threat beyond the walls. Every day, they faced the possibility of another horde, of the dead breaking through their defenses. It wasn't just about fighting them off. It was about staying one step ahead, learning from every battle, and strengthening their position.

That's what Frank had always been good at, thinking ahead, anticipating the worst. And now, more than ever, those skills were being put to the test.

"Let's head to the command center," Reynolds said, breaking the silence. "We've got some new recon reports to go over. Seems like there might be another group of survivors holed up near Savannah. Could be worth checking out."

Frank nodded, feeling that familiar sense of purpose settle over him again. There was always work to be done, always another mission to plan. But this time, he wasn't just fighting for survival. He was fighting for a future.

As they walked back toward the heart of Beaufort, Frank couldn't help but smile. It was a small victory, but it was one he was going to hold onto. They were alive. They were thriving. And with every step they took, they were proving one undeniable truth.

They would survive.

Chapter 47: Expanding Horizons

The makeshift town hall, originally a storage shed for a nearby marina, was buzzing with activity. Frank leaned against the wall, arms crossed as he surveyed the room. It was filled with a mix of Marines, civilians, and recently arrived survivors, all gathered to discuss the next phase of their survival. The mood was tense but focused. People were ready for action, but they also knew the risks that came with it.

A map of the southeastern United States was pinned to the wall, dotted with red and green markers indicating cleared zones and areas still overrun with the undead. Beaufort was a green dot in a sea of red. But it was growing, pushing outward inch by inch. They had already expanded their perimeter by several miles, turning the once-vulnerable town into a near-impenetrable fortress.

Sergeant Reynolds stood at the front of the room, his voice calm but commanding as he outlined the latest reconnaissance missions and supply needs. "We've managed to clear most of the immediate areas around Beaufort, but we're running low on essential resources—fuel, medical supplies, and long-term food sources. We need to start thinking about expansion, not just for land, but for sustainability."

Frank nodded along with the others. This meeting wasn't just about the logistics of surviving the next few weeks; it was about ensuring they could last for months, even years, in this new world. The Marines had kept them safe, but it was the community that would keep them alive in the long run.

As the discussions continued, Frank's mind drifted to his own family—Annie, Colt, Nash. They had all found their places here, each contributing in their own way. Annie had become a key part of the medical team, organizing and training new arrivals with basic first-aid skills. Colt was now a leader among the younger group, helping to manage supply runs and assist the Marines with patrols. Nash, though younger, had grown more confident, spending his days working in the community gardens, learning how to farm and care for the livestock they had recently acquired.

He thought about the future they were building. It wasn't just about holding on anymore; it was about creating something more, something better.

"Frank," Reynolds called out, pulling him back to the present. "What's your take on the Savannah situation?"

Frank straightened, his focus returning to the task at hand. Savannah, once a bustling city, had become a potential gold mine for resources—if they could clear it out. Recon teams had reported signs of survivors, but they had also noted large groups of undead still roaming the outskirts.

"I think it's worth the risk," Frank said. "If there are survivors, they could have supplies we need, and we can bring them into the fold. But we'll need a solid plan—air support, ground teams, and a fallback strategy if things go south."

Reynolds nodded. "Exactly. We're not going in blind. We'll send a small recon unit first, see what we're dealing with. If the situation looks promising, we'll launch a full operation. But we need to be prepared for the worst."

Frank's eyes scanned the faces in the room. Some were hardened veterans, others were civilians still adjusting to their new reality. But they were all committed. They all knew what was at stake.

"We'll need volunteers," Reynolds said, his gaze sweeping the crowd.

Frank raised his hand without hesitation. "I'm in."

Several others followed suit, including Colt, who stood at the back of the room next to Cecilia. Frank caught his son's eye and gave him a nod. They had been on enough runs together now that Frank trusted Colt's instincts. He had grown into a capable young man, and Frank couldn't have been prouder.

As the meeting wrapped up, people began to filter out, heading back to their respective duties. Frank stayed behind, going over the logistics with Reynolds and a few of the other key leaders. They discussed fuel depots, possible choke points, and alternative routes into Savannah.

When the meeting finally ended, Frank stepped outside into the fading light of the late afternoon. The air was warm, with a slight breeze blowing in from the coast. He saw Annie walking toward him, her expression calm but curious.

"How did it go?" she asked, slipping her arm around his waist.

"Good. We're planning a recon mission to Savannah. Could be a big score for us if we find what we're hoping for."

Annie nodded, her eyes thoughtful. "And if you don't?"

Frank shrugged. "Then we regroup, try again. We don't have the luxury of giving up anymore."

She smiled, a soft but determined look in her eyes. "No, we don't."

They walked together for a while, passing by groups of people finishing up their tasks for the day. The community was thriving, but the work was never-ending. Every day was a new challenge, a new decision to make.

As they approached the community garden, Frank spotted Colt and Cecilia sitting on a bench, deep in conversation. Nash was nearby, working with one of the older men to plant seedlings. Frank couldn't help but feel a swell of pride.

"You think they're ready for this?" Annie asked, following his gaze.

"Ready for what?" Frank replied.

"For the world they're growing up in. For the future we're trying to build."

Frank was quiet for a moment, watching as Colt laughed at something Cecilia said, the weight of the world seemingly forgotten for a brief second.

"They're stronger than we give them credit for," he said. "They'll be ready."

Annie squeezed his hand. "And what about us?"

Frank looked down at her, his heart full. "We've made it this far. We'll keep going. We'll survive."

As the sun dipped below the horizon, casting a golden glow over the town of Beaufort, Frank felt a renewed sense of purpose. They had faced the worst the world could throw at them, and they were still standing. Now, it was time to push forward, to reclaim more of the world they had lost.

And no matter what came next, Frank knew one thing for certain: they would survive.

Chapter 48: Mission to Savannah

The early morning fog clung to the ground like a veil, muffling the sounds of boots crunching on gravel as Frank led his team toward the waiting convoy. The Marines had worked through the night to prepare for the mission to Savannah, and now it was time to move. The operation had been meticulously planned—air support, ground patrols, escape routes, and fallback positions. But no plan survived first contact, and Frank knew that better than anyone.

He climbed into the lead Humvee, the familiar smell of diesel fuel and gun oil filling his nostrils. Across from him sat Reynolds, the Marine commander, checking his gear one last time. The tension in the vehicle was thick, but it was a controlled tension, the kind that comes from seasoned men and women who'd been in the fire before.

"We're as ready as we'll ever be," Reynolds said, meeting Frank's eyes.

Frank nodded. "Let's hope we don't need to use half of what we're bringing."

"Hope for the best, prepare for the worst," Reynolds replied, echoing the old Marine adage.

Outside, the convoy was assembling—Humvees, supply trucks, and even a few civilian vehicles retrofitted with armor plates. The plan was to head out early, reach the outskirts of Savannah by noon, and have the recon teams sweep the area while the convoy secured a safe perimeter. They had no idea what they'd find—survivors, supplies, or a whole city of undead. But they couldn't afford to leave Savannah unchecked.

Frank glanced out the window and spotted Colt, standing by one of the supply trucks with Cecilia. They were talking quietly, and Colt had the same look of focus Frank had seen in himself so many times before a mission. Colt wasn't the kid he used to be. He had grown into a man, a leader, and today he was coming along for his first major mission outside Beaufort.

Frank opened the door and stepped out, walking over to them. "You ready, Colt?" he asked.

Colt turned, his face serious but steady. "Yeah, I'm ready, Dad."

Cecilia smiled, though there was a hint of worry in her eyes. "Bring him back safe, Frank," she said, half-joking, but her voice was strained.

Frank gave her a reassuring nod. "We'll bring everyone back safe. Don't worry."

The reality of the situation weighed on all of them. This mission wasn't just a supply run—it was a turning point. If they could clear out Savannah, it would open up a wealth of resources and territory, but it also meant taking on more risk than they had in months.

Frank slapped Colt on the shoulder. "Stay sharp. Follow orders. We'll be fine."

"I got this, Dad," Colt replied, his confidence steady. Frank could see the determination in his son's eyes. He trusted him, but as a father, that nagging worry never completely disappeared.

The convoy roared to life, engines revving as they started down the road. The sun was just beginning to burn through the fog, casting long shadows across the landscape. Frank climbed back into the lead Humvee, feeling the familiar weight of his rifle across his lap. The ride would be tense, but they had a job to do.

The journey toward Savannah was eerily quiet. The roads had been cleared of debris, and the once-busy highways were now empty. As they passed through abandoned small towns and gas stations, it was a stark reminder of how much the world had changed. These were the places people had fled, or died trying to escape, and now they were nothing but ghost towns.

After a few hours, they reached the outskirts of Savannah. The air changed, the tension thickening as they neared the city limits.

From the distance, Savannah looked almost untouched—a beautiful, haunting reminder of the old world. But they knew better. The recon teams had reported large groups of undead roaming the streets, and the mission was to clear as much as they could, find any survivors, and secure vital supplies.

"Air recon spotted a few clusters moving near the river," Reynolds said, checking the map. "We'll move in from the west, keep the river to our left, and set up a forward base at the old armory. From there, we'll send out the teams."

Frank nodded, his eyes scanning the horizon as the convoy slowed. The Humvees came to a stop just outside the city, and the Marines began to fan out, securing the area. The tension was palpable now—every movement felt deliberate, every sound amplified. Frank's instincts were on high alert.

They made their way into the city, staying in tight formation as they moved block by block. The streets were eerily deserted, cars abandoned, buildings left in disarray. Occasionally, they would come across a handful of shamblers—former citizens of Savannah, now nothing more than empty, rotting husks. The Marines made quick work of them, their rifles cracking in the stillness of the morning.

As they approached the armory, Frank's radio crackled to life. "This is Echo Team, we've got movement in the north quadrant. Looks like a larger group, maybe 50 to 60. Over."

Reynolds frowned, signaling for Frank to follow him. "Let's go check it out."

They moved quickly, making their way through narrow alleyways and side streets until they reached the north side of the city. When they got there, Frank's heart sank. A horde, larger than they had anticipated, was ambling its way toward them. Easily 100 or more.

"We need to move fast," Reynolds said. "Set up a defensive perimeter, get the heavy weapons in place. We're gonna have to hold them off here."

Frank nodded, quickly taking command of the situation. The Marines moved with practiced precision, setting up barricades and positioning themselves at key choke points. Frank directed a team to the rooftops, giving them a better vantage point for picking off the undead as they approached.

Within minutes, the first of the horde was on them. The air was filled with the crack of rifle fire, the thud of rounds hitting rotting flesh. The Marines held the line, but the horde was relentless, surging forward like a tide.

Frank fired round after round, his heart pounding in his chest. He glanced over at Colt, who was holding his own, picking off zombies with controlled bursts. Pride mixed with fear as Frank watched his son in action. Colt was good, better than Frank had expected, but this was no time for fatherly pride.

"Reloading!" Colt shouted, dropping behind cover to swap out his magazine.

Frank ducked behind a barricade, doing the same. The horde kept coming, and Frank realized they were in for a long fight.

"Hold the line!" Reynolds shouted over the gunfire. "We're almost through!"

Hours seemed to pass as they fought, but eventually, the horde began to thin. By the time the last of the undead fell, the sun was sinking low on the horizon. The Marines stood victorious, but the cost of the battle weighed heavily on them.

As the survivors regrouped and secured the area, Frank couldn't shake the feeling that this was just the beginning. Savannah had been a hard-fought battle, but there were still more challenges ahead. They had won today, but there would always be more zombies, more fights to come.

Frank glanced over at Colt, who was wiping the sweat from his brow. Their eyes met, and Colt gave him a small, tired smile. They had survived, and for now, that was enough.

"Let's get back to base," Frank said. "We've got a lot of work ahead of us."

Chapter 49: Hostess City of the South

The next morning, the first light of dawn filtered through the crumbling streets of Savannah, casting a warm, golden hue over the ruined city. The Marines moved quietly, their boots barely making a sound as they walked through the desolate streets. Savannah, once called the "Hostess City of the South," now lay abandoned and broken, with its charm and hospitality buried beneath months of decay.

Frank led the group down Broughton Street, where storefronts sat in eerie silence. The once-bustling heart of Savannah was now a ghost town. The plan for the day was straightforward: clear out any remaining undead in the area, locate survivors, and search for supplies. The city was vast, and the Marines had barely scratched the surface the day before.

"Remember," Frank said to the group, his voice low and commanding, "we move slow, we move quiet. Anything we miss could cost us later. Colt, you're with me. Sergeant Taylor, take your squad and sweep River Street. We're gonna check the warehouses near the port."

Colt stood close by, his rifle slung over his shoulder. He had grown more confident with each mission, his instincts sharper, his movements more fluid. Frank was proud of him, but he also knew that each step they took brought new dangers.

They approached the port district, where the tall, rusty cranes loomed over the empty docks like silent sentinels. Massive warehouses lined the waterfront, their steel doors slightly ajar, as if they had been abandoned in haste. If there were supplies left in Savannah, this was where they'd find them.

"This place looks promising," Colt said, glancing toward the warehouses.

"Yeah, but we've gotta be careful. These buildings are a perfect place for the dead to pile up."

Frank signaled to the rest of the team, and they spread out, rifles raised, eyes scanning every shadow. The air was thick with tension as they entered the first warehouse. Inside, pallets of goods sat stacked high, untouched. Dust motes danced in the air as the team moved in formation.

Suddenly, a low growl echoed from the far end of the building.

"Contact!" Frank shouted, raising his rifle.

A group of undead, hidden among the shadows of the warehouse, emerged, their decayed forms shuffling toward the Marines. Colt took position next to his father, his hands steady as he fired off precise shots. The sound of gunfire echoed in the cavernous space as the team eliminated the threat.

"Clear!" Frank called out, lowering his weapon.

"Dad, look at this," Colt said, motioning toward one of the stacks.

Frank approached and saw what had caught Colt's attention. It was a row of sealed crates labeled "Medical Supplies." His heart skipped a beat. This was exactly what they needed.

"Looks like we hit the jackpot," Frank said. He turned to the rest of the team. "Get these loaded up. We need everything—medical supplies, food, whatever we can carry. This is going to make a big difference back in Beaufort."

As the Marines began to move the crates outside, Frank and Colt continued to sweep the building. In the back, they found more shelves lined with canned goods, dried rations, and bottled water. It was clear that this warehouse had been a distribution center before everything went to hell. Frank felt a surge of hope. They hadn't just found supplies—they had found enough to sustain their growing population for months.

Colt's voice broke through his thoughts. "Dad, over here."

Frank followed Colt's gaze to a steel door near the back of the warehouse. Faint sounds—almost like whispers—emanated from behind it. Frank raised a hand, signaling for silence, and approached cautiously.

He knocked on the door gently. "Is anyone in there?"

A pause. Then a voice, weak and trembling, called out from the other side. "Help... please."

Frank exchanged a look with Colt, then motioned for one of the Marines to stand by. With a nod, Frank pulled the door open.

Inside, huddled in the dark, were six survivors—three adults and three children. They looked exhausted, their clothes tattered and their faces gaunt. They had been hiding for God knows how long, too afraid to leave the warehouse in search of food.

"You're safe now," Frank said, his voice gentle. "We're clearing out the city. We've got a safe place back in Beaufort. We'll get you out of here."

Tears welled in the eyes of one of the women as she pulled her children close. "Thank you," she whispered.

Frank signaled for his men to help the survivors outside. As the team escorted them to the convoy, Frank looked at Colt, who had a somber expression on his face. This was the reality of the world they lived in now—people surviving in the dark, hiding from the horrors outside. But at least they were finding them, saving them.

"That was a good find," Frank said. "You're getting better at this."

Colt shrugged, his eyes scanning the streets as they walked. "I just wish we could've found them sooner."

Frank nodded. "Me too. But we're here now, and that's what matters."

The convoy spent the rest of the day clearing out other warehouses and abandoned buildings near the port. They found more survivors—most of them in bad shape but alive. By the time the sun began to set, they had cleared a significant portion of the area and loaded the trucks with food, medical supplies, and equipment.

As the convoy rumbled back toward their base camp in Savannah, Frank couldn't help but feel a sense of accomplishment. It had been a long time since they had made a find this significant. The supplies they had collected would keep Beaufort going for months, and the survivors they rescued would add to their growing community.

As they drove, Frank looked over at Colt, who was sitting quietly in the passenger seat, staring out the window. He had changed so much in the past few months—grown harder, more focused. But there was still a flicker of the boy he used to be, a part of him that hadn't fully accepted this world.

"You did good today," Frank said.

Colt turned to him, a small smile tugging at the corner of his mouth. "Thanks, Dad."

Frank returned the smile, then turned his attention back to the road. They still had a long way to go, and the fight was far from over. But for now, they had a victory. And in this world, that was worth everything.

Savannah might have fallen, but Frank and his team had found a way to bring life back to Beaufort. And as long as they kept pushing forward, they would continue to survive—one day, one mission at a time.

Chapter 50: The Human Threat

The air was thick with tension as the convoy made its way back toward Beaufort, the setting sun casting long shadows over the marshlands. The mission in Savannah had been a success in more ways than one: they had found food, medical supplies, and survivors. But Frank had learned to never let his guard down, especially on the road. The world was no longer just a place haunted by the dead. The living could be just as dangerous, if not more so.

Frank sat in the lead Humvee, Colt next to him, scanning the horizon. The mood in the vehicle was somber but alert. They had encountered a few scavengers along the way, but nothing that had posed a serious threat. Yet.

"How much farther?" Colt asked, breaking the silence.

"About an hour, if the roads stay clear," Frank replied, his eyes on the road ahead. "Stay sharp. We're not out of the woods yet."

Colt nodded, gripping his rifle a little tighter. He had grown into his role quickly, but there were still moments when Frank could see the tension in his son's face, the weight of it all pressing down on him. Frank didn't have the luxury of easing his mind. His instincts told him something wasn't right, and he trusted those instincts.

A sudden burst of static came over the radio, and Sergeant Taylor's voice crackled through. "Sir, we've got something up ahead. Could be a roadblock."

Frank grabbed the receiver. "What do you see?"

"Looks like vehicles, but they're old. Could be abandoned. No movement yet."

Frank cursed under his breath. "Hold position. We're coming up."

As they approached the intersection, Frank could see what Taylor had reported. A line of beat-up cars stretched across the road, blocking their path. Some had their hoods open, others were tilted on flat tires. It looked like a makeshift barricade, and Frank didn't like it one bit.

"Eyes open," he said to Colt and the other Marines. "This doesn't feel right."

They stopped the Humvee about fifty yards from the blockade. Frank climbed out, scanning the area with binoculars. The trees lining the road were dense, and the underbrush provided perfect cover for an ambush. His gut told him they were walking into a trap.

Suddenly, gunfire erupted from both sides of the road.

"Contact!" someone shouted.

Frank hit the dirt, rifle raised, scanning for targets. The sound of bullets cracking through the air sent adrenaline surging through his veins. The ambush had come fast and without warning. Shadows moved between the trees, muzzle flashes lighting up the woods. These weren't just scavengers—they were organized.

"Colt, get down!" Frank shouted.

Colt hit the ground next to him, his rifle at the ready. Frank could see the fear in his son's eyes, but there was no time to reassure him. They had to act.

"Return fire!" Frank yelled into his radio. "Suppress those shooters!"

The Marines responded quickly, their disciplined volleys of gunfire cutting through the chaos. Frank and Colt took cover behind the Humvee, firing into the trees where they saw movement. The firefight was intense, and for several long minutes, it felt like they were pinned down, outgunned by an enemy they couldn't even see clearly.

One of the Marines near the back of the convoy shouted in pain, dropping to the ground as a bullet tore through his shoulder. Another went down moments later, the firefight growing more desperate by the second. Frank's heart sank. They were taking casualties, and they needed to break free of this ambush before they lost more men.

"Push forward!" Frank ordered. "Get to the barricade!"

The Marines began to move, advancing under fire toward the blockade of cars. Frank covered them, taking careful shots at the shadowy figures in the trees. He saw a man drop as one of his bullets found its mark, but the ambushers weren't retreating. They were well-trained—or at least experienced in this kind of combat.

As they closed in on the barricade, one of the Humvees rammed through the line of abandoned cars, clearing a path. The ambushers must've realized they were losing ground because the gunfire started to die down. A few moments later, the woods went silent.

Frank didn't trust it. He signaled for the Marines to fan out, keeping their weapons ready as they cleared the area. Slowly, they moved into the trees, searching for any stragglers.

"Got one!" Colt shouted from a few yards away.

Frank hurried over to find Colt standing over a man lying on the ground, a bloody wound in his leg. He wasn't dead yet, but he wasn't going anywhere. The rest of the ambushers had either fled or were lying dead in the underbrush.

"Keep your weapon on him," Frank ordered.

The man groaned, clutching his leg. He was rough-looking, his face weathered by more than just time. He looked up at Frank with a sneer, even as his blood pooled on the ground.

"Who are you?" Frank demanded.

The man coughed, spitting blood onto the dirt. "Doesn't matter. You're already dead. You just don't know it yet."

Frank knelt down, gripping the man by his shirt. "Who are you working with? There's more of you, isn't there?"

The man laughed weakly. "You have no idea what's coming. There's more of us than you can handle. And they're coming for your little town next."

Frank's stomach twisted. "What do you mean?"

"They let us out, you know," the man continued, his voice hoarse. "The prisons. They opened the doors and let us all out. Said we were free to go. But we're not like you. We didn't go home to play house. We took control. We formed something bigger."

Frank exchanged a look with Colt. His worst fears were being realized. This wasn't just some ragtag group of scavengers—they were up against something far more dangerous.

"How big is your group?" Frank asked, his voice cold.

The man grinned, teeth stained red from the blood in his mouth. "Big enough to wipe out your little stronghold. We own this area now. And we're coming."

Frank stood, his mind racing. If what this man was saying was true, Beaufort was in serious danger. They had enough to worry about with the undead, but this new threat could be even worse. Armed, organized, and desperate men were far more dangerous than a horde of zombies.

"We need to get back to base," Frank said to Colt. "Now."

They left the man where he was, taking no chances. As they regrouped with the rest of the Marines, Frank saw the toll the ambush had taken. Three Marines were dead, and several more were wounded. The mood was grim as they loaded up the vehicles and prepared to move out. Every loss weighed heavily on Frank's heart, but there was no time to mourn.

As the convoy sped toward Beaufort, Frank's mind was already racing with the implications of the man's words. A "mega-gang" of escaped prisoners, roaming the area unchecked, could destroy everything they had built in Beaufort. The undead were one threat, but this? This was a whole new level of danger.

When they reached Beaufort, Frank would have to alert the Marine commander and the rest of the town. They would need to bolster their defenses, increase patrols, and prepare for the possibility of a full-scale attack. The battle for survival had just taken a dark and dangerous turn. And now, it wasn't just the undead they had to fear—it was the living.

The human threat was real, and it was coming.

Chapter 51: How to Prepare for Unwelcome Guests

The Humvee rumbled back through the gates of Beaufort as Frank and the team returned from their mission to Savannah. The sun was setting, casting a crimson glow across the horizon, but the beauty of the moment was lost on Frank. His mind was already racing with thoughts of the threat that loomed on the horizon—one far worse than the undead.

As soon as the convoy came to a stop inside the stronghold, Frank wasted no time. He hopped out of the vehicle, giving Colt a nod to follow him. Together, they made their way to the command center where Captain Ruiz, the Marine commander, and a few other key leaders were waiting.

Inside, the air was thick with tension. Maps of the surrounding area were spread across the table, marked with areas of interest and known zombie concentrations. But now, they would need to add a new threat to their list.

"Captain," Frank began, stepping into the room. "We have a situation."

Ruiz looked up from the map, his expression unreadable. "I assume you're not just talking about the dead."

Frank nodded, taking a deep breath. "We ran into a group of armed men on the road back from Savannah. It was an ambush. Well-coordinated, and not just a bunch of scavengers. They're part of something bigger."

Ruiz straightened, eyes narrowing. "What do you mean, 'bigger'?"

Frank gestured to the map. "We took one of them alive. He said they were part of a larger gang—prisoners released when the world fell apart. He claimed they've formed what he called a 'mega-gang' and that they're coming for us. They know about Beaufort."

The room fell silent, the gravity of Frank's words sinking in. The threat of zombies was one thing—they could be anticipated, managed, fought off. But an organized, armed, and motivated group of humans? That was a different kind of threat entirely.

"They've got numbers, weapons, and the will to take what we have," Frank continued. "If we don't act now, they'll be on us before we even know it."

Ruiz cursed under his breath, looking down at the map. "How many are we talking?"

Frank shrugged, his face grim. "We don't know exactly. But if what the prisoner said is true, we're looking at hundreds, maybe more."

Ruiz exchanged a glance with his second-in-command. "We'll have to assume the worst-case scenario. That means we need to prepare for a siege."

Frank nodded. "We need to start reinforcing our defenses right now. Claymores, tripwires, trenches, barbed wire—anything that can slow them down and give us a fighting chance."

Ruiz stood, his expression resolute. "Then we'll do just that. Let's put a plan together."

The next morning, the entire community was briefed on the new threat. There was a mix of fear and determination in the air as Frank and the other Marines outlined the plan. Beaufort had to be ready for anything, and that meant fortifying every inch of their stronghold.

The first order of business was expanding the perimeter. They needed to create a buffer zone—an area around Beaufort that was cleared of obstacles and vegetation, giving them clear fields of fire. The Marines estimated a 500-meter circle around the town would give them enough space to see any approaching threats before they got too close.

Frank led a team of Marines and civilians to start clearing the area. Trees were cut down, bushes and underbrush were burned away, and anything that could provide cover for an attacker was removed. It was backbreaking work, but everyone knew it was necessary.

As they worked, Frank couldn't help but notice how Colt had stepped up in recent weeks. His son was no longer just a boy—he was becoming a man, and a damn good soldier. Colt worked alongside the Marines, hauling debris and helping set up defensive positions without complaint. Frank felt a surge of pride, but also a gnawing worry. He had always hoped his sons wouldn't have to live through something like this, but here they were, fighting to survive in a world gone mad.

Next came the trenches. Marines and civilians dug deep into the hard South Carolina soil, creating defensive ditches that would slow down any attackers. The trenches were designed to funnel enemies into specific kill zones, areas where they could be easily targeted by the defenders. Barbed wire was strung up along the perimeter, creating a web of obstacles that would make it nearly impossible for anyone to approach the town undetected.

"We'll need tripwires too," Frank suggested during one of the planning sessions. "They'll help alert us if anyone tries to sneak in under the cover of darkness."

Ruiz nodded. "We've got claymore mines, but we need to be strategic with them. We can't just set them off at the first sign of movement. We'll place them in key choke points—areas where the attackers are forced to bunch up."

Over the next several days, the Marines deployed the claymores along the outer edges of the perimeter. Each mine was carefully concealed, its tripwire invisible to the naked eye. They would be the first line of defense, designed to inflict maximum damage on any attackers who made it past the trenches and barbed wire.

Meanwhile, the helicopters were constantly in the air, patrolling the area for signs of the mega-gang. The Marines knew that staying on the defensive wasn't enough—they had to take the fight to the enemy before they reached Beaufort. Reconnaissance missions were launched daily, with pilots scouring the surrounding areas for any signs of movement.

"Any word on their location?" Frank asked Ruiz one evening, after a particularly grueling day of work.

"Nothing definitive yet," Ruiz replied, his face etched with concern. "But we've picked up some chatter on the radio. Sounds like they're moving, but they're keeping their distance for now. Could be they're waiting for reinforcements."

Frank clenched his jaw. The waiting was the worst part. Every day that passed without an attack felt like a blessing, but also a countdown to something worse. They were doing everything they could to prepare, but the enemy had the advantage of surprise.

"We'll be ready," Frank said, more to himself than anyone else.

"We have to be," Ruiz replied, his tone grave.

As the days stretched on, Beaufort began to resemble a fortress more than a town. Defensive positions were manned 24/7, with rotating shifts of Marines and armed civilians. The clear-cut perimeter gave them a commanding view of the surrounding area, and every field of fire was carefully calculated. Frank had drilled the defenders on overlapping fields of fire, ensuring that no one area was left unprotected.

Colt and Nash took turns on watch, their eyes scanning the horizon for any sign of movement. The tension was palpable, but there was also a sense of determination in the air. They had survived the undead. Now, they would survive the living.

Frank stood on one of the newly constructed observation towers, his rifle slung over his shoulder. He looked out over the perimeter, the trenches, the barbed wire, the carefully placed claymores. Beaufort was as ready as it would ever be.

The question was, would it be enough?

"We've done all we can," Frank muttered to himself.

"Yeah," Colt said, stepping up beside him. "Now we just wait."

Frank looked at his son, then back at the horizon. They were as prepared as they could be. But in a world where chaos reigned, sometimes even the best-laid plans weren't enough.

The enemy was out there, somewhere. And soon, they would come.

But when they did, Beaufort would be ready.

Chapter 52: A Southern Welcome

The morning mist clung to the marshes surrounding Beaufort like a veil, as if the land itself was trying to hide from the chaos that had taken over the world. Frank stood atop the observation tower, his sharp eyes sweeping across the clear-cut perimeter that now surrounded the town. It had been weeks since they'd encountered the mega-gang's scouts, and the tension hung heavy in the air. Today, though, there was a calmness, an eerie stillness that reminded Frank of the calm before a storm.

Behind him, the town was waking up. The people of Beaufort had grown used to the new way of life—early mornings, long days spent either fortifying the stronghold or scavenging for supplies, and evenings where families clung to each other, trying to find some semblance of normalcy. They were getting stronger, more united, but the looming threat had cast a long shadow over their newfound stability.

Frank descended from the tower, heading to the main square where the makeshift command center had been set up. Captain Ruiz and a handful of Marines were waiting for him, along with a few key community members. Annie had taken on a leadership role in coordinating civilian efforts, helping organize food supplies, and keeping the people calm. She was standing next to Colt, who, despite his youth, had earned respect among the Marines and civilians alike. Nash was nearby, already working on some project with a group of younger kids.

"Anything?" Ruiz asked as Frank approached.

Frank shook his head. "Quiet. Too quiet."

Ruiz frowned but didn't say anything. They both knew what quiet could mean. The enemy was out there, somewhere. Whether they were planning their next move or biding their time, no one could say. All Frank knew was that Beaufort had to be ready for anything.

Just as he was about to suggest another sweep of the area, the sound of distant engines broke the silence. It was faint at first, but it grew louder, coming from the south. Everyone in the square froze, eyes turning toward the source of the noise. Frank's hand instinctively went to his rifle as he exchanged a glance with Ruiz.

"Helos?" Ruiz asked.

Frank shook his head. "No. Ground vehicles."

In seconds, the entire town was on high alert. Marines scrambled to their positions, and civilians who had been training with makeshift weapons took up their posts. The sound of the engines grew closer, rumbling toward them like the low growl of an approaching predator.

Frank moved quickly, taking Colt with him to the southernmost section of the perimeter. They reached the trenches just in time to see the first vehicle break through the tree line—a large, rusted pickup truck, its bed loaded with men holding rifles. Behind it, two more vehicles appeared, one an armored van and the other a jeep with a heavy machine gun mounted on top.

"Prison gang," Frank muttered under his breath. He glanced at Colt, who had his rifle raised and ready, his face a mix of concentration and tension.

"Remember your training," Frank said, his voice calm despite the storm building inside him. "Stay low. Breathe."

Colt nodded, his jaw set with determination. Frank was proud of his son, but he wasn't ready to lose him. Not today. Not ever.

The vehicles rumbled closer, the men inside clearly unaware that they were driving straight into a well-prepared stronghold. Frank watched them carefully, counting heads, estimating their numbers. A dozen, maybe fifteen. Not the full force of the mega-gang, but enough to cause serious damage if they made it through.

"Hold your fire," Frank ordered quietly as the vehicles approached the outer edge of the cleared perimeter.

Ruiz, who had joined them on the line, crouched down beside Frank. "Think they're scouts?" he whispered.

"More like a welcoming party," Frank replied. "They're testing us, seeing what we're made of."

As if to confirm his theory, the lead truck skidded to a halt just outside the range of the claymores. One of the men in the back jumped down, swaggering toward the town's defenses with a cocky grin on his face.

"Who's in charge here?" the man shouted, his voice carrying over the open space. "We've got a message from our boys. You can hand over your supplies, your guns, and your women, or we can take 'em by force. Your choice!"

Frank felt his blood boil. He knew the type—the kind of man who thrived in the chaos, who saw the downfall of civilization as an opportunity to take whatever he wanted by force. But what this guy didn't realize was that Beaufort wasn't some unprotected settlement. It was a fortress now, and Frank had no intention of giving these men anything except a one-way trip back to whatever hellhole they'd crawled out of.

Ruiz looked at Frank. "We ready?"

Frank nodded. "Let's give them a southern welcome."

Ruiz raised his hand, signaling to the Marines manning the trenches. Frank had already mapped out the kill zones with precision, making sure that every inch of the perimeter was covered by overlapping fields of fire. The second Ruiz dropped his hand, all hell broke loose.

The first shots came from the snipers positioned in the observation towers. Two of the men in the back of the truck dropped before they even realized what was happening. The rest scrambled for cover, but there was none to be found in the cleared zone. Within seconds, the vehicles were lit up with gunfire from multiple angles.

Frank and Colt stayed low, picking off targets as they moved through the chaos. The driver of the jeep tried to turn around, but a well-placed shot from one of the Marines hit the fuel tank, causing the vehicle to explode into a fireball. The heavy machine gun was never even fired.

The men who had survived the initial onslaught made a desperate run for the tree line, but they were mowed down before they could make it more than a few feet. By the time the last shot was fired, the entire gang had been wiped out.

Frank stood slowly, his rifle still raised as he surveyed the carnage. The vehicles were smoking wrecks, and the bodies of the gang members were scattered across the open field. The fight was over in less than five minutes.

"Is that it?" Colt asked, his voice filled with disbelief.

Frank glanced at him, giving him a small nod. "For now. But don't get too comfortable. This was just a test. They'll be back, and next time, they'll bring more."

Ruiz approached, his face grim. "They thought we were soft," he said. "Thought we'd roll over and give them whatever they wanted."

Frank shook his head. "They underestimated us. That won't happen again."

He turned to look at the town behind them. Annie was standing at the edge of the square, her eyes locked on him. He gave her a small, reassuring wave. She smiled, but Frank could see the worry behind her eyes.

As Frank and Colt made their way back to the command center, Ruiz spoke up. "We need to be ready for the full force of their gang. This was just the beginning."

CANE BAY ZOMBIES

Frank nodded, his mind already racing with the next steps. They had sent a clear message today—Beaufort wasn't going to be an easy target. But the fight was far from over.

The real war was just beginning.

Chapter 53: Fortifying for the Future

The victory over the gang's scouts had been swift, decisive, but Frank knew better than to let his guard down. Beaufort's defenses had held, but there was no question that this was just the first skirmish in what could become a larger, more sustained attack. The real fight was on the horizon, and Frank could feel it in his bones.

For now, the town was abuzz with cautious optimism. People felt proud, even hopeful, after hearing how the Marines and volunteers had handled the gang's raiders. But Frank was already planning the next phase of fortification. He knew that this initial victory would draw attention, good and bad.

The next morning, Frank gathered his leadership team. Captain Ruiz, Colt, Nash, Annie, and several civilians who had stepped up to help with logistics sat around a long table in the repurposed town hall.

"We got lucky yesterday," Frank started, his voice low and serious. "Those scouts weren't the full force, and if their leaders have any sense, they'll regroup and come back with everything they've got. We need to be ready. There's no doubt they'll attack again."

Ruiz nodded in agreement, arms crossed. "We've got our defenses in place, but we're still too exposed in a few areas. We need to reinforce the barricades, get more eyes on the perimeter."

"We can get more volunteers to patrol," Annie added. "We've trained most of the civilians, but there are plenty of people who want to do more than just guard duty. If we train them right, we can set up rotating shifts."

Colt leaned forward, clearly deep in thought. "We should also focus on supply runs. We've been lucky with what we've scavenged so far, but with more people coming in, we'll burn through it faster. If we can find another warehouse or another store like we did in Savannah, we can keep building up our food and medical supplies."

Frank nodded, appreciating the practicality of his son's thinking. Colt had been maturing rapidly, not just physically but mentally. His leadership was growing stronger by the day. "Agreed. We need to secure another food source soon. But first, we've got to lock down Beaufort."

Ruiz leaned forward. "I'm thinking we expand the perimeter by another hundred meters. Clear out everything in that zone, trees, brush, anything that could give cover. I want to see them coming from a mile away."

Frank looked around the table. "We can start that today. I'll need half of the Marines on perimeter defense while the rest help with the clearing and building."

Annie spoke up next. "We also need better communication. We've been relying on runners and short-range radios, but that won't cut it if we're attacked on multiple fronts. If we can get some solar panels working and boost our radios, we could coordinate more effectively across the town."

"That's a good idea," Frank said. "Anyone have leads on equipment?"

Nash chimed in for the first time. "I've been talking to some of the older guys who used to work at the naval base in Charleston. They said there might still be some comms gear left there. It wasn't fully looted when everything went down."

Frank raised an eyebrow. "Charleston's a risk. Big city, lots of undead. But if we can get the right gear, it'll be worth it. Let's put together a team and hit it in a few days."

Ruiz looked at Frank. "We've got another concern too—the river."

Frank's brow furrowed. "The river?"

Ruiz nodded. "We've been focused on ground attacks, but if those gangs have boats, they could come up the river and hit us from the water. We don't have much in the way of defenses along the shoreline."

Frank hadn't thought about the water threat, but it made sense. Beaufort was surrounded by marshlands and rivers, and while the waterways had provided a natural barrier against the undead, they could be a vulnerability if someone knew how to use them.

"We'll need to set up a watch along the river," Frank said. "Maybe even fortify a few key points along the shore. We'll use the marsh to our advantage—set up traps, use the natural bottlenecks to slow them down."

The group spent the next hour hammering out the details. Teams would be assigned to clearing the new perimeter, setting up traps along the river, and scouting for better communication gear in Charleston. By the end of the meeting, everyone had their marching orders.

As the room cleared out, Frank stayed behind with Annie and the boys. Colt and Nash had been quiet for the last few minutes, clearly thinking about something.

"What's on your mind?" Frank asked, looking between his sons.

Colt spoke first. "Dad, we're talking a lot about defenses, but what happens when the fighting stops? When the gangs are gone?"

Frank raised an eyebrow. "You think the fighting's going to stop?"

Colt shrugged. "It has to, eventually. At least against people. The zombies... they're a different problem. But I'm thinking about the future—how we keep building, how we make sure this isn't just about surviving day to day."

Frank exchanged a glance with Annie. Colt was starting to think beyond the here and now. "We'll deal with that when the time comes, Colt. Right now, we focus on keeping everyone safe."

Colt nodded but didn't seem satisfied with the answer.

Nash, ever the quieter of the two, finally spoke up. "If we make it through this, maybe we could be something more than just a stronghold. Maybe Beaufort could be the start of something bigger."

Frank placed a hand on his son's shoulder. "One step at a time, Nash. But you're right. We're not just surviving here. We're building something."

Annie smiled softly. "We'll make sure it's a world worth living in. Not just for us, but for the people coming after."

Frank looked out the window, toward the marshes and the town they had worked so hard to protect. The work was far from over, but Beaufort had become more than just a haven—it was the beginning of a new chapter in human survival.

"We'll survive," Frank said, his voice steady. "But we'll also thrive. And if anyone tries to take that from us, they'll get a Southern welcome they won't forget."

Chapter 54: First Line of Defense

The morning after the strategy meeting, Frank was already in the thick of preparations. The air in Beaufort felt different, there was a sense of purpose, of determination, but also an underlying tension. Everyone knew the gangs wouldn't stay away for long. The town had become too valuable, too fortified to go unnoticed. If the mega-gang had any intention of expanding their control, Beaufort would be their first target.

Frank stood at the edge of the cleared perimeter, now expanded an additional hundred meters around the town. The last remnants of trees and overgrowth were being bulldozed by a team of civilians, their bodies working in a rhythm of survival. What was once the untouched beauty of the Lowcountry now lay as a vast, flat expanse of exposed earth, a battlefield waiting to happen.

"Good work, everyone," Frank said, his voice raised over the roar of machinery. "We've got to get this done by sundown. I don't want anyone caught outside when darkness falls."

He turned to Ruiz, who was overseeing the placement of claymore mines and tripwires along the newly cleared section. "How's it looking?"

Ruiz wiped sweat from his brow. "We're making progress. Got about half of the explosives in place. We'll have interlocking fields of fire set by tomorrow morning. That should give us enough stopping power to keep any large group of raiders at bay."

Frank scanned the area, noting the spread of trenches being dug in front of the perimeter. The dirt walls were deep enough to force any attackers to funnel into specific kill zones—exactly what they needed. Above the trenches, sniper nests were being erected with sandbags and wooden frames, providing vantage points to rain down fire on any approach.

"I'll get Colt and the others up on those nests for drills later today," Frank said. "We need them sharp."

Ruiz nodded. "Agreed. If that gang is as big as we think, we'll need every able body on the line."

Frank caught sight of Colt in the distance, working alongside Nash to carry supplies to the snipers. He felt a surge of pride seeing his sons step up, but there was always a knot of worry in his chest—one that had grown tighter since the firefight against the gang's scouts. They were both strong, capable, but this was war. Frank knew how unpredictable battle could be, and he hated the thought of them having to face more of it.

He pushed the thought aside and walked over to the riverbank, where Annie and a group of civilians were installing traps along the marsh. The natural bottlenecks in the terrain provided ideal spots for slowing down any attackers who might try to use the river as an entry point.

"You've been busy," Frank said, stepping up beside Annie.

She glanced up from the wire she was securing to a tree. "You know me, can't just sit around waiting for the end of the world."

Frank chuckled softly. "This is impressive. I think we might actually have a fighting chance if they try to come by water."

Annie stood up and wiped her hands on her jeans, surveying the area. "I just want to make sure we're covering all angles. We've got the river and the marsh, but we can't forget the smaller inlets either. If they've got boats, they could slip through."

Frank nodded. "We'll patrol it. We've got enough people now that we can keep eyes on everything, at least for the short term."

Annie gave him a sidelong glance. "How's it going with the perimeter?"

"It's getting there," Frank replied. "We've got the trenches almost finished, and the mines are going in. I want to get the snipers up and running by tonight. Make sure we've got enough firepower ready."

She paused, her expression softening. "You think they'll come soon, don't you?"

Frank didn't answer right away, looking out over the river. "Yeah, I do. They're not going to let this place go. We've built something too strong. They'll want it."

Annie stepped closer, resting a hand on his arm. "We'll be ready, Frank. You've made sure of that."

He looked down at her, grateful for her unwavering support. Even in the face of everything, Annie was his rock. They were in this together, and that made all the difference.

As the day went on, Beaufort became a hive of activity. Civilians worked alongside Marines, digging trenches, placing explosives, and setting up barricades. Every corner of the town was being fortified, every weak point shored up. The air buzzed with the hum of preparation, a mix of fear and hope intertwining as everyone worked toward a common goal: survival.

By nightfall, the perimeter was complete. The trenches were dug, the explosives in place, and the sniper nests manned. Frank stood at one of the newly built lookout posts, his rifle slung over his shoulder as he scanned the horizon through his binoculars. In the distance, beyond the cleared land, he could see the dark outline of the forest. Quiet for now, but hiding potential threats.

Colt approached, his own rifle in hand, and stood next to his father. "Perimeter's set," he said, his voice calm but alert. "We're ready."

Frank nodded, glancing at his son. "Good. You did well today."

Colt didn't say anything, but there was a quiet satisfaction in his expression. He had grown into a leader, whether he realized it or not.

As the night stretched on, the town fell into a tense silence. Guards patrolled the perimeter, their eyes sharp in the darkness. Frank remained on watch, his senses attuned to every sound, every movement. He knew the next attack would come—it was just a matter of when.

But for now, Beaufort stood strong, fortified and ready for whatever came next. And as long as Frank was breathing, he'd make sure it stayed that way.

Chapter 55: Safer, Finally

Morning in Beaufort broke with a heavy fog rolling in from the marsh, the sun a dim light hidden behind thick clouds. The air was damp, almost stifling, as if it carried the weight of the uncertainty that had gripped the town. Frank stood on the edge of the fortified perimeter, looking out across the flat, barren stretch of land they had cleared over the past few days. The trenches, mines, and razor wire created a jagged circle of protection around Beaufort, a place that had once been a peaceful, scenic town now turned into a fortress.

Behind him, Beaufort's streets were busy with people moving supplies, securing buildings, and keeping themselves occupied. The civilians and Marines alike had settled into a routine. They all knew that the threat from the mega gang of ex-prisoners was coming. But for now, it was eerily quiet—just the steady hum of daily work, preparation, and a collective bracing for what was next.

Frank turned as Colt approached, his rifle slung over his shoulder and a focused look in his eyes. Colt had grown so much in the last few weeks—stronger, more serious. The boy who once spent hours glued to a screen now carried the weight of their survival on his young shoulders.

"Scouts just came back," Colt said. "Nothing yet. No sign of movement from the south."

Frank grunted, nodding. "That's good. We'll keep up patrols. They're watching us, though. I can feel it."

Colt glanced out toward the distant tree line, his brows furrowed. "It's weird, Dad. We've been building defenses for days, and still, nothing. You really think they'll come?"

"They will," Frank replied. "They're waiting for the right time. They'll want to strike when we least expect it, but we'll be ready."

Colt nodded, but there was a flicker of doubt in his eyes. Frank could see it—his son was trying to stay strong, trying to be brave.

And he was doing a damn good job. But the weight of responsibility was starting to press down.

"You're doing great, Colt," Frank said, putting a hand on his shoulder. "I know this is a lot, but you're handling it better than most grown men would. Just keep your head clear and stay focused."

Colt managed a small smile. "Thanks, Dad. I just... I don't want to screw up."

"You won't. You've got a good head on your shoulders." Frank gave him a reassuring squeeze before letting go. "Now go check in with Ruiz. Make sure everyone's got enough ammo and see if we can rotate the night watch a bit more. People are getting tired."

Colt nodded and jogged off, heading back toward the central part of town where Ruiz was organizing the shifts. Frank watched him for a moment, his chest swelling with pride. Colt was becoming a leader, and in a world where survival depended on strength and trust, that meant everything.

Frank continued his patrol, making his way toward the eastern edge of town where Annie was stationed. She had taken charge of setting up a small command center there, working with some of the civilians to manage supplies and communications. When he reached her, she was busy directing people, her calm and steady voice cutting through the noise of the bustling streets.

"Everything going smoothly here?" Frank asked, leaning against a makeshift barricade.

Annie looked up, her eyes bright despite the exhaustion etched on her face. "As smoothly as it can, I suppose. We've got enough food and water for now, but if those supply lines get hit, we'll be in trouble."

Frank nodded grimly. "I know. That's why we need to keep expanding our safe zone. I want to send out another team in a couple of days, check for more survivors, supplies, maybe even more vehicles."

Annie wiped her brow and sighed. "It never ends, does it?"

"Not until this is over," Frank replied. "But we're doing it, Annie. We're surviving."

She gave him a tired smile and reached out, squeezing his hand. "As long as we're all together, that's all that matters."

Frank leaned in and kissed her forehead, his rough fingers brushing against her cheek. "We'll make it, I promise. I'm not letting anything happen to you or the boys."

They stood in silence for a moment, the chaos of the town fading into the background as they found a small sliver of peace in each other's presence.

"Frank," Annie said quietly after a pause, "do you think they'll really attack? The prisoners, I mean."

He sighed, running a hand through his short-cropped hair. "I don't know when, but yeah, I do. They know we've got something worth taking, and they're not the type to just let us be. We need to be ready for them."

Annie nodded, her expression hardening. "Then we'll be ready."

The rest of the day passed in a blur of activity. The town buzzed with the sounds of hammering, sawing, and the occasional bark of orders from the Marines. They fortified the gates, double-checked their ammo reserves, and prepared the civilians for the worst-case scenario. Beaufort had transformed into a well-oiled machine of defense, and Frank could only hope it would hold up when the time came.

As the sun set, casting an orange glow over the marshlands, Frank gathered with Colt, Ruiz, and a few other key leaders in the command center. A map of the surrounding area was spread out on the table, marking their patrol routes, sniper positions, and possible avenues of attack.

"We've got all our lines of defense in place," Ruiz said, his voice low and measured. "The tripwires and mines are good to go. We've got sniper teams stationed at every entry point. If they come, we'll have at least a few minutes of warning."

Frank nodded, scanning the map. "Good. Keep rotating the patrols. No one stays in one spot for too long. We can't afford to have anyone caught off guard."

Colt, standing beside him, looked over the map with a sense of purpose. "And what about the helicopters? Are we still using them for recon?"

"Yeah," Frank replied. "They're our eyes in the sky. As long as we've got fuel, we'll keep sending them out. But we need to be smart about it. They're not infinite."

The group continued discussing their plans late into the night, every contingency examined, every possible scenario prepared for. Frank could feel the weight of it all pressing down on him, but he knew they had done everything they could.

As the meeting broke up and people headed back to their posts, Frank lingered a moment longer, staring at the map. He traced a finger along the perimeter, imagining what it would look like when the prisoners came. It wasn't a matter of if—it was when.

"Frank?" Colt's voice cut through the silence.

Frank looked up at his son, who was standing by the door. "Yeah?"

"We're gonna be okay, right?" Colt asked, his eyes searching his father's face for reassurance.

Frank walked over and put a hand on his son's shoulder. "Yeah, Colt. We're gonna be okay. We've got each other, and that's more than most people have right now."

Colt nodded, a quiet determination in his eyes. "Alright. I'll see you in the morning."

As Colt walked away, Frank stood there for a moment, letting the silence settle in. Tomorrow would be another day of fighting, surviving, and waiting. But for now, the calm held. And Frank intended to make the most of it.

Chapter 56: Going to Charleston

The decision was made at dawn. Frank stood on the edge of the marina in Beaufort, staring out at the still waters. The light mist hung low over the river, giving the scene an almost peaceful aura, a stark contrast to the reality of the world they lived in. Behind him, the town was waking up, civilians and Marines moving through their morning routines, preparing for the day. But today wasn't just another day—it was the beginning of a critical mission. Charleston Naval Base was the target, a place that might hold the resources they needed to survive, and the team had to reach it by water.

Frank had weighed the risks. Taking the roads to Charleston was a death sentence. Zombies were everywhere, and the looming threat of the mega gang meant every mile of land between Beaufort and Charleston was dangerous. But the water—while not without its dangers—offered the safest route. They could avoid the undead hordes and circumvent potential ambushes.

Annie approached from behind, her boots crunching on the gravel as she joined him at the water's edge. "You're really doing this, aren't you?"

Frank nodded, not taking his eyes off the river. "We need what's in Charleston, Annie. Weapons, food, maybe even more survivors. The base could have supplies that could sustain us for months, maybe longer."

Annie looked out at the boats docked in the marina, the sleek, unused vessels that had once been a symbol of leisurely coastal living now repurposed for survival. "And you think it's safer on the water?"

"It's the best shot we've got," Frank said. "No roadblocks, no ambushes. The zombies can't swim. If we stay close to the coast, we'll avoid the open sea and any storms. The only thing we have to worry about are other people."

Annie sighed, folding her arms. "It feels like we're walking a fine line, Frank. Every mission, every supply run, it's like tempting fate. I just don't want to lose you."

Frank turned to her, his expression softening. He reached out and pulled her into his arms, the weight of the moment pressing down on them both. "I'll be back," he whispered. "We're doing this for all of us. For Colt, for Nash, for you."

Annie rested her head against his chest, her grip tightening. "Just come back. That's all I need."

Frank kissed the top of her head, holding her for a long moment before gently pulling away. He knew the risks, but there was no other choice. They needed what the naval base might offer.

By midday, the team was assembled. Frank had handpicked the Marines for this mission, along with Colt, who had insisted on coming along. Colt was 18, but he had earned his place beside the men. He was growing stronger, more capable every day, and Frank could see the man he was becoming.

Ruiz, ever dependable, stood by the boat, going over the equipment one last time. They had loaded up with enough fuel, weapons, and supplies to make the trip, but they needed to travel light. Speed and stealth were their greatest assets.

"Everyone's ready," Ruiz said, looking up from his checklist. "Boat's good to go, fuel tanks are full. We've got radios, but there's no guarantee we'll have a signal the whole way."

Frank nodded. "We'll use the radio sparingly. We can't afford to draw attention, and I don't want anyone tracking our location."

Colt was standing nearby, adjusting his gear. He looked nervous but determined. Frank walked over and clapped a hand on his son's shoulder. "You good?"

Colt nodded, his jaw set in a firm line. "Yeah. I'm ready."

"Good," Frank said, his voice steady. "This is a big mission. Stick close to me and Ruiz. Keep your head down and stay focused."

Colt gave a sharp nod, his eyes flicking to the boat. "You think the base is still intact?"

Frank sighed, glancing at the horizon. "I don't know, son. But we're about to find out."

The boat was a modest but sturdy vessel, large enough to carry the team and their gear, but small enough to navigate the coastal waters with ease. The plan was simple: head north along the coast, avoiding the open ocean, and keep an eye on the shoreline for any signs of danger. They would move quickly, stopping only if necessary, and reach Charleston within a few hours.

The group boarded the boat, and Frank took his position at the helm. The engine rumbled to life, cutting through the quiet of the marina as they began their journey. The water was calm, the boat cutting through the river with ease as they left Beaufort behind.

For the first few hours, the trip was uneventful. The coastline slipped past them, deserted and quiet, the remnants of civilization just barely visible through the mist. Abandoned homes and businesses dotted the shoreline, the world left in a state of decay. Occasionally, they would spot a few scattered zombies wandering the beaches, aimless and unaware of the boat passing by.

Ruiz kept a watchful eye on the horizon, his rifle at the ready. "So far, so good," he muttered, scanning the water. "No signs of other boats or threats."

Frank nodded, but he kept his focus sharp. This was only the beginning.

As they approached the halfway point, the radio crackled to life. "Boat team, this is Beaufort. How's it looking out there?" The voice was distorted but recognizable—it was one of the Marines back at base, checking in.

Frank picked up the radio. "This is Frank. So far, everything's clear. No signs of activity. We'll check in again when we're closer."

"Copy that. Stay safe."

Frank set the radio down and glanced back at Colt, who was sitting at the rear of the boat, watching the water. "You doing alright back there?"

Colt nodded. "Just... wondering what we'll find at the base."

Frank didn't have an answer for that. No one knew what they would find in Charleston. The naval base had been a major hub of military activity before everything went to hell, but now it could be anything. Zombies, gangs, survivors—it was impossible to predict.

By late afternoon, they could see the outline of Charleston on the horizon, the naval base just barely visible in the distance. The tension on the boat rose as they got closer, everyone on high alert.

"We're getting close," Ruiz said quietly. "Let's be ready for anything."

Frank cut the engine as they neared the docks of the naval base, the boat coasting quietly into position. The silence was oppressive, broken only by the soft lapping of water against the hull. Frank scanned the shoreline through his binoculars—no movement, no signs of life. But that didn't mean it was safe.

"Alright," Frank said, turning to the team. "We go in quiet. No unnecessary noise. Our priority is supplies like food, weapons, medical equipment. If we find survivors, we help them. But we're not staying long. Get in, get what we need, and get out."

The team nodded, and they disembarked, stepping onto the dock with their rifles at the ready. The naval base loomed ahead, a ghostly, abandoned relic of what had once been a stronghold of military power.

Frank took a deep breath, the weight of the mission pressing down on him. They had made it this far, but the real challenge was just beginning.

"Let's move," he ordered, and they moved toward the base, their footsteps silent against the cracked concrete, ready for whatever awaited them inside.

Chapter 57: The Ghosts of Charleston

The silence inside Charleston Naval Base was thick, oppressive, as if the air itself was waiting for something to break it. The team moved cautiously, their rifles raised, scanning every shadow, every abandoned structure. Frank took point, his senses sharpened from years of training and recent months of fighting both the undead and the living. Behind him, Colt followed closely, his steps mirroring his father's, his young face set in grim determination.

The base was eerily still. Abandoned military vehicles were scattered throughout the lot, some turned over, others sitting idle, covered in grime and dust. Buildings, once bustling with activity, now stood hollow, windows broken and doors ajar. The place looked like it had been deserted in a hurry.

"Looks like no one's been here in a while," Ruiz muttered under his breath as he scanned the area with his rifle, moving close to Frank.

"Or someone left it this way on purpose," Frank replied quietly. His instincts told him this wasn't just an empty base. There was always a reason for places like this to be left behind.

They had chosen to dock farther up the river to avoid drawing attention, walking their way deeper into the base. Now, standing near what appeared to be the old command center, Frank gestured for the team to stop. The sound of footsteps echoed off the concrete, and the soft shuffle of the wind carried with it distant creaks from rusted metal.

"Hold up," Frank whispered, kneeling to the ground. He glanced at the ground, noticing something that made his blood run cold—footprints. Not just one or two, but several sets. Some were large, heavy boots. Others were smaller, likely from civilian shoes.

Colt knelt beside him, following his gaze. "What do you think?" he asked, his voice barely a whisper.

"People have been here," Frank replied. "And recently."

Ruiz, standing a few feet away, nodded in agreement. "We need to be careful. Could be survivors. Or worse."

The team pressed on, moving with even more caution now. Every corner they turned felt like it could reveal a threat, every sound amplified by the weight of uncertainty. They passed several large warehouse buildings, some with massive steel doors, others with smaller entrances for personnel.

Finally, they reached what Frank believed to be the supply depot. It was a massive building, its structure looming over them like a giant. The doors were locked, but the lock itself was old and rusted. Frank motioned for Ruiz, who pulled out a pair of bolt cutters and snapped the lock off in seconds.

"Alright, let's make this quick," Frank said, pushing the door open slowly.

The smell hit them first. It wasn't the rot of decay they had become all too familiar with, but more like the stale, stagnant air of something left untouched for too long. They stepped inside, the beams of their flashlights cutting through the darkness, revealing rows upon rows of crates and shelves.

"Jackpot," Ruiz muttered, his voice laced with relief.

Colt was the first to start opening crates. Inside were MREs, Meals Ready-to-Eat, hundreds of them. Another crate held medical supplies, and further back they found ammunition, still sealed in military-grade containers.

"We've hit the mother lode," Colt said, grinning for the first time since they'd arrived.

Frank smiled grimly. "We load up everything we can carry. Prioritize the food and medical supplies. Ammo, too. Let's not waste time."

The team split up, grabbing as much as they could. They worked in silence, but the air felt heavier now, a creeping sense of being watched.

Just as Frank was sealing up a box of antibiotics, a noise broke the silence—a clatter from somewhere deep inside the warehouse. Everyone froze, exchanging tense looks.

"What was that?" Colt whispered, gripping his rifle tighter.

Frank held up a hand, signaling for silence. His heart raced, adrenaline pumping through his veins as he listened. There it was again—a faint shuffling sound, the kind that made his stomach twist. He gestured for the team to spread out and move toward the source of the noise.

They approached cautiously, their rifles aimed and ready. As they turned a corner, Frank's flashlight caught a flicker of movement, and for a split second, he thought they'd come across another group of survivors.

But as the figure came into full view, it became clear—this wasn't a survivor.

A zombie, its decaying body draped in tattered military fatigues, lunged at them with a sudden burst of speed. Its lifeless eyes locked on Frank, its mouth hanging open in a grotesque snarl. Frank didn't hesitate. He squeezed the trigger, and the sound of gunfire echoed through the warehouse, the creature dropping to the ground.

"More incoming!" Ruiz shouted from the other side of the warehouse, his voice laced with urgency.

The shuffling grew louder, more distinct. The sound of dozens, maybe hundreds, of undead moving through the building, drawn by the noise.

"Fall back!" Frank ordered. "Get to the boat. Now!"

The team scrambled, their mission now one of survival. As they rushed toward the exit, more zombies appeared from the shadows, some dressed in civilian clothes, others in remnants of military uniforms. It was a horrifying reminder of what had become of the world.

Colt fired at a pair of zombies that were closing in, dropping them with precision. He turned to follow his father and the rest of the team, his heart pounding in his chest.

They burst through the warehouse doors, the fresh air hitting them like a wall. But they couldn't stop. The undead were pouring out behind them, and they needed to get to the boat fast.

"Come on, come on!" Frank shouted, urging his team forward as they sprinted toward the docks.

By the time they reached the boat, the zombies were dangerously close. Ruiz jumped aboard first, starting the engine as Frank and Colt fired off a few final shots to hold the horde back. Colt leaped onto the boat, and Frank followed, the engine roaring to life just as the first wave of undead reached the water's edge.

The boat sped away from the dock, leaving the zombies behind, their decaying forms stumbling into the water as if they could follow.

Frank let out a breath he hadn't realized he was holding. They had made it, but just barely.

Ruiz turned to him, shaking his head. "That was too close, man."

"Yeah," Frank agreed, looking back at the now distant naval base. "But we got what we came for."

Colt sat down, breathing hard, but there was a determined gleam in his eyes. "We're going to survive this, Dad. All of us."

Frank nodded, his gaze steady on the horizon. "Damn right we will."

Chapter 58: One More Stop

The boat rocked gently on the water as the team sped away from the Charleston Naval Base, adrenaline still coursing through their veins after the close encounter with the undead. Frank stood at the helm, his eyes scanning the horizon, but his mind was already working on the next move. They had come for supplies, but Frank knew there was still more they could do.

"Ruiz," Frank called over the wind. "What's the situation at the port of Charleston?"

Ruiz glanced at a map he had spread out over his lap, his brow furrowing. "It's a risk, but we might find more supplies. The port's likely been abandoned, but we might encounter more survivors—or worse."

Colt, sitting beside his father, looked up. "Another stop means more supplies. We need everything we can get."

Frank nodded. "We'll check the port. But we need another boat. We can't carry all this back to Beaufort on just one run."

Ruiz turned back to Frank. "There's a marina a little north of the port. Might be worth checking out. Could find a second boat there."

"Good idea," Frank said, making the decision quickly. "We'll stop there first."

The team made their way to the marina, keeping a sharp lookout as they docked. The place was eerily quiet, with only the sound of the water lapping against the boats. The docks were lined with vessels, most of them abandoned and showing signs of neglect. Frank scanned the area for any movement but saw none.

"Let's make this quick," he ordered, motioning for Colt, Ruiz, and the others to follow. They split up to inspect the boats, and after about ten minutes, Colt waved them over to a mid-sized vessel that seemed to be in decent shape.

"This one's got fuel, and it looks like it'll hold up," Colt said.

Frank examined it, giving a nod of approval. "Good find. Let's get it ready to go."

Once the second boat was prepared, the team split between the two vessels and headed toward the Port of Charleston. The closer they got, the more Frank's instincts told him to be cautious. Large ports like this were always a gamble—there could be supplies, survivors, or the undead. Possibly all three.

When they finally arrived at the port, they saw it was in a state of disrepair. Massive cargo ships were docked haphazardly, some tilted or partially submerged in the water. Cranes that had once loaded and unloaded goods stood like skeletons against the gray sky. The area looked deserted, but the team knew better than to trust appearances.

"Stay sharp," Frank warned as they docked the boats. "We don't know what we're walking into."

They moved through the port cautiously, checking the warehouses and containers. It didn't take long to find what they were looking for—food, medical supplies, and even some weapons. It was a goldmine, but Frank was wary. This much untouched material meant the place had been abandoned in a hurry.

"Got enough here to last Beaufort for months," Ruiz said, grinning as he inspected a container full of canned goods.

Colt nodded, but his eyes were scanning the area, alert for any sign of danger. "Feels too easy," he muttered.

Suddenly, a noise echoed from one of the nearby buildings, causing everyone to tense up. Frank raised a hand, signaling for the team to move in quietly. They approached the building, weapons ready, and peered inside.

What they found was unexpected.

A group of survivors, huddled together inside the warehouse, looked up at them with wide eyes. They were dirty, disheveled, but very much alive. Among them was a man in his mid-thirties, his face pale but determined, and an older man with graying hair who held himself with the authority of someone used to being in charge.

"We're not infected," the younger man said quickly, holding up his hands in a gesture of peace. "We've just been trying to survive here."

Frank lowered his weapon slightly but kept his guard up. "How many of you are there?"

"Just us," the man replied. "There were more, but... well, you know how it is."

Frank nodded, understanding all too well. "Who are you?"

The man stepped forward. "My name's Tim. I'm—well, I was an emergency room doctor at MUSC before all this happened." He gestured to the older man beside him. "This is George. He's... he was the mayor of Charleston."

Frank's eyes narrowed slightly at that. A mayor. That complicated things. Bringing survivors back to Beaufort was one thing, but a politician? Politics had no place in the world they were trying to build, not with everything at stake.

"You're both coming with us," Frank said after a moment. "We're taking you back to Beaufort. But I'll warn you now, we run things differently there."

Tim looked relieved, but the mayor's face remained impassive. "I understand," George said. "We're not here to cause trouble. We're just trying to survive like everyone else."

"We'll see about that," Frank muttered under his breath.

The team loaded up the survivors and the supplies onto the boats, making the return trip to Beaufort. The mood on the boat was tense, especially with the mayor sitting quietly in the corner, watching everything. Frank caught Colt's eye and nodded, silently telling him to keep an eye on the newcomers.

When they arrived back in Beaufort, they were greeted by Annie and the other members of the community. Frank explained the situation quickly, introducing Tim and George to the leadership team.

"A doctor," Annie said with a smile. "That's good news. We could always use more help in the medical tent."

Tim nodded gratefully, clearly eager to contribute. "I'll get to work right away."

But George remained silent, his eyes scanning the growing stronghold. Frank didn't miss the calculating look in his eyes.

As the day went on, Frank gathered the marines and the leadership team for a meeting. They had to address the potential complications of bringing a politician into their midst. George had yet to say much, but Frank knew that men like him always had a plan.

"He could be trouble," Ruiz said bluntly when they were alone. "A guy like that, used to being in charge... he might try to stir things up."

Frank nodded in agreement. "We'll have to keep a close eye on him. But for now, we focus on what's important. We've got supplies, we've got more survivors, and we're building something strong here. We can't let politics get in the way."

Annie, sitting beside Frank, squeezed his hand. "We've survived this long because we've stayed united. We won't let anything change that."

Colt, who had been listening quietly, spoke up. "We'll handle it, Dad. Whatever comes next, we'll be ready."

Frank looked at his son, seeing the man he was becoming. He smiled, nodding. "We will. We've faced worse. And we'll keep fighting, no matter what."

But as he glanced toward where George stood talking with some of the other survivors, Frank couldn't shake the feeling that this new chapter in their survival was going to be more complicated than any fight with the undead.

Chapter 59: Politics Is Not Polite Dinner Conversation

The sun was setting over Beaufort, casting a warm, golden glow across the stronghold. People were gathering for dinner, grateful for another day of safety and survival. Frank, Annie, Colt, and Nash sat at one of the long wooden tables set up in the open-air dining area. Around them, marines, civilians, and newly arrived survivors enjoyed their meal, the mood light despite the underlying tension of their situation.

Across the table from Frank sat George, the former mayor of Charleston. Tim, the doctor they'd rescued, was engaged in conversation with Annie, clearly eager to contribute to the medical team. But George was quieter, his sharp eyes observing everything, particularly the way the community operated. Frank had noticed it too, the way George asked questions without actually asking them. He was gathering information, and Frank didn't like it.

"So, Frank," George finally said, breaking the relative silence between them. "What's the plan for the long term? You've built something impressive here, but we both know it won't last unless there's structure. Leadership. Governance."

Frank didn't look up from his plate. "We've got leadership," he said gruffly. "The marines and the community work together. We make decisions as a group."

"Sure, for now," George continued, his tone conversational, but there was a hint of challenge in his eyes. "But as this place grows, as more people come in, you'll need more than that. You'll need laws. A system to keep order. Otherwise, it's chaos."

Colt, sitting beside Frank, shifted uncomfortably. He didn't trust George either, and the way the man spoke reminded him too much of the old world. The world where people like George were in charge, pulling strings behind the scenes.

Annie noticed the tension rising and tried to diffuse it. "We've been doing just fine without politics," she said gently. "People here know what's at stake. We work together because we have to."

George smiled, but it didn't reach his eyes. "That's all well and good, Annie, but sooner or later, human nature takes over. People will want more—more control, more security. It's inevitable. And when that happens, you'll need someone who knows how to manage it."

"Someone like you?" Colt asked, his voice edged with suspicion.

George met his gaze steadily. "Yes, someone like me. I've been in leadership roles before. I know how to keep people together, how to make hard decisions when the time comes. You're going to need that."

Frank finally looked up, his eyes cold. "What we need, George, is to survive. We're not rebuilding the old world here. We're not going back to the way things were. What you're talking about... it sounds like politics. And politics doesn't belong at this table."

"Frank's right," Ruiz chimed in from a few seats down. "We've managed without all that so far, and we're better off for it. The last thing we need is someone trying to bring back bureaucracy when what we need is action."

George chuckled, leaning back in his chair as if he found the entire situation amusing. "You can't avoid it forever. As this place grows, as more survivors come in, they'll want more than just a military operation. They'll want a future, a community. You can only govern with guns for so long."

Frank's hand tightened on his fork, but he kept his voice level. "We're not governing with guns. We're protecting people. There's a difference."

Tim, sensing the growing tension, cleared his throat. "I think what George is trying to say is that structure is important, but so is keeping the spirit of cooperation alive. We don't want to repeat the mistakes of the past."

Annie nodded, grateful for Tim's attempt to steer the conversation back to a calmer place. "Exactly. We've all seen what happened to the old world when politics and power got in the way. We can't let that happen again."

George didn't respond immediately, but Frank could see the wheels turning in his mind. He was calculating, assessing the room, figuring out his next move. Frank had seen men like him before—men who thrived on control, who couldn't stand not being in charge. He knew George wasn't going to give up on his idea of taking over, not without a fight.

"I hear you," George said after a moment, his tone conciliatory. "But I'm just saying, keep an open mind. This place is growing, and it's only going to get more complicated. I've got experience that could help you. That's all I'm offering."

Frank's eyes narrowed. "We'll keep that in mind."

The rest of the meal passed in tense silence, the usual easy conversation muted by the unspoken conflict brewing at the table. When dinner was over, George excused himself and walked toward the makeshift housing area, leaving Frank, Annie, and the others to sit in uneasy quiet.

Colt leaned toward his father, lowering his voice. "I don't trust him."

"You're not alone in that," Frank said, his voice grim. "Men like him don't give up power easily. He's testing the waters, seeing how far he can push before someone pushes back."

Annie sighed, resting her head on Frank's shoulder. "Do you think he'll try to take over?"

"He'll try something," Frank replied. "We just have to make sure he doesn't get the chance."

Nash, who had been quiet throughout the conversation, finally spoke up. "Do we really need politics, Dad? Can't we just keep doing things the way we've been doing them?"

Frank looked at his youngest son, his heart heavy. Nash was still young, still hopeful, and Frank wanted to protect that for as long as he could. But he also knew that as their community grew, the challenges would only become more complex.

"I don't want politics here any more than you do, Nash," Frank said softly. "But the bigger this place gets, the harder it's going to be to keep it simple."

Colt crossed his arms, his expression resolute. "Then we make sure it stays simple. We don't need someone like George running things."

Frank nodded, but he knew it wasn't that easy. George wasn't going to sit back and let others lead. He'd push, and when the time came, Frank would have to push back.

Annie, ever the peacemaker, stood up and placed a hand on Frank's shoulder. "We'll figure it out, like we always do. For now, let's focus on what's important—keeping everyone safe."

Frank smiled at her, grateful for her steadiness. "You're right. We'll handle George when the time comes. But right now, we've got more important things to worry about."

As the family got up to leave, Frank cast one last glance in the direction George had gone. He didn't know when the former mayor would make his move, but he knew it was coming. And when it did, Frank would be ready. Politics might not belong at their dinner table, but it was knocking on their door, nonetheless.

And Frank wasn't about to let it in without a fight.

CANE BAY ZOMBIES

Chapter 60: Storm on the Horizon

Frank stood on the makeshift lookout tower, his eyes scanning the horizon as the early morning sun painted the sky in shades of orange and pink. The air was still, but there was an unmistakable tension that seemed to permeate everything. It wasn't just the zombies or the looming threat of the prison gang that had his gut churning—it was the unease that had settled in Beaufort since George's arrival.

Down below, the stronghold was coming to life. Marines were preparing for the day's patrols, civilians were setting up for their morning duties, and the newly arrived survivors were starting to integrate into the community. Frank could see Colt with Cecilia near the entrance, talking quietly before Colt headed out for another scouting mission. Even from a distance, Frank could sense the weight on his son's shoulders. The boy was becoming a man faster than Frank had ever imagined.

"Storm coming?"

Frank turned at the voice and saw Ruiz climbing the ladder to join him at the top of the lookout. The marine's easygoing grin was a stark contrast to the seriousness of his question.

"Feels like it," Frank muttered, turning his gaze back to the horizon. "Something's brewing, that's for sure."

Ruiz joined him, leaning on the railing and letting out a sigh. "We heard the whispers last night. George is making his rounds, talking to people, planting seeds. He's smart about it, though. Doesn't come off as a threat—just a guy with ideas."

"That's what makes him dangerous," Frank said, his jaw tightening. "He's not here to help. He's here to take control."

Ruiz nodded. "Yeah, but the thing is, some of the new folks... they might not see it that way. They didn't know what it was like out there before we built this place. They think maybe George has a point."

Frank clenched his fists, fighting the urge to punch the railing. It wasn't just George's ambition that bothered him—it was the thought of people actually listening to him. This was a community built on trust, on mutual survival. Politics had no place here. But Ruiz was right. Not everyone understood that.

"Keep an eye on him," Frank said, his voice low. "I don't trust him, but I'm not going to make a move until he does something. We don't need to stir the pot unless it's necessary."

Ruiz gave a sharp nod. "You got it, Sarge."

Just as Ruiz started to head back down, Frank's radio crackled to life. It was Colt's voice, calm but with a hint of urgency.

"Base, this is Colt. We've got movement to the west. A lot of it."

Frank grabbed the radio and pressed the button. "What kind of movement, son?"

"Zombies. A horde, looks like. Maybe a hundred, maybe more. They're about five clicks out, moving slow, but they're headed our way."

Frank cursed under his breath. "Stay put. We'll send reinforcements your way. Keep eyes on them, but don't engage until we're in position."

"Roger that," Colt replied, his voice steady.

Frank turned to Ruiz, who was already reaching for his own radio. "Get a team ready. We need to intercept that horde before it gets any closer."

Ruiz was already moving, shouting orders as he descended the ladder. Frank quickly made his way down as well, his mind racing. A horde this size wasn't unheard of, but it was dangerous, especially if they were already dealing with potential unrest in Beaufort. They couldn't afford any distractions.

By the time Frank reached the ground, the marines were mobilizing. Hummers were being prepped, weapons loaded, and men and women were getting into formation. Frank found Annie near the medical tent, organizing supplies with Tim.

"We've got a horde coming," he said as he approached her.

Annie straightened, her eyes widening slightly, but she didn't panic. "How big?"

"Big enough to be a problem. Colt spotted them. We're heading out to deal with it."

Annie wiped her hands on her pants and gave him a quick nod. "Be careful."

Frank leaned in and kissed her forehead. "Always."

He turned to leave but hesitated, glancing back at her. "Keep an eye on George while we're out. I don't trust him not to stir things up while we're gone."

Annie's face darkened, but she nodded. "I'll keep him busy. Just come back in one piece."

Frank gave her a tight smile before hurrying toward the convoy. The hummers were already loaded, and Ruiz was at the wheel of the lead vehicle. Frank climbed in next to him, scanning the small group of marines who were coming with them. They were good men, tough, but the horde was unpredictable. They'd have to be smart about this.

"Let's move out," Frank ordered, and the convoy roared to life, heading toward the western perimeter.

As they drove, Frank's mind kept drifting back to George. The man hadn't done anything overt yet, but Frank could feel the tension building. Sooner or later, George would push too far, and when that happened, Frank would be ready. But first, he had a horde to deal with.

Colt crouched behind the remains of an old truck, binoculars in hand as he watched the horde slowly shamble toward Beaufort. Cecilia was beside him, her eyes scanning the distance. They were both quiet, the weight of what was coming hanging heavily between them.

"How many do you think there are?" Cecilia asked softly.

"Too many," Colt replied, lowering the binoculars. "But we'll handle it. We always do."

Cecilia gave him a small smile, but there was worry in her eyes. "I know. It's just... things feel different now, you know? With George here and everything changing."

Colt didn't answer right away. He knew exactly what she meant. Beaufort was growing, and with growth came new problems. George was one of those problems, but so was the simple fact that they couldn't stay hidden forever. The world was still dangerous, and now, with the prison gang and the constant threat of the undead, it felt like they were always one step away from disaster.

But he couldn't let himself dwell on that right now. He had a job to do.

"Whatever happens, we'll face it together," Colt said, turning to look at her. "You and me. And the rest of us. We'll get through this."

Cecilia nodded, her hand finding his and squeezing tightly. "I know we will."

In the distance, the sound of engines rumbled through the air, and Colt spotted the convoy approaching. His father was coming, and with him, the marines who would help stop the horde.

The fight wasn't over yet—not by a long shot—but Colt knew one thing for sure: no matter what came next, they wouldn't face it alone.

Chapter 61: Admin Isn't for Everyone

George sat at the old, wooden desk inside the makeshift admin office, tapping his fingers impatiently on the surface. Outside, the camp bustled with the usual sounds of preparation: vehicles being fueled, weapons checked, civilians gathering supplies, and the low hum of the marines going about their day. But George, former mayor of Charleston, was stuck in here, overseeing inventory reports and supply lists. He felt like he was wasting away, buried under paperwork that didn't matter to anyone except maybe a bureaucrat.

This was not the role he envisioned when he agreed to come to Beaufort. He imagined himself part of the leadership, guiding the community with wisdom and experience. After all, he had run a major city—he knew how to lead, how to organize people, how to strategize for the long term. But instead, Frank and the others had assigned him to administrative duties. Inventory control, food distribution, keeping records—mundane tasks that made George feel like he was being sidelined.

He was above this. He *should* be above this.

"Ridiculous," George muttered under his breath, flipping through another stack of inventory sheets. He barely scanned the items listed: canned food, medical supplies, ammunition counts—all of it insignificant compared to the bigger picture in his mind. He didn't need to be counting cans; he needed to be in the war room, making decisions that affected their future.

The door to the admin office swung open, and Sergeant Ruiz walked in, carrying a clipboard and a notepad. His face was set in a serious expression, though George could tell he was in no mood for pleasantries.

"You're late," George snapped, not even bothering to look up from the paperwork. "I've been waiting for that list for an hour. Time is a valuable commodity, you know."

Ruiz stared at him, his expression cold. "You'll get the list when I'm done with my rounds, George."

"Mr. Mayor," George corrected, leaning back in his chair with an air of condescension. "You seem to forget that I used to run the largest city in South Carolina. I expect a certain level of respect."

Ruiz cut him off, his voice as sharp as a blade. "No one cares what you used to be. Out here, you do your job like everyone else. You don't get to pull rank just because you're not happy with your assignment."

George's face flushed with anger. "You people have no idea what it takes to lead! I built Charleston into a powerhouse."

"You built Charleston into a bureaucratic mess," Ruiz shot back. "And that's exactly why you're in here, counting beans, instead of making decisions. You can't even handle a basic inventory job without complaining."

George slammed his hand down on the desk, standing up abruptly. "I am not some errand boy, Sergeant! I don't belong in this office. I belong out there, with the leaders. I should be planning our next moves, not cataloging supplies like some pencil pusher."

Ruiz didn't flinch. "We already have leaders out there. Frank, the Commander, the Marines, they're the ones keeping this place running. Your job is to make sure we know what we have and what we need. It's important. And if you can't handle that, well, maybe it's time we reconsider your position here."

The implication hung in the air like a heavy weight. George bristled, his ego wounded. But before he could fire back, the door opened again, and this time, it was the Marine Commander who entered.

Colonel Hastings was a man of few words, but when he spoke, people listened. He was in his mid-fifties, with graying hair and a steely demeanor that radiated authority. He looked between Ruiz and George, his eyes narrowing slightly.

"Problem?" Hastings asked, his voice calm but carrying the unmistakable edge of someone who didn't tolerate nonsense.

George took a breath, trying to regain his composure. "Colonel, I believe my talents are being wasted here. I've been assigned to administrative duties, but I could be doing so much more. I have experience leading large populations, making strategic decisions."

Hastings cut him off with a raised hand. "You've been assigned to admin because we need someone to handle inventory and logistics. It's a crucial role, and it's not optional."

George's jaw tightened. "With all due respect, Colonel, I think my abilities would be better suited elsewhere. Out in the field, perhaps, or..."

"You think I care where you *think* your abilities are best suited?" Hastings interrupted, his voice low and dangerous. "Out here, you're only as useful as the job you can handle. And right now, your job is to make sure we know what supplies we have, where they're going, and how long they'll last."

George's face turned red with frustration, but Hastings didn't stop.

"You don't like it? Fine. I've got a patrol heading out tomorrow morning. How about you join them? See what it's like to actually be out there in the field, where every decision means life or death. Maybe that'll give you some perspective on why we need people handling admin tasks."

Ruiz's eyes flicked to George, a barely-contained smirk tugging at the corner of his mouth. George, on the other hand, looked horrified at the idea.

"Out on patrol?" George stammered. "That's—Colonel, I don't think that's—"

"You don't think, George," Hastings said coldly. "That's the problem. So either you get back to doing your job, or I'll put you on the next patrol, just for fun."

The office fell silent. George stared at the Colonel, trying to gauge if he was serious. But the look in Hastings' eyes told him everything he needed to know.

Without another word, George sat back down at the desk, grabbing the nearest clipboard and pretending to focus on it. Ruiz gave a slight nod of satisfaction and handed over his own list of supplies before leaving the room.

Colonel Hastings lingered for a moment, watching George with that same unflinching gaze.

"Remember," Hastings said quietly, "everyone has a job to do here. Do yours."

With that, he turned and left the office, the door closing behind him with a decisive click.

George sat there in silence for a long time, his mind racing. The anger still simmered beneath the surface, but there was something else now—something colder, more calculating. He wasn't going to stay in this role forever. He'd bide his time, play his part, but eventually, he'd find a way to rise above this.

For now, though, he was stuck counting cans.

Chapter 62: The Mayor of the Clipboard

George shuffled through the camp, clipboard in hand, his expression darker than the gathering storm clouds above. He had never been a man to blend into the background, but out here in Beaufort, amidst the grit and survival, he felt like a shadow of his former self. The survivors had started calling him "The Mayor of the Clipboard" behind his back, and the nickname had spread like wildfire. No one said it to his face—yet. But George could hear the whispers, the quiet laughter when he passed by.

"Mayor of the Clipboard," one of the younger survivors had muttered just loud enough for him to hear when he walked past the supply tent that morning. The others chuckled, and George clenched his jaw, his hand tightening around the clipboard so hard his knuckles turned white.

He knew it was a joke. He knew they didn't respect him. They saw him as a bureaucrat, a relic of the world before everything fell apart. But George wasn't about to accept that fate. No, he had plans—he just needed time to put them in motion. Until then, he had to tolerate this humiliation, even if it made his blood boil.

As he walked past the rows of tents and make-shift shelters, George's eyes scanned the camp, watching the marines at work, the civilians chatting and moving supplies. All the while, the muttering continued behind him. "Here comes the mayor... better get that inventory right." More laughter, another jab. George's nostrils flared, but he didn't respond. Not yet.

He'd get his respect back. One way or another.

Meanwhile, in a quieter corner of the camp, Frank and Annie finally had a rare moment to themselves. For the first time in weeks, the demands of survival had eased just enough to allow them some time alone, away from the chaos of organizing, planning, and fighting.

They sat by the edge of a calm creek that bordered the camp, the sound of the water trickling over rocks providing a peaceful backdrop. The late afternoon sun filtered through the trees, casting a soft golden light over them. Annie leaned against Frank, her head resting on his shoulder, and for a moment, it almost felt like life was normal again.

"This feels nice," Annie said softly, breaking the silence. "Like we're just on some quiet camping trip, far away from everything."

Frank nodded, his arm wrapped around her waist. "Yeah... for a minute, it's easy to forget about the world out there."

They hadn't had much time to just be a couple since the collapse. Every day had been about survival—keeping their family safe, making sure the camp was secure, helping the marines and the other survivors. But out here, for just a little while, it was only them.

"I miss this," Annie murmured. "Just us."

Frank kissed the top of her head, a rare smile playing at his lips. "Me too. Maybe we'll get more moments like this soon."

Annie let out a soft laugh. "You're always the optimist."

"Gotta be, right?"

She looked up at him, her blue eyes searching his face. "Do you think we're really safe here? I mean, with the prison gang out there, the zombies, everything... are we ever going to feel like this again, really safe?"

Frank sighed, his eyes drifting to the tree line. "I don't know, Annie. I really don't. But I do know we've got people we can trust. The marines, the folks here in camp. We're all working together, and that's something. We'll keep building, keep fortifying. We'll survive."

Annie nodded, though worry still clouded her features. "I just... I don't want to lose this. Or you."

"You won't," Frank said, pulling her closer. "I promise."

Back in camp, Colt and Cecilia sat on the hood of one of the Humvees, their fingers intertwined. The past few weeks had changed them both. They had grown up fast in this new world, forced to navigate life and death situations daily, but even in the midst of all the chaos, their relationship had deepened.

Cecilia rested her head on Colt's shoulder, her dark hair cascading over her face as they watched the sun set in the distance. There was something unspoken between them, a tension that had been building since they had decided to take the next step in their relationship. They had talked about getting engaged, but the prospect of actually starting a family in a world like this seemed... surreal.

"I've been thinking," Colt said, breaking the silence. "About us. About... you know, the future."

Cecilia looked up at him, her eyes soft but serious. "Me too. It's crazy, isn't it? Thinking about the future when everything around us is falling apart."

"Yeah." Colt let out a nervous laugh. "But I want it. I want us to have a future. I don't care what's happening out there... I want to be with you."

Cecilia smiled, but there was something bittersweet in her expression. "I want that too, Colt. But with everything going on, how do we even plan for something like that? How do we get married in a world where everything's a fight for survival?"

Colt took a deep breath. "I don't know. But maybe we don't wait. Maybe we do it now, before... before things get worse."

Cecilia raised an eyebrow. "Are you saying...?"

"I'm saying let's do it. Let's get married. Now."

Cecilia stared at him for a moment, her heart racing. It was sudden, impulsive—but then again, everything about their lives was unpredictable now. Nothing was guaranteed. If they wanted a future together, maybe they needed to grab it now, while they could.

"Colt..." she began, but before she could finish, he took her hand and pulled out a small ring from his pocket. It wasn't much—a simple silver band, something he had found during one of their scavenging missions—but it was enough.

"I know it's not what you deserve," Colt said, his voice soft but determined. "But it's all I've got right now. I love you, Cecilia. And I don't want to waste any more time."

Tears welled up in her eyes as she looked at the ring, then back at Colt. She didn't need some grand gesture or a perfect proposal. All she needed was him. And in that moment, despite the world falling apart around them, love seemed like the only thing that still made sense.

"Yes," she whispered, her voice barely audible. "Yes, Colt. Let's get married."

As they kissed, the sun dipped below the horizon, and the camp around them carried on as usual. But for Colt and Cecilia, everything had changed. They had chosen to create something beautiful in the midst of the chaos. And that was enough.

Later that evening, Frank and Annie returned to camp, their brief moment of peace behind them. Colt and Cecilia found them by the fire, exchanging glances.

"Mom, Dad," Colt said, standing in front of them, his hand gripping Cecilia's. "We need to talk to you about something."

Frank raised an eyebrow. "What's up, son?"

"We... we've decided to get married," Colt said, his voice steady, but his eyes searching his parents' faces for a reaction.

Annie blinked, stunned. "Married? Now?"

Colt nodded. "We don't know what's going to happen tomorrow. We love each other, and we don't want to wait."

Frank looked at Annie, a mix of surprise and understanding in his eyes. This world had forced them to grow up fast, and as much as he wanted to protect his son from the harshness of it, he knew this was a decision they had to make for themselves.

Annie's face softened, and she reached out to take Colt's hand. "If this is what you want... then we'll support you."

Frank nodded in agreement, his voice gruff but sincere. "You've got our blessing, son."

Colt and Cecilia smiled, and for the first time in what felt like forever, there was a moment of pure happiness in their small camp.

In the midst of the chaos, love had found a way to thrive.

Chapter 63: Impending Nuptials

The mood in Beaufort had shifted. Where tension and survival once dominated every conversation, a new topic had taken over—the wedding. Colt and Cecilia's upcoming nuptials had injected a much-needed spark of hope into the camp, and suddenly, everyone was buzzing with excitement.

For the first time since the collapse, it felt like people had something to look forward to that wasn't just about surviving the next zombie horde or the looming threat of the prison gang. It was about life, love, and the future. Even George, who had been simmering with frustration in his role as "The Mayor of the Clipboard," seemed to have found a new purpose.

"Well, I'll be damned if I'm not honored," George had said with a grin when Colt and Cecilia asked him to officiate their wedding. The man who once ruled Charleston now found himself unexpectedly touched by the request. It had softened him—if only a little—and gave him something to focus on beyond inventory and logistics.

The camp was transformed overnight. Where there was once dread and a grim focus on defense, now there was a flurry of activity as the wedding planning began. Cecilia, with Annie at her side, was making lists, talking about dresses, flowers, and a cake. Colt was busy rounding up help, making sure the location—an old church just outside Beaufort's borders—was safe and secured for the ceremony.

Cecilia sat by the campfire with Annie, her notebook open and a pen furiously scribbling away. She was sketching out a rough list of everything they would need for the wedding. Her face was lit up with excitement, the weight of the world seemingly forgotten for the moment.

"I know it sounds silly," Cecilia said, glancing up at Annie, "but I've always dreamed of having flowers—roses, lilies, something beautiful. I want it to feel like a real wedding, not just something thrown together."

Annie smiled warmly. "It's not silly, sweetheart. You deserve this day. We all do." She paused, then added, "And if there's anyone who can make a supply run happen, it's Frank."

Cecilia's smile brightened. "You think so?"

Annie chuckled softly. "Oh, I know so. When Frank sets his mind to something, he doesn't stop until it's done. I'm sure he's already thinking about how to make this wedding everything you want."

Just then, Frank strolled up to the fire, dusting off his hands from the day's work. "What are we talking about?"

"Your next supply run," Annie teased, tilting her head toward Cecilia. "Looks like you've got your work cut out for you."

Frank raised an eyebrow as Cecilia handed him her list. It was extensive—more than he'd anticipated for a wedding in the middle of the apocalypse. Flowers, a wedding dress (or something close to it), food, wine, candles, a few decorations... and the cake. Frank let out a low whistle as he scanned the page.

"You sure you're not asking for a little too much here, kid?" Frank asked with a teasing grin.

Cecilia laughed. "I know, I know. It's a lot. But... it's worth a shot, right?"

Frank smiled, nodding. "Hell, if anyone can find a way to make this happen, it's me." He winked at Annie, who gave him a knowing look.

Colt joined them, his usual stoic expression replaced with a rare smile. "Dad. Don't tell me you're gonna make this harder than it needs to be," he said with a grin, nudging his father.

Frank shook his head. "No way, son. I want this wedding to be perfect for you two. We'll make it happen, one way or another. Might take some creative scavenging, though."

"Well, I'm here to help however I can," Colt said. "What's the plan for the supply run?"

Frank folded up the list and tucked it into his pocket. "I've been thinking about that. There's a few stores and warehouses we haven't touched yet on the outskirts of Savannah. Could be some good supplies left. I'll take a team out in the morning."

Colt nodded. "I'm coming with you."

Frank smirked. "I figured as much. But we'll need to move fast. Can't risk running into any more trouble, especially not with that prison gang still lurking out there."

The next morning, the supply run was in full swing. Frank, Colt, and a small team of marines loaded up the Humvees, armed and ready. Cecilia and Annie waved them off, nervous but hopeful. Cecilia couldn't hide her excitement, her mind swirling with thoughts of what her wedding day could look like. It was strange to be planning something so joyful in such a bleak world, but it gave her something to hold onto—a future that was worth fighting for.

As they drove toward Savannah, Frank's mind was focused on the task at hand. The last few runs had been risky—too many close encounters with both zombies and other hostile groups. But this one felt different. This wasn't just another mission for survival. This was personal. He wanted to make sure his son and Cecilia had the day they deserved, even if it meant taking a few extra risks.

They reached the outskirts of Savannah just before noon, the city eerily quiet. The undead were scattered, moving sluggishly through the streets. Frank motioned for the team to keep their distance, moving in carefully as they approached the first store on their list—a large general goods warehouse that had once supplied grocery stores all over the region.

Inside, the air was stale, but there were still supplies to be found. Food, canned goods, some decorations—nothing fancy, but enough to add a little flare to the wedding. Colt and the marines worked quickly, gathering everything they could find that wasn't spoiled or damaged.

As they moved through the aisles, Colt spotted something unusual in the back corner of the warehouse. He motioned for Frank to follow, his expression a mix of curiosity and excitement. Frank moved up beside him, squinting into the dim light. There, tucked behind some crates, was a large box labeled *"Event Supplies."*

Colt knelt down, prying open the box with the tip of his knife. As the top popped off, his eyes widened in surprise. Inside were neatly packed white tablecloths, strings of decorative lights, plastic champagne flutes, and—best of all—several unopened boxes of wedding decorations. Small faux bouquets, ribbons, and even a set of candles meant for a wedding altar.

"You've got to be kidding me," Colt muttered, half laughing as he pulled out one of the bouquets.

Frank grinned, shaking his head in disbelief. "Looks like we hit the jackpot, kid. Cecilia's gonna lose her mind."

Colt nodded, unable to suppress the grin spreading across his face. "She'll love this."

The team loaded up the supplies as quickly as they could, keeping an eye on the shadows for any signs of movement. Though the streets were mostly empty, the silence felt uneasy. Frank kept his hand on his rifle, scanning the area as the last of the gear was stowed in the vehicles.

"All right, let's move," Frank ordered, climbing into the driver's seat. Colt hopped in beside him, and with a quick rev of the engine, they were heading back to Beaufort.

Back at the camp, the atmosphere was electric with anticipation. Word had spread about the upcoming wedding, and the entire community was chipping in to make the event something special. Despite the hardships they faced every day, people found a way to come together, using what little they had to help Colt and Cecilia celebrate their love.

As the Humvees pulled back into camp, Annie and Cecilia were there waiting. Frank and Colt stepped out, their faces lit up with pride as they opened the back of the vehicle, revealing the supplies they'd gathered.

Cecilia gasped when she saw the decorations. "You found all this?" she asked, her eyes wide with amazement.

Colt nodded, handing her one of the small bouquets. "We did. Might not be exactly what you had in mind, but I think we're gonna have one hell of a wedding."

Tears welled up in Cecilia's eyes as she looked at Colt, her heart full. "It's perfect," she whispered.

Annie wrapped an arm around Frank, smiling as she watched Colt and Cecilia embrace. "You really outdid yourself this time," she said softly.

Frank grinned, his hand resting on her shoulder. "It's worth it. They deserve something good—something real. We all do."

The days leading up to the wedding were filled with preparations. People who had been hardened by survival found themselves laughing and working together, piecing together the best celebration they could manage. The old church was cleaned up, the broken windows boarded, and the makeshift decorations were hung with care. The smell of freshly baked bread and roasted meat filled the air—a rare treat, but one the community agreed was worth it for the occasion.

Chapter 64: Gravity

Colt and Cecilia planned on settling down in a small house on the outskirts of the camp. It wasn't much—just two rooms and a garden—but it was theirs. Frank smiled, remembering how proud his son had been to take on the responsibilities of marriage, something he never thought he'd witness in such a chaotic world.

The ongoing wedding preparations that had taken weeks to put together. They seemed to be going smoothly. The community was coming together like a well-oiled machine, people who had been at each other's throats weeks before now working hand in hand. It gave everyone a sense of purpose—something to fight for beyond just survival. Love, family, the future.

But the brief respite from fear wasn't going to last forever.

Annie stepped onto the porch with two mugs of coffee, her quiet presence a steadying force. She handed me one, settling next to me, and we sat in silence for a moment, watching the town.

"They're happy," she said, her voice soft but thoughtful. "Colt and Cecilia... they need this, something to hold onto. We all do."

I nodded, but the unease lingered. "It feels like the calm before the storm."

Annie's brow furrowed as she turned to face me. "What are you thinking?"

I took a sip of the coffee, letting the warmth calm me. "Everything's been going too smoothly. There's always something around the corner, waiting."

They sat in silence for a moment, both lost in their thoughts. Annie finally spoke again, her voice soft. "Do you think we're prepared? If something happens?"

Frank sighed. "We've done what we can. The walls are strong, the patrols are steady, and we've cleared the area. But if that mega gang comes this way... or if something worse is out there... I don't know if we can ever be fully prepared for that."

Annie reached for his hand, squeezing it gently. "We'll face it together. Like we always have."

Frank gave her a small smile, appreciating her quiet strength. But even her reassurance couldn't shake the unease settling deep in his bones.

Later that afternoon, Frank gathered the leadership of Beaufort for a meeting. The Marine Commander, Colonel Harrington, sat at the head of the table, flanked by George, the former mayor of Charleston, and a few key members of the town's council. Colt had joined them, newly married but still keenly focused on his duties to the town.

"We've received intel from one of our helicopter recon teams," Colonel Harrington began, his voice calm but firm. "There's movement along the southern perimeter, near Savannah. A large group. Could be zombies, could be something else."

Frank leaned forward, his instincts on high alert. "How large?"

"Several hundred, maybe more. We couldn't get an exact count, but they're organized. That's not something we've seen with zombies before."

George frowned, leaning back in his chair. "Organized? You mean it could be that gang?"

Harrington nodded. "It's possible. We haven't made direct contact yet, but we need to prepare for the worst. They're moving slowly, but steadily. If they're heading our way, we've got maybe a week before they're at our doorstep."

The room fell silent as the gravity of the situation set in. The wedding had been a bright spot, but now they were back to the harsh reality of survival. Frank felt that familiar tension coil in his chest. They couldn't afford to be caught off guard.

"What's our plan?" Frank asked, breaking the silence.

"We reinforce the walls," Harrington replied. "Double the patrols, set up more traps around the perimeter, and fortify the town as much as possible. If this gang is as big as we think it is, we're going to need every able-bodied person ready to fight."

Frank nodded, his mind already racing with preparations. "We should also stockpile supplies—ammo, food, medical gear. We need to be able to outlast them if it comes to a siege."

George spoke up, his voice tense. "What about diplomacy? Can't we send someone to negotiate? Maybe offer them something in exchange for leaving us alone?"

Harrington shook his head. "We can't negotiate with people like that. They're scavengers, killers. They'll take what they want and leave nothing behind. We have to be ready to fight."

The tension in the room thickened. No one wanted war, but it seemed inevitable. Frank's gaze drifted to Colt, who sat silently, his face grim.

"We'll be ready," Frank said finally. "Whatever it takes, we'll be ready."

That evening, Frank and Colt walked the perimeter of Beaufort, checking the defenses. The sun was setting, casting an orange glow over the town. As they reached the north gate, Colt broke the silence.

"Do you think we can win, Dad? If they come?"

Frank looked at his son, seeing the worry etched on his face. Colt had grown up so much in the past few months, becoming a man faster than Frank ever thought possible.

"I don't know," Frank admitted. "But we'll give them hell trying."

Colt nodded, his jaw set with determination. "We're not gonna let them take this place. We've built something here, something worth fighting for."

Frank smiled, proud of the young man his son had become. "That's right. We fight for what's ours. And for the people we care about."

As they stood there, watching the sun dip below the horizon, Frank couldn't shake the feeling that this was only the beginning. The calm before the storm, as he'd always known it.

But this time, he was ready. They all were.

C.F. HAYES

Chapter 65: Under Attack

The night was too still. The soft thud of my boots on the packed dirt echoed through the silence, tension pressing down like the weight of the stars above. Beaufort lay quiet, but I could feel the anticipation, it clung to the air like a storm waiting to break.

Colt and a group of Marines were stationed at the north gate, rifles in hand, eyes scanning the darkness for any sign of movement. The recent patrol reports had been ominous—a group was coming, and they were organized. The former prisoners had finally made their move.

Frank checked his watch. 0200 hours. The time felt like it stretched on forever as he waited for something, anything, to happen. He hated this—the waiting. It was the moments before the storm that rattled him more than the fight itself.

Suddenly, a distant explosion shattered the silence, its echo rippling through the night. Frank's radio crackled to life.

"Contact! We've got movement on the southern perimeter—repeat, movement on the south!" one of the scouts reported, his voice strained.

My pulse quickened as I grabbed my rifle, motioning for the two Marines with me. "Move!"

We sprinted to the southern wall, where chaos had already begun. Flashes of gunfire lit up the horizon like flickering embers. The prisoners were here.

By the time Frank reached the wall, the sound of heavy machine gun fire filled the air. Marines had manned the mounted guns, laying down suppressive fire into the night. Shadows shifted in the tree line, moving erratically as the enemy advanced, using the cover of darkness and the natural terrain to get closer.

Frank raised his rifle and squinted through the scope. The prisoners weren't moving like zombies—there was no mindless shuffling, no disorganized mass. These were men who knew how to fight. In the dim light, he saw them weaving between trees, taking cover, returning fire with semi-automatic rifles. Frank's gut twisted.

"They're coming in hard," one of the Marines beside him muttered, crouching low as bullets whizzed overhead.

Frank ducked behind a barrier and radioed in. "Colonel, they're here. Looks like at least a hundred, maybe more. They're hitting us hard."

Colonel Harrington's voice was calm but clipped, as always. "We expected this. Keep them pinned down. Reinforcements are en route."

Frank barked orders to the men around him, directing fire towards the advancing attackers. The prisoners were smart, using the trees for cover and splitting their forces to hit multiple points along the wall. Beaufort's defenses were strong, but they'd never faced anything like this.

Explosions rocked the ground as a group of prisoners lobbed homemade grenades over the barrier. The ground trembled, and Frank's ears rang with the deafening noise. He dove behind a sandbag pile just as shrapnel tore through the air.

"Reload!" someone shouted, and the Marines worked swiftly, slamming fresh magazines into their rifles and keeping the pressure on the advancing horde.

Through the chaos, Frank's eyes caught movement near one of the tripwires. He squinted, adjusting his scope to get a clearer view. The prisoners were trying to breach the fence, cutting through the barbed wire as quickly as they could.

"They're at the wire!" Frank yelled, pointing towards the breach. "Focus fire on the fence line!"

The Marines redirected their fire, mowing down anyone who got close to the wire. But for every one prisoner that fell, it seemed like two more took his place. The numbers were overwhelming, and the prisoners were relentless.

In the distance, Frank saw the glow of headlights as a convoy of Humvees roared towards the southern wall. Reinforcements. About time, he thought, but even with backup, this was going to be a hell of a fight.

Colt's voice crackled over the radio. "Dad, we've got movement at the north gate too. Smaller group, but they're trying to draw our attention."

Frank cursed under his breath. The prisoners were smart, hitting both sides at once to stretch their defenses. "Hold them off, Colt! We've got our hands full down here."

Another explosion rocked the ground, this one much closer. Frank rolled to his feet, rifle at the ready, scanning for the source. His heart pounded in his chest as he saw a group of prisoners breach the southern fence, sprinting towards the inner defenses.

"Breach! They're inside!" Frank shouted, raising his rifle and firing off quick, precise shots. The first two prisoners dropped instantly, but more kept coming.

The Marines fell back to secondary positions, setting up choke points and using the narrow streets to funnel the attackers into kill zones. Frank fired round after round, moving with practiced precision. His training kicked in, instincts guiding his every move.

But no matter how many they took down, the prisoners kept pushing. They were desperate, driven by something more than just hunger or survival. These men were here for blood.

As Frank reloaded, he saw a flash of movement out of the corner of his eye. A prisoner had made it past the line and was charging straight towards him, knife in hand. Frank barely had time to react. He swung his rifle around, catching the man in the gut with the butt of the weapon. The prisoner grunted, staggering back, but he didn't stop. Frank fired a single shot, dropping him at his feet.

"Frank! Watch your six!" a Marine shouted, and Frank spun just in time to see another attacker lunging at him. A burst of gunfire rang out, and the man crumpled to the ground. Frank glanced up and saw Colt, rifle smoking, standing a few yards away.

"Thanks," Frank said, breathing heavily.

"Don't mention it," Colt replied, his face grim. "We've got more coming."

The attack continued for hours, the sky gradually lightening as dawn approached. The prisoners were relentless, but Beaufort's defenders were holding the line. By the time the first rays of sunlight broke over the horizon, the attack had begun to wane. The prisoners, realizing they couldn't breach Beaufort's defenses, began to retreat.

Frank watched them disappear into the tree line, his heart still pounding in his chest. They'd survived the night, but barely.

As the smoke cleared and the sun rose higher, Frank looked around at the carnage. Bodies littered the ground, both prisoner and Marine. The southern wall was heavily damaged, and the fence had been torn apart in several places. But Beaufort still stood.

Colt walked up beside him, his face streaked with dirt and sweat. "We made it," he said quietly.

Frank nodded, but his mind was already racing ahead. This attack was just the beginning. The prisoners had tested their defenses, and now they knew where the weaknesses were.

"They'll be back," Frank muttered. "And next time, they'll be stronger."

Colt looked at him, determination in his eyes. "So will we."

Frank glanced at his son, then out at the horizon where the prisoners had retreated. The fight wasn't over, not by a long shot. But they'd survived one hell of a night, and for now, that was enough.

Chapter 66: The Aftermath

The sun's first rays crept over the marshes, casting an eerie glow on the smoldering remains of the battlefield. Smoke still rose from the charred barricades, and the air reeked of gunpowder and blood. After a night of chaos, the silence was deafening.

Frank stood by the southern wall, his body aching from the fight, but the weight on his mind was heavier. Bodies littered the field, both friend and foe. Marines were already moving, silently collecting their dead and clearing away the fallen prisoners.

He wiped a hand across his face, the grit of ash and dirt mixing with sweat. This wasn't just another skirmish; it had been a full assault. And it had taken everything they had to survive it.

Colonel Harrington approached, exhaustion etched into every line of his face. His uniform was torn, streaked with dirt and blood. "We lost 12 Marines," he said bluntly. "Nearly 30 civilians were injured. Could've been worse."

Frank nodded, jaw tight. "It's too many. But we held the line."

The Colonel's gaze drifted over the battlefield. "They were better organized than we thought. Smarter too. We'll need to tighten up everything. Barriers, patrols, communication. They'll be back."

"Yeah," Frank agreed. "And we need to be ready."

Harrington sighed, looking at Frank. "Get some rest, Sergeant. You've done more than enough for one night."

Frank grunted. Rest was impossible. His gaze drifted to the southern wall, where Colt and the younger Marines were already at work, repairing the damage. He saw the same look on Colt's face he had seen in his own reflection so many times—exhaustion, the weight of loss, the bitter realization that the fight wasn't over.

"Keep an eye on him, Harrington," Frank said, nodding toward Colt. "He's a good kid, but he's carrying a lot."

Harrington followed Frank's gaze and gave a small nod. "I'll keep him close. You've raised a good Marine, Frank."

Frank didn't answer. His eyes shifted toward the heart of Beaufort, where civilians huddled in makeshift triage centers. Somewhere in that crowd was Annie, moving tirelessly between the injured. She'd been up all night, fighting to save lives, her quiet strength anchoring the broken. Even in the darkest moments, she never wavered.

As he made his way through the wreckage, the weight of what had happened began to sink in. The town had been scarred—emotionally and physically. The once orderly streets were littered with debris, broken weapons, and torn-up sandbags. Civilians looked shell-shocked, many of them sitting in small clusters, trying to comprehend the carnage they had witnessed.

He found Annie near the town square, her hands bloody and her face lined with exhaustion. She was wrapping a bandage around an older man's leg, her movements precise but weary. When she saw Frank, her eyes softened, though the exhaustion behind them was unmistakable.

"You alright?" he asked softly, crouching down beside her.

Annie nodded, tying off the bandage and brushing a strand of hair from her face. "I've been better. We lost some good people, Frank." Her voice wavered, but she held it together. "But we saved a lot too."

Frank took her hand, squeezing it gently. "You did good, Annie. You always do."

She leaned into him for a moment, drawing strength from his presence. "What about Colt? Is he okay?"

"He's fine," Frank reassured her. "Tired, but he's alright. He handled himself well."

Annie nodded, a mixture of pride and worry crossing her face. "He's growing up too fast. I hate that this is the world he's inheriting."

Frank didn't have a response to that. He hated it too, but there was no changing the reality they were living in. All they could do was survive.

The morning dragged on, the cleanup efforts in full swing. Marines and civilians worked together to clear the debris, repair the walls, and tend to the wounded. It was a grim reminder of what they were up against—not just the dead, but the living threats too. The prisoners had tested their defenses, and they had barely held.

By midday, the triage area was mostly cleared out, with the seriously injured moved to makeshift medical tents. Frank found himself back at the southern wall, staring at the freshly patched-up breach. Claymore mines and additional fortifications were being installed, but he knew it wouldn't be enough. They needed more than just better defenses—they needed a long-term strategy.

Colonel Harrington joined him once again, his face grim. "We need to track these bastards down. Cut them off at the source."

Frank nodded. "They'll regroup. They know they did some damage. Next time, they'll come in harder."

Harrington sighed. "Agreed. I'm going to pull in the air assets. Start scanning the areas around Beaufort. If there's a base of operations out there, we'll find it. And we'll crush it before they have a chance to hit us again."

Frank crossed his arms, watching as more sandbags were stacked along the wall. "We can't just wait for the next attack. We have to go on the offensive."

Harrington's eyes narrowed as he turned to Frank. "That's exactly what I'm thinking."

The two men stood in silence for a moment, the gravity of what lay ahead settling between them. The prisoners had pushed Beaufort to the brink, but Beaufort had survived. Now, it was time to push back.

Later that evening, as the sun set and the town settled into an uneasy quiet, Frank returned to the small house he shared with Annie, Colt, and Nash. He found Colt sitting on the porch, rifle across his lap, staring out at the horizon.

"You should be resting," Frank said as he sat down beside his son.

Colt shrugged, his face unreadable. "Can't sleep. Too much on my mind."

Frank understood that feeling all too well. He leaned back, letting the cool evening air wash over him. "You did good today, Colt. I'm proud of you."

Colt didn't say anything for a moment. When he finally spoke, his voice was quiet. "Do you ever think it'll end, Dad? This fighting? The running? The fear?"

Frank sighed, staring out at the horizon where darkness was quickly taking over. "I don't know, son. I hope so. But until then, we keep fighting. We keep surviving."

Colt nodded, his jaw set in determination. "Yeah. We survive."

As they sat in the gathering darkness, the weight of the day finally began to lift, if only slightly. The battle was over, for now, but the war was far from won. And tomorrow, the fight would begin again. But tonight, they could rest. Even if only for a moment.

Chapter 67: Wedding Day

The morning of Colt and Cecilia's wedding dawned warm and clear, a perfect southern day in the midst of everything that had gone wrong with the world. The bright sun was a welcome contrast to the heaviness of recent weeks, as if the weather itself was offering a small blessing to the young couple. In the heart of Beaufort, people bustled around in preparation, their spirits lifted by the prospect of a celebration—something rare and precious in their new reality.

Frank stood by the small garden that had been transformed into a makeshift venue for the wedding. Rows of wooden chairs had been lined up, some salvaged from nearby homes, others crudely built by hand in the days leading up to the ceremony. Flowers—wild and scrappy, but beautiful—adorned the altar, their vibrant colors a stark reminder of life persisting even in the darkest times.

He tugged at the collar of his cleanest shirt, which still didn't feel quite right. He hadn't dressed up like this in what felt like forever, and part of him couldn't believe the day had come. His son was getting married. In the middle of a world teetering on the brink of collapse, Colt had found something real, something pure.

Annie appeared beside him, looking radiant despite the stress that had been etched on her face over the last few weeks. She wore a simple dress, the soft blue fabric swaying in the light breeze. Her hair was pulled back, showing off the faint lines of worry that had settled in over time, but her smile was brighter than Frank had seen in a long time.

"He's going to look so grown up," Annie said softly, her eyes scanning the preparations. "Our baby boy..."

Frank smiled and wrapped his arm around her waist, pulling her close. "Yeah, he's not a baby anymore. He's a man. I'm proud of him, Annie. Of both of them."

The thought of Colt and Cecilia together, young, in love, and choosing hope in a world where so much seemed lost—stirred something deep inside him. It wasn't just about survival anymore. It was about building something, about living for more than just the next battle.

As guests started to arrive, the air filled with soft murmurs of excitement. Civilians and Marines alike gathered, dressed in their best, some even sporting freshly washed uniforms. There was an air of celebration, a reprieve from the constant tension of survival.

Cecilia's parents had arrived first, looking both proud and emotional. Frank had noticed over the past few months how much Colt had become a part of their lives. In many ways, the young couple had given their parents something they desperately needed—hope for a future.

Near the front, George, the former mayor of Charleston, stood with a clipboard in hand, ready to officiate. His demeanor had softened considerably since his arrival in Beaufort. There was no denying the tension that had arisen between him and the Marines, but this day was different. He seemed genuinely honored to have been asked to perform the ceremony, and his usual bureaucratic frustration had been replaced by a rare warmth.

"Everything's going smoothly," George said as Frank passed by, his voice tight with anticipation. "We'll be starting soon."

Frank nodded, giving George a pat on the shoulder. "Thanks for doing this, George. It means a lot to Colt and Cecilia, and to us."

George's face softened further. "It's an honor, Frank. They're good kids. This is something worth fighting for."

Soon enough, it was time. The buzz of conversation quieted as the crowd took their seats. Frank stood by Colt near the altar, his son looking uncharacteristically nervous. Colt was dressed in a simple white button-up shirt, his hair combed neatly—a stark difference from his usual combat-ready appearance. Frank caught his son's eye and grinned.

"Still time to make a run for it," Frank joked lightly.

Colt rolled his eyes but chuckled. "I'm good, Dad. No running. This is the best thing I've done since this whole mess started."

Frank's grin widened with pride. His son was strong, level-headed, and ready for what lay ahead, not just in the fight for survival but in building a future with Cecilia.

The ceremony began as Cecilia appeared at the edge of the garden, her arm linked with her father's. She was breathtaking, her white dress flowing softly as she walked down the aisle. It wasn't much—just a simple gown that someone had managed to sew together in time—but on her, it was perfect. The entire crowd seemed to hold its breath as they watched her approach, her face radiant with happiness.

Colt's eyes locked on her, and Frank could see the emotion welling up in his son. This was it—the moment they had all fought for, in some way. It wasn't just about a wedding; it was about hope, love, and the belief that life could still hold beauty, even in a world ravaged by destruction.

When Cecilia reached the altar, Colt took her hand, his expression full of love and gratitude. George cleared his throat and began the ceremony, his voice carrying over the quiet crowd.

"We gather here today to witness the union of Colt and Cecilia, two souls who have found love in the midst of chaos, who have chosen to stand together against the darkness that surrounds us," George began, his tone solemn but hopeful. "In times like these, love is not just a luxury; it's a necessity. It reminds us why we fight, why we endure, and why we continue to hope."

Frank found himself nodding in agreement. This was what they needed—a reminder of what made life worth living.

The ceremony continued, simple and heartfelt, as George led the young couple through their vows. Colt's voice wavered slightly as he spoke, but his sincerity was undeniable.

"I promise to love you, to protect you, and to fight for our future, no matter what comes," Colt said, his eyes locked on Cecilia's. "We'll face this world together."

Cecilia's response was just as moving. "I promise to stand by your side, through everything. We'll build something beautiful, Colt. Something that lasts."

When George pronounced them husband and wife, the crowd erupted in applause. Cheers and shouts of joy echoed through the garden as Colt and Cecilia kissed, sealing their vows. It was a moment of pure joy, a rare light in the darkness.

As the newlyweds made their way down the aisle, hand in hand, Frank and Annie exchanged a glance, their hearts full. They had survived so much, and now, they had something to celebrate.

For the first time in what felt like forever, it wasn't about the fight. It wasn't about survival.

It was about love.

And that, Frank thought, was worth everything.

Epilogue

Months had passed since Colt and Cecilia's wedding, and the once fragile stronghold of Beaufort had blossomed into something no one could have imagined when they first arrived. The town, once battered by the chaos of the undead and the violence of humanity, now stood fortified, a symbol of survival and hope. Its walls were strong, its people stronger, and its future—though uncertain—was no longer something to fear but something to build toward.

Frank sat on the porch of their modest home, his eyes scanning the horizon. Beyond the walls, the world was still broken, but here, within the boundaries of Beaufort, life had found a way to carry on. Gardens had been planted, homes repaired, and a community born out of the ashes of a ruined civilization. It wasn't perfect, but it was a start.

Annie stepped outside, holding two cups of coffee. She handed one to Frank before sitting beside him, the two of them settling into the comfortable silence they had learned to share. She looked content, but Frank could sense the same lingering questions that weighed on him—what comes next? How long could they keep this peace?

"The boys are down by the water," Annie said, breaking the silence. "Colt and Cecilia are teaching Nash how to fish. You should see them, Frank. They look... normal. Like kids should."

Frank smiled at the thought. He hadn't seen Nash so carefree in a long time. The boy had grown up faster than any twelve-year-old should have, but here, he had the chance to be a kid again—if only for a moment.

"And Colt?" Frank asked, though he already knew the answer. His son had embraced this new life, just as he had embraced the responsibility of marriage and family. Colt was a natural leader, someone the other survivors looked up to, just as Frank had always known he would be.

"Colt's doing great," Annie replied, pride evident in her voice. "He's got the makings of someone who can help keep this place going long after we're gone."

Frank nodded, his mind drifting to the future. They had come so far, but he knew the challenges would keep coming. The world wasn't going to fix itself overnight, and there were still dangers lurking beyond their walls—zombies, rogue human factions, and the ever-present threat of running out of supplies. But for now, in this moment, they had peace. And for Frank, that was enough.

"We've done well, Annie," Frank said, turning to look at her. "I wasn't sure we'd ever get to this point, but here we are."

Annie smiled, her hand resting on his arm. "We have. And we'll keep going, Frank. Together."

Their bond had been tested over the years, through the hardships of raising a family in an apocalyptic world and the strain of constant survival. But they had come out the other side stronger, their love deepened by every challenge they had faced.

The sound of footsteps approached, and Frank looked up to see Colt and Cecilia walking toward them, Nash trailing behind with a fishing pole slung over his shoulder. The young couple looked happy, despite the world they had inherited. They had found something rare—a future worth fighting for.

"Catch anything?" Frank asked as they reached the porch.

"Just a couple," Colt said with a grin. "But we'll try again tomorrow. It's peaceful down by the water."

Frank nodded, watching as Nash bounded into the house, leaving the four of them alone on the porch. Colt and Cecilia exchanged a glance, and Frank knew what was coming before they even spoke.

"Mom, Dad," Colt began, his voice steady but filled with excitement, "we've got news."

Annie sat up straighter, her eyes widening. "What is it?"

Cecilia smiled, placing a hand on her stomach. "We're going to have a baby."

The words hung in the air for a moment, sinking in. Frank felt a swell of emotion he hadn't expected, a mix of joy, pride, and the faintest hint of worry. But more than anything, he felt hope. In the midst of everything, life was continuing. His son and daughter-in-law were building the future.

Annie was the first to react, pulling them both into a hug, tears in her eyes. Frank stood, his heart pounding, and wrapped his arms around the group. It was a small moment, but it was everything.

As they pulled away, Frank looked at his son—the man he had raised, the man who had found love and hope in a world that had tried to take everything from them. Colt was ready for this, just as he had been ready for everything else.

"We'll be here for you," Frank said, his voice thick with emotion. "All of us. This is what we've been fighting for."

Colt nodded, his expression serious but filled with gratitude. "I know, Dad. And we're going to keep fighting. For the baby, for everyone."

Frank glanced out at the horizon again, the sun beginning to set over Beaufort. The world was still dangerous, still uncertain, but for the first time in a long time, Frank felt like they were building something lasting—something real.

As the sun dipped lower, casting the town in a golden glow, Frank squeezed Annie's hand. The fight wasn't over, but they had each other. They had family. They had love.

And for Frank, that was enough.

The world had fallen apart, but they had found a way to survive. To live. To build.

And maybe, just maybe, that was how the human race would endure—one family, one town, one moment of hope at a time.

The future was theirs to shape, and Frank was ready for whatever came next.

The End

Milton Keynes UK
Ingram Content Group UK Ltd.
UKHW040308181024
449757UK00005B/399